# If Only They Could Talk

*Ian Walker*

Clink
Street

London | New York

# Chapter 1

"We have entrusted our brother Miles Goodyear to God's mercy, and now we commit his body to be cremated: earth to earth, ashes to ashes, dust to dust: in sure and certain hope of the resurrection to eternal life through our Lord Jesus Christ who will transform our frail bodies that they may be conformed to his glorious body, who died, was buried, and rose again for us. To him be glory for ever. Amen."

The service was nearly at an end and mindful that there was another cremation in ten minutes' time the vicar continued:

"Before we depart, the family has asked me to inform everybody that you are invited for drinks and a buffet at the George Stephenson on Newbold Road immediately after this service."

The George Stephenson was a large brick-built pub dating from the 1950s. It stood on a main thoroughfare less than a mile from Chesterfield town centre and had been named after 'the father of the railways' and inventor of the Geordie miner's safety lamp.

George Stephenson had resided in Chesterfield for the final years of his life. He was buried in the graveyard at Holy Trinity church, just down the road from the pub that now bore his name.

"We will finish by singing one of Miles's favourite hymns, 'Praise My Soul the King of Heaven'," the vicar continued.

Mind you no one present could remember Miles ever going to church, let alone having a favourite hymn.

Once the service was over the congregation filed out of the crematorium and gathered shivering by the flowers, which had been laid out at the back of the main building. It was early January and the temperature was close to freezing on a dull, overcast day, a fact that only served to add to the overall gloom of the occasion.

"Well, it was a lovely service," said Emma. "It's just a pity that there weren't more people here."

"He was 92 and it's an unfortunate fact of life that most of his friends died years ago," commented Nigel.

Nigel and Emma were brother and sister, nephew and niece of the deceased and his closest living relatives. Although both of them had been born in Chesterfield, neither of them lived locally anymore. Nigel was the nearest as he lived in Ashbourne along with his wife Molly and Bruce, their black Labrador.

He was formerly the financial controller for Rolls Royce in Derby, joining straight from university. It was one of those good old-fashioned jobs for life, or so he thought until they offered him early retirement in 2018. Not that he'd been disappointed. It was manna from heaven where Nigel was concerned, as he'd worked for them for nearly forty years by then. So after receiving a six-figure severance payment he was able to start drawing his pension and spend more time pursuing his hobby restoring classic cars. In fact he'd just completed his latest project, a 1948 MG TC, which he'd discovered in a friend's barn. It was in a truly dreadful state of repair and had taken eighteen months of painstaking work, but he'd finally got it back to its original showroom condition.

Nigel loved his hobby and the same was true of Molly who nowadays enjoyed one of her own. She'd taken up making pottery after the hotel where she'd worked as a receptionist closed back in 2017. Fast forward three years and she now designs and makes her own range of vases, which she sells locally at various craft fairs.

Nigel and Molly had been married for 35 years and although their interests didn't overlap, they always made sure they supported each other's pastimes. Molly attended classic car rallies and Nigel helped his wife at the monthly artisan market in Bakewell.

The two of them may have retired, leaving them free to pursue other interests, but the same was not true for Nigel's sister and her husband. Emma was four years younger than her brother and was employed as a school secretary at a large comprehensive in Guildford. She was married to Ralph, a consultant orthopaedic surgeon working at the Royal Surrey County Hospital. He had just turned sixty and was considering retiring himself in two to three years time. But in the meantime his work kept him busier than ever.

Neither Emma nor Ralph had made any plans for their retirement. Work and children had taken up all their time for the past thirty years. But with the children now having fled the nest and retirement looming large for both of them, they knew they had to make some decisions pretty soon. Perhaps they'd travel. After all neither of them had taken a gap year when they were younger. They could always buy a campervan, just disappear and spend months travelling around Europe. Or if they were really adventurous they could go even further afield.

But all that was for the future. Today was about family.

In truth the turnout at the crematorium was pitiful. If they had known it was going to be so poor, Emma and Nigel would have insisted that their children attend in order to make up the numbers. But the fact was that their kids barely knew their great-uncle. They hadn't seen him since the funeral of their grandmother back in 2006.

Also Emma's three all lived in London, Nigel's son Jacob was in Devon and his daughter Flo in New Zealand. As a result it was always going to be difficult to persuade any of them to attend.

Miles's death had brought to an end a long family connection with Chesterfield. Emma and Nigel's parents had also lived there until their deaths – their father from dementia in 2002, and their mother from cancer in 2006. Whilst they were alive, there was always a reason for the two of them to visit the town, and sometimes they would pop in to see their uncle. He was not the easiest of men to talk to. In fact both of them remember their mother referring to him as old misery guts.

"We should have made more of an effort to see him over the years," said Nigel. "Especially me. After all I only live forty minutes away."

"Look, he never wanted to see us," replied Emma. "We never even got a card from him at Christmas, so I wouldn't get too upset about it if I were you. Mum was the only one of us that he was ever close to and since she died we haven't heard a thing from him. Mum told me he got really depressed following Aunty Sarah's death and the closure of the brewery back in the 1960s. She said he never fully got over his double loss."

"It's amazing. I'd forgotten all about Aunty Sarah," said Nigel. "Mind you, I never really knew her being as I was only three when she passed away and you weren't even born. Aunty Sarah would only have been 33 when she died. I remember now that Mum always said Uncle Miles was totally devastated by her death. That's probably why he was so miserable and never remarried."

As they were talking, an elderly gentleman wearing the customary dark suit and black tie wandered over and interrupted their conversation.

"It's Mr Nigel, isn't it?" he asked.

"Good grief, it's a long time since anyone called me that," Nigel replied. "I'm afraid you're going to have to remind me."

"Alf Parkes," said the man. "I used to be chief clerk at the brewery back in the 1960s."

Goodyear's of Chesterfield had been one of three breweries in the town and the last one to close after it was taken over by Sheffield Brewery in 1967. Emma and Nigel's mother had been a Goodyear and they had both been allowed to visit the family business on special occasions when they were young. These were mainly for events such as the company Christmas party and the annual summer outing.

They were always referred to as Mr Nigel and Miss Emma by the brewery staff. This was a common practice amongst employees of family run companies throughout England in the twentieth century. With so many members of the same family involved in a business, it would have been confusing to refer to them all by their surname. And since it was considered too familiar to use their Christian names alone, the tradition was to call them Mr or Miss followed by their first name instead.

Mind you, Emma and Nigel's surname wasn't Goodyear. It was Friedrich. Goodyear had been their mother's maiden name. Additionally, there were no other children from the owning family at that time, but this made no difference to the brewery employees. The two of them were part of the Goodyear dynasty, and therefore would always be known as Mr Nigel and Miss Emma.

"Mr Parkes," said Nigel. "I remember you. You always used to lead the singing on the bus back from the seaside during the staff summer outing."

"They were happy days Mr Nigel," said Parkes. "It was the worst day of my life, the day your uncle sold the brewery. My father and grandfather had both worked for Goodyear's and all of a sudden I had to find myself another job. Eventually I got one as steward of Chesterfield Miners Welfare Club, but it was never the same."

"Well, it was really good of you to come, Mr Parkes," said Nigel.

"I never held it against your uncle," Parkes continued. "He didn't want to sell the business. The banks forced him to. Bloody banks, they never did anything for anybody. Look at the mess they've got the country into nowadays. Mind you, it would never have happened if your grandfather had still been alive. He would have known how to save the brewery. Of course some of us could have transferred to work in Sheffield. But that was twelve miles away. At Goodyear's I could walk to work in the mornings and stagger back home again in the evenings after a few pints in the brewery cellars. In the end very few members of staff decided to transfer and most of those who did, didn't like working there. By the end of 1968 there wasn't a single one of them left.

"Of course there aren't many of us old employees who are still alive nowadays. There's Jim Stuart over there who used to work on the drays and next to him is Eileen Greenbank who used to work in the empties store. They're the only ones of your uncle's old workforce who are here. Bill Steadman, who used to work in the brewhouse is still going, although he uses a Zimmer frame these days and doesn't get out much. I see him every now and again when I take a few bottles of beer around to his house and we talk about the old times. It allows his wife to go and do a bit of shopping and stops him from getting under her feet for a few hours."

"That's very good of you, Mr Parkes," said Emma. "Tell

me, are you going to join us at the George Stephenson?"

"Oh yes, I'll be there," said Parkes. "I wouldn't miss my last opportunity to drink to the memory of Mr Miles. Mind you the beer they serve these days is bloody awful. It's a bit like drinking someone's dirty bathwater after they've been farting in it. Of course it was your family that built the George Stephenson, you know. It used to be one of your pubs."

"Of course it was. I'd forgotten that," said Nigel.

"Yes, it was your family's flagship outlet when it opened in 1954," continued Parkes, "two bars, a restaurant and six letting bedrooms. It was billed as a new beginning for the brewery. A move away from male boozers towards the type of pub you could take your wife to. Or somebody else's wife for that matter, bearing in mind the letting bedrooms."

He chuckled a little, obviously amused by his own joke before continuing.

"Look at it now, it's owned by Sizzling Steak Shacks. You can't even go in there without someone saying, 'Are you dining with us tonight sir?'

"No I'm bloody well not, I came in for a pint of mild and a game of darts. Not that they sell mild or have a dartboard anymore. It's all lager and two for one steaks these days cooked in a bloody microwave. I asked for a medium rare sirloin in one of their pubs once and do you know what the man behind the bar said to me?"

"No, what did he say?" said Nigel pretending to be interested.

"He said, 'I'm awfully sorry sir but we've just sold the last medium rare sirloin. I can offer you a medium one instead though.'

"What do you think of that? Nothing in that bloody pub is cooked to order. It's all prepared in a bloody big factory in Scunthorpe and then reheated by some spotty youngster on the minimum wage. I'll never ask for a sizzling steak in one of their pubs again. Your uncle would turn in his grave."

Nigel considered saying that their uncle didn't actually have a grave to turn in and was probably sizzling himself at that precise moment. But then he had second thoughts, deciding it wasn't appropriate to be making jokes at a funeral. Instead he just said,

"Well, it's been really nice talking to you, Mr Parkes. Hopefully I'll catch up with you again later, but Emma and I really need to get to the George Stephenson in order to greet our guests."

With that Nigel, Molly, Emma and Ralph went over towards the stretched black Jaguar that had brought them to the crematorium and which was now going to take them to the George Stephenson.

However, just as they were getting in Nigel apologised to the others. He had spotted a couple of his former teachers from his days at the Grammar School and wandered over to talk to them. They were both in their eighties and had been colleagues of his uncle's after he got a teaching job there following the closure of the brewery. Nigel had been a pupil at the time, which is how he came to recognise them.

Nigel had never been taught by his uncle, but Beaky King had taught him history. Nigel remembered him as a stern man who wouldn't take any nonsense from his pupils. Pansy Potter had been the art master back then and Nigel had also been in his class in years one and two. Old Pansy had been the exact opposite of Mr King. He was a man with his head in the clouds who let his pupils run rings around him.

"Mr King, Mr Potter," said Nigel. Then seeing that they didn't recognise him continued by saying. "It's Nigel Friedrich, Miles's nephew."

Suddenly the penny dropped. "Young Friedrich, I haven't

seen you since you left school," said Mr King before adding. "That would be in 1977 wouldn't it?"

"1976," replied Nigel.

"And what are you doing these days?" asked Mr King.

"Well, I was the financial controller for Rolls Royce in Derby until two years ago. But I was offered the chance of early retirement and jumped at the opportunity."

"There's nothing that makes you feel older than seeing the boys you once taught getting old themselves and retiring," Mr Potter replied.

"I'm sorry about your uncle," said Mr King. "He had a good innings but he was unlucky in love. I asked him once why he never remarried and he told me that he'd been let down by women on too many occasions. He said that he was happy with just his garden and the odd pint in the Nags Head. He told me that his dick had got him into all kinds of trouble over the years and that he'd learnt his lesson and was going to keep it in his trousers from now on."

This statement by his old history master came as a bit of a shock for Nigel who had never thought of his uncle as a ladies' man before. However, he soon composed himself and asked them if they were coming to the George Stephenson. When they confirmed that they were, Nigel said he hoped to speak to them both again later.

With that he rejoined the others who were waiting for him in the stretched Jaguar. A few seconds later the chauffeur pulled out of the crematorium gates bound for the George Stephenson.

"Who were those two men you were talking to?" Molly asked him as they were heading towards Newbold.

"Beaky King, my old history master, and Pansy Potter who taught me art."

"So did you have nicknames for all your teachers when you were at school?" she asked.

"Most of them. Beaky got his nickname because of his initials. His real name is Brian King, so his initials are BK, which is where Beaky comes from. Mr Potter got his nickname from a character in the Beano.

Mind you, the talk amongst some of the boys was that he was called Pansy for another reason. But I'll not go into that now."

Molly wasn't too impressed by Nigel's schoolboy reminiscences, so instead she decided to change the subject.

"I think we've over-catered," she announced. "There couldn't have been more than twenty people at the crematorium and I doubt if they will all come to the George Stephenson."

She was referring to the fact that when the pub manager had asked her how many he had to cater for, she'd told him that they were expecting between 35 and 40 guests. It now seemed that there would be less than half that number and consequently most of the buffet would be wasted.

"Oh, I don't know," added Ralph. "Perhaps we'll get some professional mourners attending."

"Pardon?" said Molly.

"Professional mourners," he repeated, "people who scour the papers for details of funerals that are going to take place. Then they go along for the free food even though they'd never met the deceased."

"Do people really do such things?" enquired Molly.

"Of course they do," Ralph replied. "Some of them even do research into the person who's died so that they can join in conversations about them."

"Well, I think that's awful," said Nigel. "If we get any of them today I will personally throw them out."

"Ah, but how would you recognise them?" Ralph continued. "If someone came up to you in the George Stephenson who you've never met before and said that they used to live in the same street as your uncle back in the 1940s, how would you know if they are genuine or not?"

Before Nigel had the chance to answer, the Jaguar arrived in the car park of the George Stephenson and the four of them got out. The pub looked pretty garish in its red and yellow livery and was plastered with boards advertising the pub's various offers, such as two-for-one Tuesdays and free-bottle-of-wine Wednesdays. It hadn't been chosen for its décor. It had been chosen because it was next door to their uncle's house.

As it turned out Nigel needn't have worried about inter-lopers, as there were only eighteen people in the small func-tion room they'd hired for the wake and that included the four of them. He recognised the other fourteen, as all of them had been at the crematorium.

The four members of the family helped themselves to tea and coffee and then started to chat to the assembled guests. Most of them were really old and had known their uncle, either from his time as a schoolmaster or from the days before the brewery had closed. As well as Beaky, Pansy, Alf, Jim and Eileen there were also a couple of former Goodyear brewery tenants and a local farmer. He'd known their uncle because he used to buy spent grains from him to feed to his pigs.

There was also John Blenkin, their uncle's next-door neighbour and one of the few friends he'd had in recent times. John was joint executor of their uncle's will along with their uncle's solicitor. In addition he was the person who'd raised the alarm that led to their uncle's body being discovered.

On seeing Nigel and Emma, John walked over to have a word with the two of them.

"Please accept my condolences," he said. "He had a long life, but death is never a pleasant experience for the family, all the same."

"That's true," said Nigel. "Even though we rarely saw our uncle in the past few years, we all have happy memories of him from when we were children."

Nigel was not being completely truthful of course, but saw no point in besmirching his uncle's memory now that he was dead.

"I have to say that you have been very good," said Emma, "arranging the funeral and dealing with his solicitor."

"Unfortunately it's a poor turnout," John replied. "But I suppose you have to bear in mind that your uncle was 92 when he died and most of his friends and former work colleagues are now dead themselves. Anyway talking about the legal side of things I've got a copy of his will for both of you."

"Oh, I thought his will would be read out by his solicitor after his funeral," said Emma.

"That sort of thing only happens in films," replied John whilst opening the folder he had brought with him. "No, with most estates a copy of the will is merely sent to the beneficiaries by the solicitor handling probate."

With that John produced two photocopied pieces of paper from the folder he was carrying and handed one to Nigel and one to Emma.

"As you can see," John went on. "Your uncle's will is very straightforward. He leaves everything to the two of you as his only living relatives."

"We never discussed his will with him," said Nigel. "Neither of us ever presumed that he would leave his entire estate to us. However, we did realise that he didn't have any other relatives."

"Well, it's not all good news I'm afraid," John went on. "I have to tell you that Miles was not a wealthy man when he died. In fact he barely had enough money in his bank account to cover his funeral costs. That is why we are having finger buffet number one, the cheapest they do here. Mind you, given the poor turnout I'm glad we didn't have more money to spend."

"You surprise me," said Nigel. "After all, our family used to be quite wealthy back in the 1960s when we owned a brewery and 35 pubs. The whole lot must have been sold for a tidy sum when Sheffield Brewery bought it back in 1967."

"He should have sold it earlier," said John. "It was one of Miles's biggest regrets that he didn't sell it in 1961 when he had the opportunity. The brewery was haemorrhaging money in its final years. In the end he sold it for a knockdown price following pressure from the bank, which was threatening to call in the receivers. Your uncle was a proud man and very few people know the full story."

"Really?" said Nigel whilst remembering that Alf Parkes had told them a very similar story half an hour earlier. Then he said, "Still, I guess his house must be worth quite a bit?"

"There's one problem with that," added John. "Your uncle didn't own his house. He'd been living there as a tenant since 1967. The house is owned by Sizzling Steak Shacks and they've been waiting to get their hands on it for years. It seems they want to knock it down in order to build a Barmy Barn, which I'm told is a children's indoor play area. I believe they also intend to use the garden for extra car parking. They already have planning consent and want to start demolition in a couple of weeks' time. I'm afraid you will need to clear out your uncle's stuff by then."

Nigel and Emma remained quiet. They were both too shocked by the news they had just heard to say anything.

# Chapter 2

Once they had recovered from the shock of discovering that the value of their uncle's estate was virtually zero, Nigel and Emma had to decide what to do. In the end it was Nigel and Molly who volunteered to clear out Miles's house. Emma and Ralph couldn't do it as they lived three hours away and both of them had work commitments. So it was either going to be Nigel and Molly who took on the task, or they would have to pay a house clearance company to do it.

There were other reasons why they had volunteered. Since the value of their uncle's estate was almost nothing it meant that they, along with Emma and Ralph, would have to pay if they used a house clearance company. Also they felt they owed it to their uncle to go through his things carefully to see if there were any family mementos worth keeping. Finally, there was the fact that they only lived a short drive away and being retired, had the time to do the job.

So, the following Monday the two of them got up early, put on old clothes and drove to Chesterfield.

"You know I worked out that it's been fourteen years since I last visited this house," said Nigel as they approached the suburb where their uncle had lived. "And on that occasion it was only for half an hour. When I was young I used to visit every week. We'd come with Mum and Dad every

Sunday and listen to the radio whilst the grownups all had a sherry. It was one of those old radios with valves in it. The last time I came here he'd still got it, although I think it had stopped working years ago. At 12.30 on the dot we'd all troop next door to the George Stephenson for Sunday lunch. I guess it was one of the perks of owning a brewery and a string of pubs."

Soon afterwards they arrived at their uncle's house. Nigel had driven past it the previous week when the two of them had been to the George Stephenson. But on that occasion he hadn't noticed what a poor state it was in, with peeling paintwork and a hedge that looked as if it hadn't been trimmed in years.

"The garden's in a right old state," said Nigel. "Uncle Miles used to love his garden, but it looks as if he neglected it in recent years, probably because he suffered from arthritis. I always wondered why he didn't pay somebody to look after it for him. I guess we know the reason now. He almost certainly couldn't afford to."

"Well there's no point in worrying about it now," said Molly. "It will be covered in tarmac and marked out into parking bays in a few weeks' time."

John had given Nigel the front door key at the funeral so he and Molly could let themselves in.

"It's just as I remember it," announced Nigel as the two of them wandered into the living room. "In fact I don't think it has changed at all in the sixty odd years I've been coming here."

"By the looks of it your uncle didn't throw anything away for sixty years either," added Molly who was casting an eye around the room.

Every space seemed to be taken up with items that had ceased to be of use years ago. These included an old record player, the radio, which Nigel had referred to a few minutes earlier, and an old black and white TV. Even if it was still in working order it couldn't be used any more. It was an old 405 lines model and the service had been discontinued in 1985. In recent years it had been used as a stand for the modern flat screen TV that stood on top of it.

"This job is going to be bigger than we thought," Molly added.

She pointed at the sideboard before continuing, "And that's just based on what I can see. God knows what's stored in all those drawers and we've got another seven rooms plus the attic, shed and garage to tackle."

With that she suggested that they start after having a cup of tea. Molly had brought tea and milk from home and so she went to find the kettle.

"Good grief, has nobody been in this house since your uncle died?" she shouted from the kitchen. "Only I've just looked in the fridge and wished I hadn't."

"No, I should have warned you that nobody has been here since his body was discovered," Nigel shouted back. "I guess that clearing out the fridge isn't top of anybody's priority list when you've just discovered a corpse."

Nigel's uncle had died of a heart attack just before Christmas. He'd collapsed on the kitchen floor after opening a can of beans.

On Boxing Day, John from next door had returned after spending Christmas at his daughter's and had noticed that the curtains were still drawn. He'd immediately raised the alarm by contacting the police who'd broken in and discovered their uncle's body.

They had replaced the door lock in order to make the house secure. But nobody had cleared up the mess and three weeks later the open can of beans was still exactly where Miles had put it on the kitchen worktop. The only difference was that in the intervening weeks, it had grown a coat of green mould. Not only that but the fridge was now full of rotten food and rancid milk. It was enough to make even people with the strongest of stomachs retch.

"I think the first job we should do is to clear out the kitchen," said Molly before adding that tea would have to wait a little longer.

Nigel nodded in agreement, even though he was not looking forward to this job at all. Molly had brought several black bin liners and numerous cardboard boxes with her and the two of them started clearing out the fridge. It was not a pleasant task, but pretty soon the worst of it was behind them and after Molly had cleaned the inside with a disinfectant spray they were able to put their own milk into it.

"Before we continue I'm going to have a quick look upstairs," Nigel announced and promptly headed for the three upstairs bedrooms.

The largest of these was obviously the one that his uncle had been using since it was the only one that contained a made up bed. It was quite a large room with a couple of chests of drawers, a row of built-in wardrobes and a bedside cabinet with an old fashioned wind-up alarm clock on it. The electric fire in the corner looked as if it had come from the ark and probably should have been condemned as a fire hazard years ago.

A few minutes later Nigel was back downstairs in the kitchen carrying a moth-eaten teddy bear with him.

"Hey look what I've found," he said. "This is Edward, Uncle Miles's old teddy. I found him in his bedside cabinet. This brings back memories; I remember him telling me that he was given it as a boy and then he lost him for fifty years. It's amazing when you think about it. Where did he go? How did he find him again? I guess we'll never know now."

"He looks well loved," replied Molly. "He's definitely

been through the wars. Just imagine what stories he could tell us if only he could talk?"

\*\*\*\*\*\*\*

"It's your turn Miles," said Mother as the whole family sat in front of the fire on Christmas Day.

It had been the words I'd been waiting to hear for over two hours and I immediately squeezed the gift that was neatly wrapped in festive paper.

"It's soft," I said. "Is it a new jumper?"

"'Of course it's not," said my brother Rupert whilst looking at the ceiling in disbelief. "It's the wrong shape for a start. Anyway you didn't put a jumper on your list for Father Christmas did you? Go on, open it."

The year was 1933. It was a family tradition to open our presents one by one after checking that Father Christmas hadn't forgotten to visit the Goodyear family the previous night. I woke up at 6.30 in the morning but had to wait until after 8.30 before the other members of my family had finally risen from their beds. It was only then that we could unwrap all the presents that were under the Christmas tree.

There was my mother Emily and my father Thomas. Father was also known as 'The Major' by many of his friends and all the staff at the brewery, even though he had left the army in 1919. My parents had met during the Great War after Father was wounded as he led the charge into no-man's land during the Battle of Amiens in 1918. He was sent to Striding Hall just outside Chesterfield, which had been requisitioned as a hospital for officers. It was there that he met my mother who was the daughter of a local vicar. He was 25 and she was a volunteer nurse and only seventeen years old at the time. He'd fallen for her hook, line and sinker, although it was another four years before she finally agreed to marry him.

After the army, Father had gone to work in the family brewery, firstly in charge of the tied pubs, then as Managing Director taking over from his father who'd moved to the role of Chairman. It was a role in which he could enjoy his retirement whilst at the same time keeping a watchful eye on the family business. Rupert was born in 1924 and I followed three years later. Finally our sister Rebecca was born in 1930.

All three of us were born in September, which later on gave rise to the joke between my brother, my sister and I that Mother and Father only had sex once a year on Christmas Day. If that was the case then Father was due to get his present that very evening and it wasn't the type that came gift-wrapped.

We lived in a fine Georgian house close to the centre of town within easy walking distance of the brewery and opposite the Market Place Station. We were also very close to the Star Inn, which was not one of our pubs, much to Father's consternation. Instead, it belonged to our great rivals Brimington Brewery. We could clearly see their advertising slogan from our upstairs front windows. It said 'Drink Brimington Bitter; a beer fit for heroes'.

The slogan had been devised during the Great War and Father said they had only put it there to wind him up. He'd been awarded the Distinguished Service Order for leading the charge at Amiens, which was why he believed the sign had been put up in full view of his bedroom window. Brimington wanted to say that he drank their beer.

"Beer not fit to wash your socks in, is what it should say," was one of the kinder comments he used to make about it.

The house had five bedrooms plus another one in the attic, which was home to Evans, our maid.

Every Christmas, Father would decorate the house so that it resembled a scene from a Dickens novel. We had a huge Christmas tree in the front room and crêpe paper streamers hung between the corners of the ceiling, meeting in the middle where they were tied to the chandelier. We had candles on the mantelpiece and a holly wreath on the front door. In addition there was always mistletoe hanging from the light fitting in the hallway. People entering the house wouldn't even notice it until they discovered my mother or father giving them a sloppy wet kiss underneath it.

Christmas was one of the best times in the Goodyear household. We'd have special things to eat, things we never saw at any other time of the year, like dates, mince pies and sugared almonds. We'd have crackers with bad jokes in them that always made us laugh even though they were pathetic. Best of all though were the presents. I really enjoyed the presents and couldn't wait to discover what Father Christmas had brought me that year.

I tore the paper from my gift and to my delight, I discovered that my main present was a teddy bear that growled when I tilted it.

"You must have been a very good boy this year for Father Christmas to bring you such a wonderful teddy," said Mother. "What are you going to call him?"

"Edward," I replied. "I will call him Edward."

My two other presents were the *Pip, Squeak and Wilfred Annual* for 1934 and a bag of marbles. My sister got a doll and a cradle to put it in. However, it was my brother who got the best present of all, a Hornby clockwork train set, complete with a model station and signals that really worked. I was over the moon because Rupert allowed me to be the signalman whilst he played the part of the engine driver.

It kept the two of us occupied all morning whilst our sister played with her new doll. Meanwhile Mother was busy cooking Christmas lunch. This was a job Evans usually did. But she had gone to stay with her parents in Derby for Christmas. So Mother had taken up the mantle instead, frantically chopping vegetables and stuffing the bird as Father smoked his pipe and listened to the BBC on the radio.

Then there was a knock on the door, which told us that my grandparents had arrived. Mother and Father had invited them to join us for Christmas dinner and they arrived carrying yet more presents for us to open.

The meal itself was a veritable feast, with a massive goose that Father had bought from Kirk's butchers. We also had pigs in blankets, stuffing and bread sauce, as well as parsnips, carrots and Brussels sprouts. It was followed by Christmas pudding soaked in brandy, which Father set fire to after he had closed the curtains and switched off all the lights. It was the only part of the meal that Mother allowed him to help her with, although she soon began to regret her decision when Father realised that he'd used too much brandy. This caused the flames to burn far fiercer than he had anticipated, setting fire to one of the lower hanging streamers as a result.

Rupert, Rebecca and I all thought that it was highly amusing as we watched our father frantically trying to blow the flames out. Fortunately there was no damage done and a few moments later we were all tucking into the pudding, which was accompanied by a thick yellow custard.

"It doesn't get any better than this," I thought to myself.

But then it did, as I was the lucky member of the family who found the sixpence in my pudding.

After lunch it was Mother's turn to put her feet up as Father and Rupert did the dishes. Father did suggest that they leave it until Evans got back, but Mother was having none of it.

Once that was done, Father lit all the candles in the room and the whole family settled down to play Escalado and carpet bowls.

I never wanted Christmas day to end, but all too soon it was over and I found myself tucked up in bed with Edward.

"Rupert may have received the best toy," I thought to myself. "But you can't snuggle up in bed with a train set. I'm glad I got Edward. He's the best bear in the whole world. Thank you Father Christmas. I will love him for ever and ever."

With that I fell asleep.

The following December Rupert and I fell out. Rupert had pinned me down and was flicking my ears and nostrils. To make matters worse he then farted in my face.

"You naughty boy," I said as I got up and tried to hit him. However, he was far bigger than I was so my punches had no effect.

"I will tell Father Christmas what you've done and he won't bring you any presents this year."

"Oh that makes me really worried," said Rupert sarcastically. "Didn't anyone ever tell you that Father Christmas doesn't actually exist? It's really our mother and father who buy the presents. Everybody knows that."

I went to bed that night with tears in my eyes as I cuddled up to Edward. Somehow Christmas would never be as magical again. After all I wasn't a little boy anymore. I knew a terrible secret. I knew that Father Christmas didn't really exist.

# Chapter 3

"I think we'd better divide everything into three groups," said Molly. "Things to take to the recycling centre, things that we can take to the charity shop, and things that we can sell at auction. So which pile do you want to put Edward on?"

"Can't we keep him?" asked Nigel. "Only he's part of the family. My uncle had him for over eighty years."

"Apart from the fifty years that he went missing, you mean. Anyway you'd forgotten all about him until a few minutes ago," said Molly before adding. "Look I don't want to be unkind, but we just do not have space for loads of your uncle's old junk. Why don't you and Emma choose one thing each before we take the rest to auction? That way you will have something to remember him by without cluttering up our house with loads of tat. Who knows, perhaps one of you might even choose Edward here."

Nigel realised that what she was saying made sense and after a brief moment spent thinking about it he nodded his agreement.

He looked at Edward and said, "Well he's not a Steiff bear, but he is really old so he must have some value."

With that Nigel took Edward into the living room and put him on the rug in front of the fireplace. He was the first of many items that they intended to take to auction.

It was at that point that Molly was finally able to put the kettle on to make some tea. Whilst they were drinking it they continued clearing out the kitchen.

"I don't think he ever bothered using his change," said Molly as she opened yet another drawer full of copper coins. The vast majority of them were old pennies and half pennies from the days before decimalisation. "Lets put them in this old tea caddy and we can sort them out later."

It wasn't just old coins that they were discovering as the various kitchen cupboards gave up their secrets.

"Do you know what the best before date on this tin of peaches is?" asked Nigel. "It's the 8th of November 2007."

"That's nothing," Molly replied. "There's another tin here which was made before best before dates were introduced."

"I don't know if it was because he was a hoarder or just plain lazy, but I cannot understand why he didn't throw things away," said Nigel. "There are three jars of Marmite in here. All of them have been opened and from the packaging one of them looks at least fifty years old."

The job of clearing out the kitchen was long and laborious, but eventually all the cupboards were empty and they had six black bin liners full of rubbish to take to the recycling centre. They also had a mound of kitchen utensils, pans and crockery all laid out on the kitchen table.

"Do you think that any of this stuff is worth taking to auction?" asked Nigel.

"Well, there's a Charlotte Rhead jug and a boxed set of silver fish knives and forks," said Molly. "There's also a Pearson's pottery vase, but other than that it's all junk."

Nigel decided to take a closer look at the items on the table. The Charlotte Rhead jug would probably fetch a bob or two at auction. The silver knives and forks were black because they hadn't been cleaned for so long, but they were silver so they would always sell.

"I'm not so sure about the Pearson's vase," he said. "It was obviously a wedding present as it's dated 1953 and has an inscription on it from the staff at the brewery. Things with inscriptions never sell for as much as those without. Mind you, Pearson's has closed down now so they won't be making any more. Let's take it anyway and see how it does."

With that, Molly took the three items into the living room, placing them next to Edward ready to be taken to auction.

"Right," said Molly. "We will take everything else to the charity shop. I suggest that we split up. I will wash all this stuff and clean the kitchen and you can start on one of the other rooms."

"That's okay by me," replied Nigel. "How about if I start upstairs?"

Molly agreed and after she had reminded him to take some bin liners with him Nigel headed back to the master bedroom. He decided to start with the fitted wardrobe.

"Good grief," he thought to himself as he looked inside.

It was stuffed full of all manner of ancient clothing. There were numerous shirts and jackets, five suits, several pairs of trousers and even his uncle's old dinner jacket. Then something he recognised caught his eye and he reached in and pulled it out. It was an old Grammar School blazer complete with a red house tie and school cap.

Nigel knew that a red school tie meant that his uncle had been in Lingard House. His own tie had been dark blue, signifying that he'd been in Foljambe, just like his father. Given the size of the blazer it was almost certainly the one that his uncle had worn in his first year.

"I wonder why he kept this?" he thought to himself.

*******

"Don't fidget Miles," said Mother.

It was the final fitting of my new school uniform and she still had to take up my jacket sleeves. Senior school started in two days' time and I wanted to look smart. I'd been hoping for a new blazer, but had to put up with one that had been handed down from Rupert. He was now in the fourth year and it no longer fitted him following a recent growth spurt.

"Why do I have to have hand-me-downs?" I thought to myself. "It isn't as if my family can't afford a new uniform."

After all, the Goodyears were one of the wealthiest families in Chesterfield. We lived in a fine Georgian house with a maid and we owned a local brewery. But still my mother made me wear my brother's cast-offs. It just wasn't fair.

"Right, you can take your blazer off now Miles and I'll take the sleeves up for you," said Mother. "School starts the day after tomorrow and I don't want you going in on your first morning looking like the wreck of the Hesperus."

Mind you, when Monday finally arrived, the last thing on anybody's mind was the way I looked. I started at the Grammar School on September 4th, 1939, three weeks before my twelfth birthday. It was also the day after Britain declared war on Germany marking the start of World War II. Consequently there was only one topic of conversation on everyone's lips.

"I bumped into Mrs Houghton yesterday and she says that it will all be over by Christmas," said Mother as she checked to see that my cap was on straight.

"And Mrs Houghton is a well known expert in international diplomacy, is she?" commented Father as he got ready for work. "Anyway they said that about the last lot and it lasted for four years."

"I hope it isn't over by Christmas," said Rupert. "I'd hate to miss all the fun."

"Darling, you're only fourteen and even if it isn't over by Christmas I'm sure that it will be all over by the time you reach eighteen."

"I'm fifteen later on this month," replied Rupert. "This time next year I will be planning to run away to Gretna Green in order to get married.

Mother looked horrified, which prompted Rupert to add, "Only joking Mother. I don't even have a girlfriend."

"Anyway war is not fun," said Father. "People get killed and maimed. Look at me, I've still got part of a German shell in my leg."

"Don't forget that you wouldn't have met me if it wasn't for that piece of shrapnel," replied Mother.

"That's as may be, but it still doesn't alter the fact that war causes a lot of heartache," added Father in a defiant voice that told everyone that the debate was over.

A few minutes later the four of us set off. My father left for his office whilst Mother, Rupert and I headed towards my new school. It wasn't really necessary for Mother to come with us. The Grammar School on Sheffield Road wasn't that far from our house and Rupert was more than capable of looking after me. However, she wanted to show her support on my first day in big school.

We arrived at the school gate and Mother kissed us both goodbye and told Rupert to keep an eye on me. My brother was quite embarrassed at being kissed by his mother in front of his friends, but nevertheless he promised to look after me.

We set off together across the playground, both dressed identically in our school blazers and our Lingard house ties and caps. The only difference between us was that Rupert was a foot taller than me and looked far smarter in his brand new blazer and long trousers. My blazer of course was second-hand and came complete with ink stains.

It wasn't difficult to spot who the new boys were. Most

of us were wearing short trousers for a start and we all had bewildered looks on our faces. We made easy targets for the older boys who would creep up behind us and flick the backs of our legs with elastic bands.

It wasn't long before it happened to me and I yelped with pain after being caught behind my left knee. However, a couple of seconds later it was my attacker who was yelping as Rupert whacked him across his knuckles with his ruler.

"Anyone who attacks my brother has me to answer to," he proclaimed.

Rupert may have liked to torment me by flicking my ears and farting in my face, but he sure as hell wasn't going to let anyone else bully me. He was my protector and my hero.

Pretty soon we were all filing into class. In total there were about thirty of us, the cream of Chesterfield's youth. A few of the boys already knew each other from junior school, some had even attended the prep school section of the Grammar School. However, the prep school was in a completely different building across the road from the senior school and as a result this was a brand new experience for all of us.

One thing that we all had in common was that our parents could afford the £10 and 15 shillings a year tuition fees. All of us apart from one or two boys who were on scholarships and even they were vetted to ensure that they came from good families.

The noise in the classroom was deafening, but it all quietened down when our form master, Mr Duggins entered the room. He looked intimidating in his black gown and mortarboard. He was totally unlike any of my teachers at junior school. For a start they had all been women and none of them ever carried a cane about with them. As soon as we spotted him we all stood to attention.

"Thank you gentlemen, you may be seated," he said.

Once we had all sat down he continued.

"As you are no doubt aware there are grave things happening in the world at the moment. Yesterday Mr Chamberlain, the prime minister, announced that we are now at war with Germany and I have to ask myself what terrifies me the most? The thought of Nazi jackboots in the market square or the thought of the task I now face, that of trying to educate a class full of little morons like you lot."

There was some laughter in the room at that last statement, but it was soon ended when he brought his cane down on the desk with a whack.

"I'd like to introduce you to Lord Kitchener," he said referring to his cane, before adding. "Mind you, you don't want to get to know him too well. Lord Kitchener is here to instil some discipline into you and to make sure that you turn out as fine young men. Young men that the school can be proud of. Young men who will carry on in the footsteps of our famous old boys. Old boys who went on to become giants in the fields of religion, literature and the sciences. I'm talking about men such as Dr Secker, the former Archbishop of Canterbury, Dr Bradley, the editor-in-chief of the Oxford English Dictionary and Sir Robert Robinson, professor of Chemistry at Oxford University. Or indeed even like this school's most famous old boy, Erasmus Darwin.

"Yes, Erasmus Darwin, the man who taught his grandson Charles everything he knew, was a student here and learnt all he knew at this very school. So consider this. If it hadn't been for this glorious Grammar School we never would have known that you lot were descended from apes."

He then paused for a second before continuing.

"Although by the look of you all, evolution hasn't moved us on very far. Do I make myself clear?"

There was unanimous nodding from all the boys in the room.

Nevertheless, Mr Duggins hit his desk with Lord Kitchener again and repeated the question.

"Do I make myself clear?'

"Yes sir," the class replied in unison.

"Right then," continued Mr Duggins. "I am now going to read out the register, but before I do there is one very important thing that I have to say to you."

With that he looked up and pointed at a boy towards the middle of the class and said, "You boy, what is your name?"

For a moment I thought that he was talking to me, before I realised that he was actually referring to the boy sitting next to me.

"Russell sir," he replied adding. "But my friends call me Russ."

"I am not your friend boy. I am your worst nightmare," replied Mr Duggins in a flash. Then looking at his cane he added, "Aren't I Lord Kitchener?"

I tried not to laugh.

"Sorry sir," said Russell.

"There is an important point that I want to make," continued Mr Duggins, "which is that in this school nobody uses Christian names. We only ever use surnames, so all of you may as well forget your first names until you leave school after the sixth form."

With that he turned to Russell again and said, "So boy what is your surname?"

"Russell sir," replied Russell.

"No you stupid boy," shouted Mr Duggins. "Russell is your Christian name. What is your surname?"

"It's Russell sir," repeated Russell. "My name is Russell Russell, I've got the same Christian name as my surname."

"Russell Russell," exclaimed Mr Duggins. "That really is the most stupid name I've ever heard. Were your parents having a laugh? Did they christen you Russell Russell because they couldn't think of a proper name for you, or was it just to wind me up?"

"I don't think so sir," replied Russell Russell.

"Tell me boy, did your father attend this school?"

"No sir, he went to Hasland Hall School. I'm the first in my family to go to the Grammar School."

"And what, pray, does your father do for a living boy?" added Mr Duggins.

"He's a greengrocer sir."

"I thought so," exclaimed Mr Duggins. "Is he the Russell who's got a stall on the market? He sold me a bag of plums once and one of them had a wasp in it."

"Yes sir, I mean no sir, sorry sir," replied Russell Russell.

"Sorry," exclaimed Mr Duggins. "Is the question too complicated for you boy? Which is it, yes or no?"

"Well yes, he did have a stall on the market sir. Only now he's got a shop on Low Pavement instead."

"Moving up in the world, eh. Bettering himself and his family. No doubt that's why he wants to pay for you to attend the Grammar School," added Mr Duggins. "I hope you are going to repay your father by doing well in your exams."

"I will try my best sir," replied Russell Russell.

"No doubt you will boy," said Mr Duggins adding. "But you can clearly see that I have a real problem here. I can't call you Russell because that is your Christian name and we don't use Christian names in this school. So what shall I call you?"

"I don't know sir," Russell Russell replied.

By this stage Russell Russell had been in conversation with Mr Duggins for over five minutes and he was earning the admiration of us all. I vowed to make him my best friend.

"The only option I have is to call you by a nickname,"

added Mr Duggins, "and being as though your father is a greengrocer I'm going to call you Sprout. Russell Sprout."

That caused howls of laughter in the room, which soon ended when Mr Duggins hit his desk with Lord Kitchener again.

"Nicknames are permitted in this school," added Mr Duggins. "In fact some of the masters even have nicknames. Do you know what my nickname is, Sprout?"

"No sir," replied Sprout.

"Does anyone know?" asked Mr Duggins addressing the entire class.

Of course many of us did know, especially those of us who had older brothers in the school. In fact I'd received a full briefing on the masters' nicknames from Rupert. My favourites were Mr Janus the Latin master, whose nickname was Hugh, Froggy Phillips the French master, Ratty Owen the Chemistry master who was small and resembled a rodent, Mr Fields the Physics master whose nickname was Gracie and Tinker Bell the Geography master.

Despite the fact that many of us knew what his nickname was, none of us felt brave enough to put our hands up. None of us that was except for a small kid with glasses who sat in the front row of the class. He obviously didn't realise that he was being led into a trap and instead thought that it was some kind of general knowledge test. He raised his hand and said, "Sir, I know what it is."

The rest of us felt relieved and sat back waiting for the entertainment to begin.

"And may I ask how you know?" asked Mr Duggins.

"I overheard some transitus boys talking about it, sir," said the boy.

Transitus was the name given to boys in the fifth year. Boys in the prep school were known as first formers. Boys in the first year at senior school were called second formers and so on until you reached the fifth year, which was called transitus. It was a sort of halfway house between the lower school and the sixth form.

"So go ahead boy, we are all waiting, pray enlighten us," Mr Duggins went on.

"It's Dildo sir, Dildo Duggins," replied the boy.

I really felt for him and at that point every part of me wanted to scream 'No,' but like everybody else I just suppressed a smirk and waited for the inevitable. It was quite obvious that he didn't know what a dildo was. In fact, I hadn't known what one was either until Rupert explained it to me whilst telling me about the masters' nicknames.

"It's what ladies use to pleasure themselves with," he'd informed me.

"What? Like bath salts?" I'd replied. "Only Mother says that there's no greater pleasure in life than relaxing in a warm bath full of bath salts."

"No, it's nothing like bath salts," he'd said before explaining in great detail what a dildo was.

Unfortunately for the little lad who'd put his hand up, he didn't have the benefit of an older brother to tell him things like that. He probably thought that Mr Duggins's nickname was just a play on the name Bilbo Baggins from *The Hobbit*. Which, of course, it was, albeit a rather rude version of Tolkien's famous character.

Mr Duggins walked over to the boy and grabbed him by the ear.

"And that's the last time you will ever call me that," he said whilst twisting his ear, as if he was uncorking a bottle of wine. The boy yelped in pain and got out of his chair due to the force of Mr Duggins's twisting action.

"What's your name boy?" asked Mr Duggins.

"Stanley, I mean Worthington sir," said the terrified boy.

"Well, Worthington," said Mr Duggins. "You will write

out fifty times, 'I must always show respect to the masters in the school and must always refer to them as sir.' Do I make myself clear?"

"Yes sir," replied Worthington.

"And when you have finished that you can then write out fifty times, 'I must not listen in on other people's conversations,'" Mr Duggins went on. "Do you understand me boy?"

"Yes sir," said Worthington who couldn't stop trembling.

"Right," said Mr Duggins. "Let's get on with the register."

Mr Duggins opened the large book that was on his desk in front of him and started to read.

"Arnold," said Mr Duggins.

"Sir," came the reply.

"Ashcroft."

"Sir."

"Baker."

"Sir."

"Bateman."

"Sir."

"Blubberwick, sorry Blatherwick."

Blatherwick was a large fat boy and Mr Duggins's deliberate error resulted in the whole class erupting in laughter. Now there were two boys in my class who had acquired nicknames, 'Sprout' and 'Blubber'.

"Sir," mumbled Blatherwick.

Mr Duggins continued,

"Butcher."

"Sir."

"Chamberlain."

Before Chamberlain even had the chance to reply Mr Duggins was onto him in a flash.

"Tell me Chamberlain, are you related to the Prime Minister?"

"No sir," replied Chamberlain.

"I didn't think so," said Mr Duggins. "You're far more likely to be related to a chamber pot than to the Mr Chamberlain who lives in Number 10 Downing Street."

Once again this caused howls of laughter from the boys, much to the embarrassment of Chamberlain who, from that moment on, was always referred to as 'Piss Pot'.

Mr Duggins read on, "Chippendale."

"Sir."

"Clarke."

"Sir."

"Clarke, I presume that everybody calls you Nobby," said Mr Duggins. "Am I correct?"

"No sir," Clarke replied.

"But that can't be right," Mr Duggins continued. "Every Clarke since time immemorial has been called Nobby, even the girls. You must be called Nobby."

"No sir, I don't have a nickname," he replied.

"Everybody has a nickname boy," stated Mr Duggins. "And if it's not Nobby, then I can only assume that it must be Fanny."

Which was why thousands of Clarkes all over the world may have had the nickname Nobby, but the one in our class was always called Fanny.

Mr Duggins then resumed the roll call.

"Davis."

"Sir."

"Duncan."

"Sir."

"Friedrich."

"Sir."

Mr Duggins paused and then said, "Friedrich, what kind of a name is that boy?"

"It's my family name sir," Friedrich replied.

"And are all your family fifth columnists?"

"No sir, we are all loyal British subjects sir."

"So how come you've got the name Friedrich then?" Mr Duggins went on. "Where were you born lad?"

"In Chesterfield sir," replied Friedrich.

"And where was your father born?" added Mr Duggins, unwilling to let the subject drop.

"He was born in Chesterfield as well sir."

"And your grandfather?" said Mr Duggins who now resembled a dog with a bone.

"He was born in Grindelwald, sir."

"I thought so," said Mr Duggins. "You're a bloody Hun, a Bosch, a Kraut, a Jerry, you're a pint-sized Nazi."

Friedrich was not going to take this insult lying down and replied, "Grindelwald isn't in Germany, sir. It's in Switzerland. My grandfather repairs watches for a living in our family jewellery shop, sir. He's not a storm trooper."

Mr Duggins merely brought Lord Kitchener down with a whack on his desk in the face of such insolence and said, "It may not be in Germany right now, but given that Mr Hitler has already annexed Austria, I wouldn't bet against it being part of the Third Reich by the end of the year. In which case I would suggest that you persuade your father and grandfather to change your family name from Friedrich to Frederick."

Friedrich may have got the message across that his family originally came from Switzerland, but that didn't stop him from subsequently being known as Herman, as in Herman the German.

By this stage I was becoming increasingly nervous, worried that I too would be singled out by Mr Duggins. I didn't have long to wait, as he was only two names away from me in the register.

Mr Duggins continued,

"Frith."

"Sir."

"Gleason."

"Sir."

"Goodyear."

"Sir," I replied in as strong a voice as I could muster.

There was a horrible pause.

"Oh no," I thought to myself. For a moment I thought I'd got away with it.

"Goodyear," repeated Mr Duggins. "Doesn't your family make that crap beer?"

I wasn't going to meekly roll over and let Mr Duggins insult my family's business, but at the same time I didn't want to antagonise him. After his war of words with Herman I feared that I might feel the backlash.

Our advertising slogan at the time was 'Goodyear's excellent beers' so I merely said "Goodyear's excellent beers sir."

"Goodyear's crap beers more like," he repeated. "Because that's where you end up after drinking it, in the crapper. I got a dickey tummy after a couple of pints of Goodyear's Pride in the Fox and Hounds last Friday. Serves me right though, I knew I should have gone to the Red Lion for a pint of Brimington Bitter."

And that was it. He continued with the register and I felt as if I had won a moral victory. It was short-lived however, as all my classmates started calling me Crapper.

Mind you, those of us who'd been given nicknames considered them to be a badge of honour and Sprout, Herman and I became good friends.

Later that day I told Rupert what Mr Duggins had said. He merely laughed and eventually started calling me Crapper as well. Personally I'd have expected more support from my brother, especially since he was a Goodyear himself. Later on I discovered that he'd been given the nickname 'Blimp' after the barrage balloon made by the Goodyear rubber company. Of course that had absolutely no connection with our family firm. I thought he'd got off lightly when you compared it with my nickname.

Three years later Mr Duggins was killed at El Alamein. He'd lied about his age in order to join the Desert Rats. Not in the normal way of course, Mr Duggins had said he was younger than he really was.

Even though he may have gone, his nicknames lived on long after his death at the hands of the bloody Hun.

# Chapter 4

"How are you getting on up there?"

"Fine," Nigel shouted back. "There are lots of old clothes and I've earmarked most of them for the charity shop. Mind you I feel like an intruder, what with having to go through the drawers containing his underpants, vests and socks."

"Unfortunately it is one of those jobs that has to be done though," replied Molly, before adding, "Do you want to come down for lunch as I've made you a sandwich?"

A few seconds later she heard the sound of Nigel's footsteps coming down the stairs.

"What do you think of this?" he said holding up the school blazer. "It's too old to take to the charity shop and besides which the Grammar School closed down years ago. Do you think the auction house would be interested in it?"

"It must be eighty years old at least," Molly replied. "I'd take it if I were you. After all the worst they can do is to refuse it and sometimes I'm absolutely astounded by what sells for good money on *Flog It*."

Since his retirement Nigel had joined Molly in watching quite a lot of daytime TV with *Flog It* being one of their favourite programmes.

"Anyway," she continued. "Here's your sandwich and I've also made you another cup of tea."

Nigel noticed that the kitchen was looking far brighter than it did a few hours earlier. Molly had certainly done a thorough job with her cloth and anti-bacterial spray.

Of course it was only pride that had made her do it. After all, the house was going to be demolished in a few days' time, so it didn't really matter if it was tidy or not.

However, Molly was the type of person who would tell her husband to put on a clean pair of underpants just in case he was involved in a car accident. It wouldn't save his life, but at least the staff at the hospital would know that he came from a good home. Similarly, when they came to demolish Uncle Miles's house the demolition crew would know that he came from a good family.

"Look what I've found," she said holding out a small album that looked as if it were either an autograph book or a small stamp album.

Nigel opened it only to discover that it wasn't either. What it actually contained was a complete set of mint Goodyear's bottled beer labels, probably dating from the 1940s.

"Good grief," said Nigel. "Where did you discover this?"

"It was just lying in one of the kitchen drawers beneath a load of tea towels."

"I never realised that we produced so many different beers," added Nigel as he thumbed through the album. "And I'd totally forgotten that we used to bottle soft drinks as well."

In total, the album contained 22 different labels, from Goodyear's Pride and Bottoms Up Bitter through to Goodyear's Lemonade and Chesterfield Cream Soda. It was a window on the past, a glimpse of a world that had long since disappeared. A world in which every town in England had their local favourites, favourites that nowadays have been replaced by major national and international brands.

"This might be the one thing I keep," Nigel continued.

"I'd think long and hard about that," replied Molly. "What would you do with it other than transfer it from a drawer in Uncle Miles's house to a drawer in ours? Don't you think you'd be better off taking something more practical? Something that we can use every day?"

"I suppose you're right," he replied. "Although I would like an item that will remind me both of my uncle and of my family's heritage."

"Shall we put it with the items that we are taking to the auction?" asked Molly.

Nigel thought about it for a second and then he finally replied with a nod.

*******

The war years were not great times for the brewery. For a start many of the men who formed the bedrock of our consumers joined the forces and moved away, either to fight abroad or to military bases elsewhere in the UK. Consequently, demand for our beers fell substantially.

In addition, many members of our workforce were drafted into the army leaving us short of men. Production and warehousing were particularly badly affected, making it extremely difficult for us to produce and distribute our beers.

If this wasn't bad enough, there was also a shortage of malt and hops, as agricultural land was needed for the production of food rather than beer. This improved a little after the government realised that beer was good for morale. Or to be strictly accurate, they realised that a shortage of beer was bad for morale.

However, we still ran out of beer on many occasions, which literally caused riots, especially in some of the pit villages of North Derbyshire. On one occasion, a pub that had been out of beer for three days finally got a delivery from us. Of course this didn't mean that the pub could start selling the beer straight away, as it still had to undergo its secondary fermentation in the cellar. But try telling that to the angry mob that gathered outside as news got around that the pub now had a full cellar.

They didn't understand about cask conditioning. All they wanted was a pint or twelve and in their anger they set fire to the cellar flaps. The situation was starting to get out of hand until the police arrived to restore order.

Personally the hardship caused by war only affected me in two ways. Firstly we had to let Evans go. She left us and went to work in one of the town's factories that made bandages for the army.

As a result, my brother, sister and I were all given tasks around the house and Mother took on cooking duties. Our main task was doing the washing up after the evening meal. Rupert would wash the dishes, I would dry them and Rebecca would put them away. I have to admit that I was quite a clumsy boy and after my first attempt our kitchen resembled a Greek restaurant, because the floor was covered in broken crockery.

Mother was very good about it, telling me not to worry as she could always go to Swallows department store in Packer's Row and buy some new plates. Father was less understanding though and threatened to make me clean the toilets and replace all the coal in the coalscuttles instead. Our house had seven fireplaces and the cellar was dark and full of cobwebs. So as you can imagine, this was not a job I relished and consequently I made sure I was more careful in future. Next time I dried the dishes, I didn't drop a single plate, which was precisely what my father had hoped to achieve by his threat.

The other way in which the war affected me was that

I was roped in to help in the brewery as soon as I turned thirteen. Not permanently of course, just helping out when I wasn't at school.

Rupert was already working there. He'd started during the summer holidays following his fourteenth birthday and the original plan was for me to do the same. But the labour shortage caused by the war forced my father to bring this plan forward and as a result I started in September of 1940.

At the time, the Grammar School was the only school in Chesterfield that had half days on Wednesdays and Saturdays, rather than a full day on Wednesday and a day off on Saturday. Most of the boys in the school were like Sprout and Herman, sons of shopkeepers. Consequently, the school hours mirrored the opening hours of Chesterfield shops, which were closed on Wednesday afternoons.

As a result, I worked in the brewery on my afternoons off during term time and then Monday to Friday during the holidays.

On my first day I arrived from my morning classes and went straight to my father's office. It was very impressive with its mahogany desk, its leather chairs and numerous items on the walls, most of them advertising Goodyear's beers.

Behind my father's desk was a large ornate mirror etched with the words 'Goodyear's fine Chesterfield Beers'. On another wall were several framed certificates won by the company at various brewing exhibitions dating all the way back to 1883. Some of them were from foreign exhibitions held in places such as Berlin and Strasbourg. There was even one that had been awarded in Cape Town in 1892.

Finally there were numerous signs, many of which had been painted by the company signwriter. Some of them were pub signs with names such as Valiant Soldier and Furness Inn. Others were advertising signs, some on wood and others in enamel saying things like Goodyear's Excellent Beers, or Goodyear's Pride – Makes you proud to come from Chesterfield.

Father was busy so he merely handed me over to Mr North, the bottling foreman, and told him to sort out a pair of overalls for me. He also gave him instructions that he was to treat me in exactly the same way that he would treat any other new employee.

"He's not to be given any special treatment just because he's the boss's son," Father told him as he marched me towards the men's locker room.

Mr North was a man in his sixties with a large walrus moustache. He told me that the war was the best thing to happen to him in a long time, as under normal circumstances he would have been forced to retire three months previously. But the shortage of men had meant that my father had asked him to stay on until the conflict was over. As a result he was still getting his full wage plus eight pints of beer a day, rather than trying to scrape by on his small pension.

We arrived in the locker room where he presented me with a pair of overalls that were three sizes to big for me and showed me where I could hang my school uniform.

I was a little surprised when I opened my locker and was faced by several pictures of naked ladies. Naturally I was curious. After all women hadn't featured much in my life up to that point and certainly not naked ones. In fact, my only exposure to that sort of thing came from a small art deco statue on my father's desk.

"I'll take those," said Mr North.

It seemed that the locker had previously belonged to one of the draymen who'd been sacked for fighting after drinking eight pints of Goodyear's Pride in the brewery sample room. It wasn't unusual for a drayman to consume eight pints, but it later transpired that he'd already drunk fourteen pints during the course of his deliveries.

Mr North transferred the photos to his own locker where they helped to brighten up his remaining months at the brewery before he finally retired.

He then took me into the bottling hall where the noise was deafening. To my surprise all the other people working there were women. I don't know why I was surprised. After all, women were doing all sorts of jobs during wartime. Perhaps it was my middle class upbringing, which made me think that women's work was in the home, looking after children, shopping, cleaning and cooking.

However, I soon realised that these women did all these things in addition to an eight-hour shift at the brewery.

"This is Mr Miles," announced Mr North after switching off the bottling line. "The Major says to treat him the same as you would any other new starter."

With that he left, although I am sure he winked as he went through the door.

"Who gave you them pair of overalls?" asked one of the women who I later discovered was called Marge.

"Mr North," I replied.

"They're far too big for thee, little 'un, take them off and I'll get thee a pair that'll fit thee."

I was really pleased that she was so interested in my comfort, although I was a little bit concerned about taking my overalls off in front of a room full of women. However, I didn't wish to appear rude in the face of Marge's kindness and so I stripped off down to my pants and vest.

As soon as I had done this a few of the other women grabbed hold of me whilst another one of them pulled my pants down.

"Bloody hell, what have we here?" said Marge. "I've seen

bigger maggots and it's as bald as a coot. Not a pubic hair t' be sin."

With that all the women started laughing. I say laughing but it was more a cackle than a laugh.

Naturally I was embarrassed and therefore was extremely grateful when Marge said, "Come on girls, cover him up. We can't have him wandering around with his John Thomas showing,"

before she added, "mind you, given the size of it I better call it Wee Willy Winkle rather than John Thomas."

That caused another cackle of laughter from everyone present.

I'd assumed that my ordeal was about to end, but unfortunately I'd assumed wrongly. Instead of handing me my underpants one of the women reached for a pot of glue used for sticking labels onto the bottles.

She stuck bottle labels all over my private parts. I had never been so embarrassed in my life as I looked down and saw that they had stuck a label saying 'Goodyear's Pride' on my dick, whilst my buttocks had labels saying 'Bottom's Up Bitter" all over them.

By this stage most of the women in the room were positively wetting themselves they were laughing so much. I just wanted the floor to open up and swallow me.

"We pay you to work not to hang around cackling like a coven of old witches," said Mr North who had re-entered the room much to my relief.

"Back to work all of you and as for you," he added whilst looking at me. "Go and clean yourself up."

I went to the Gents' toilet where I pulled the labels off and got rid of as much of the glue as I could. I put my overalls back on and returned to the bottling hall to a round of applause from the women.

After my initiation I thoroughly enjoyed my time in the

bottling hall where my main job was stacking the filled bottles into crates. The ladies treated me very well and I was quite sad when Father moved me to work in the warehouse a year later.

I ended up with a new nickname after my first day at work. It was 'Little Dick'. Fortunately though, it was a nickname that never took off anywhere other than amongst the staff in the bottling hall. Nevertheless some of the women still called me that even after I had become Managing Director.

On the day I moved out, Marge grabbed my arm and said, "You've done really well, Little Dick, so the girls and me want to give you this to remind you of us."

With that she presented me with a small album containing all of the company's bottle labels. I'm sure that it was no coincidence that the first two were 'Goodyear's Pride' and 'Bottoms Up Bitter'.

# Chapter 5

Molly placed the album on the pile of items they were going to take to auction.

"I think we've got enough stuff for our first trip to the recycling centre," she announced when she returned to the kitchen

Lying on the floor were several black bin liners and boxes full of ancient jars and cans that Molly had cleared out from the kitchen cupboards. There were loads of pots and pans that not even a charity shop would want. In addition, Nigel had brought the electric fire and the alarm clock from the upstairs bedroom as these were also destined for the recycling centre.

The two of them started to load up the car and once it was full, they headed to the council recycling centre on Sheffield Road. This was the first of many such journeys they would make over the next few days.

By the time they had finished it was mid-afternoon and the two of them decided they would finish clearing out the main bedroom and then call it a day.

There were lots of clothes to sort out, most of which they decided to take to the charity shop. Some though were only fit for the recycling centre. It was the same for all the bedding that was stored in the room.

"You know, given the fact that your uncle appears to have never thrown anything away I'm really surprised that there isn't anything of your aunt's still here. No clothes and no jewellery."

"You have to remember that she died a very long time ago," replied Nigel. "Perhaps he didn't want to be reminded of the happy times they had together. Maybe his sense of loss was too great."

It was at this point that Nigel discovered an old beret in a drawer.

"There you go," he said holding up the beret. "This is the first thing we've found that belonged to my aunt. Perhaps we'll discover more of her things when we clear out the loft. I wonder why he kept this though? It must be her old school beret as it has a St Helena's school badge on the front."

\*\*\*\*\*\*\*

Sprout, Herman and I were sitting on the roof of the school bike shed. It was October 1941 and it was two weeks since I'd turned fourteen.

The Grammar School was located next door to St Helena's girls' high school. We were never permitted to mix with the girls who went there, well not until we were in the sixth form when limited supervised fraternisation was allowed.

It was the school's way of introducing us to members of the opposite sex in a responsible way. Once we'd passed the age of sixteen it was felt that, if we had to show an interest in girls, it was far better if we were interested in those who came from a similar background to our own, rather than those who worked in one of Chesterfield's many factories.

However, at fourteen we were considered too young for that sort of thing. There was a massive wall that separated the two schools, which stopped us from even glimpsing the

St Helena's girls next door. We could hear them playing in the playground but, much to the frustration of the testosterone fuelled boys at the Grammar School, we could never get a glimpse of them. Well not until Sprout, Herman and I discovered that the only place where you could see over the wall was from the roof of the bike shed. It was our lunch break and we knew that in ten minutes' time some of the girls would be out to play netball. At that point the three of us would be rewarded with a glimpse of them in their navy blue knickers, the biggest treat that any teenage boy could wish for.

"What are you going to do when you leave school?" Sprout asked me whilst we were waiting.

"That's easy," I replied. "I'm going to go to university and then I'm going to work at the brewery. I will start off as Free Trade Director with my brother Rupert as Tied Trade Director, Father as Managing Director and my grandfather as Chairman. Then my grandfather will retire and Father will become Chairman. Rupert will take over from him as Managing Director and I will be promoted to Tied Trade Director. By that time our sons will have joined the firm ready to take our places when we retire."

"So your entire life is planned out for you in advance," said Herman.

"It's my destiny," I replied, "and has been ever since I was born."

"What's the difference between tied trade and free trade?" asked Sprout.

"Tied trade is the name given to everything that's sold through the pubs we own, whereas free trade is everything else. Tied trade is the most important part of the business, because it accounts for over three quarters of all our sales."

"How do you know that you and Rupert will have sons?" Herman interrupted. "Both of you might only have daughters or the two of you may never get married. After all, who'd want to marry an ugly bugger like you?"

"Oh we'll both get married. In fact I know who I'm going to marry. I'm going to marry that girl there."

With that I pointed down to one of the girls who'd just appeared in the courtyard below.

She had long blonde hair and a slightly upturned nose. Like all the other girls she was wearing her PT kit. Her white polo shirt was tucked into her navy blue knickers, knickers that revealed the full length of her perfect legs. She was Venus in a pair of pumps.

"She's a cracker," said Sprout, "and I'm going to pull her."

"No you're not," I replied. "I baggsied her first."

"Bloody hell," said Herman. "You don't baggsy girls, you have to woo them instead."

"What does woo them mean?" I replied.

"It means you have to buy them diamond rings and such like, so that when they get them they say, 'Woo that's nice.'"

Herman told us that he was an expert on the matter of wooing. After all, his family did own a jewellery shop.

"Which one are you going to marry then?" I asked Herman.

"I think I'll marry that one over there," he replied pointing to a large Amazonian girl with black hair.

Sprout and I were both shocked.

"Why on earth would you want to marry her?" I asked him.

"She's got the biggest pair of tits," was his reply.

We couldn't help but laugh, even though it put us at risk of being discovered by one of the masters. Fortunately though we got away with it on this occasion.

The three of us continued to watch the girls playing netball. We were obviously not interested in the score. In fact, we didn't have the faintest idea about the rules of the game.

We just watched the bouncing breasts, long legs and, of course, the navy blue knickers.

"So what are you two going to do when you leave school?" I asked them.

Herman said that he was going to continue into the sixth form before going to work in the family business. Sprout though was vague. He told us that the original plan had been for him to leave school at sixteen after completing his school certificate. He was then going to work in his father's shop. However, his father had recently suggested that he might be allowed to stay on and take his higher school certificate.

This was a reflection of how well Sprout's father was doing and how forward thinking he was. At that time, most pupils left school with no qualifications aged fourteen. However, parents who sent their children to a grammar school undertook to keep them in education until they were sixteen so that they could take their school certificate. Most then allowed their sons and to a lesser extent their daughters to stay on until they were eighteen in order to pass their higher school certificate.

Mr Russell was keen that his son should be able to enjoy the opportunities that he'd never had as a boy. Therefore after opening his second shop in April 1941, he was now considering the possibility of letting Sprout stay on into the sixth form. Both Herman and I hoped that he would be able to continue at school. After all, if he left it would be like splitting up the Three Musketeers.

Soon the bell was ringing to signal the start of afternoon lessons and the three of us had to climb down from the roof of the bike shed. We had to be careful not to be spotted by Froggy Philips, the master on duty that day.

Later that afternoon I was walking home when I spotted a couple of girls in front of me. They were wearing the uniform of St Helena's school and even though they had their backs turned to me I could tell from the blonde hair and long legs that one of them was the vision of loveliness. It was the girl I was destined to marry. I knew I had to get her attention. But how should I do it?

Then I had an idea. I ran up to her and grabbed her beret and ran off with it. Looking back it was a stupid thing to do and I don't know what possessed me.

All I know was that after about ten yards I stopped and looked back at her. She was sobbing and I felt really bad about what I'd just done. What on earth had I been thinking?

I slowly walked back to her with my arm outstretched, her beret in my hand. She stopped crying and took it back from me. I was just about to apologise to her when all of a sudden I was doubled up in pain.

She'd kneed me in the nuts and as a result I was in complete agony.

"Serves you right you stupid little prat," she said to me as I writhed on the floor holding my balls.

"Hey Sarah, I didn't know he was a ballet dancer," said the friend. "What's he performing down there? Is it the dying swan?

"More like the Nutcracker Suite," she replied.

They both started laughing and with that the two of them walked off leaving me to reconsider my technique for gaining her attention in future.

Still at least I'd learnt what her name was.

# Chapter 6

"Which pile do you think it should go on?" asked Molly.

"Well, I doubt if the charity shop would have any use for it," Nigel replied. "After all St Helena's school is now the Chesterfield Campus of Derby University. So it's either the recycling centre or the auction house."

"Perhaps the auction house can put it into a job lot with the Grammar School uniform," Molly suggested.

Nigel was grateful for her idea, as he really didn't want to throw the beret into one of the black bags destined for the recycling centre. Instead he took it into the living room and placed it on top of his uncle's school blazer.

The first bedroom was now completely cleared out except for the furniture. So the two of them decided to stop for the day.

It occurred to them that they hadn't chosen which charity they were going to give all the stuff to. But after a brief discussion they plumped for the local hospice, which had a collection point on the other side of town. With that decided they loaded the car up with boxes of crockery and cutlery and black bags full of clothes and bedding.

When they arrived at the industrial estate where the hospice store was located, they were pleased to discover that they also took bigger items and would even collect them from people's houses. They made a mental note to contact them regarding the larger items of furniture.

That done, they set off back to Ashbourne for a well-deserved meal and a glass of wine.

The next day they were back at their uncle's house by 9.30 in the morning, vowing to complete clearing out the house that day. That would then leave the following day to arrange for the collection of the furniture and to tackle the attic, shed and garage.

First they started in the second bedroom. It hadn't been used for years but that didn't mean that it was less of a task. In fact, there was far more rubbish in this room than there had been in the first bedroom as it seemed that Uncle Miles had used it as storage. The wardrobe and the two chests of drawers in the room were packed full of things from his past, things that hadn't seen the light of day for years.

There were yet more coins as well as postcards, thank you letters written by Nigel and Emma when they were children, and birthday cards dating back to the 1950s. In addition, there were newspaper cuttings, certificates, photographs and much more.

"Did he ever throw anything away?" asked Molly. "Or did he merely put it all in this room?"

Most of the stuff was pure junk destined for the recycling centre, but shortly after they started sorting it out, Nigel discovered some old medals and a silver hipflask in a drawer.

*******

In June 1943, Rupert left school after completing his higher school certificate. The plan had always been for him to go to university and then into the family business. The war changed all that and instead he went straight to Sandhurst and six months later he was a lieutenant commanding a unit of 46 men in Italy. I was so proud of him, he looked so grownup in his uniform.

I will always remember the day he left. Father was more worried about him than Mother was. I guess that was because of what he had experienced during the Great War. He gave Rupert a silver hipflask that his father had given to him when he'd first gone to the front in 1916. It was a battered old thing, but Father insisted that it was his lucky charm and he believed it had kept him safe during the various battles he'd fought in.

"Always keep it in your breast pocket, son," Father said to him. "It will keep you safe from sniper fire. It's made from heavy gauge silver, strong enough to stop a bullet."

Rupert had never been much of a writer, preferring sport and the sciences when he was at school. But he wrote to us every week whilst he was in Italy until one day the letters stopped.

Two weeks later I heard Mother break down in uncontrollable floods of tears. I rushed to find out what had happened only to find that she'd received a telegram from the war office. Rupert had been killed at Monte Cassino.

Father didn't say anything, he just went to his study and smoked his pipe. Later that evening as I laid in bed I could hear him sobbing his heart out. I cuddled up to Edward and clutched my old school blazer to my chest. It didn't fit me any more and Mother had bought me a new one the previous August. Of course my original blazer had first belonged to Rupert. It still had his ink stain on the pocket where his inkbottle once leaked and more importantly it still smelt of him. I started crying as well as I vowed that I would keep Rupert's blazer forever.

Later we discovered that Rupert had died whilst charging a German pillbox armed only with a wooden gun. Father was disgusted.

"It wasn't even as though he had something to protect himself with," he said when he found out. Then looking at me he added, "Miles, it's all down to you now, son. The future of the company is in your hands."

Eventually the army sent Rupert's possessions back to us. There wasn't much. There were his dog tags, his razor and the letters that Mother had sent to him. There was also the hipflask. It may have kept Father safe back in 1918 but its value as a good luck charm appeared to have ended with the end of the Great War.

Rupert is buried in Monte Cassino War Cemetery along with 4,000 other Commonwealth soldiers who gave their lives during the Italian Campaign. One day when I am older I hope to go and visit his grave.

Father says that he won't ever go because he doesn't like pasta. But the real reason is because he'd be too upset.

Father had always been proud of his medals and always wore them at army reunions and on Armistice Day. After Rupert's death, however, he threw them into a drawer along with the failed good luck charm. He never wore the medals again and I never saw them or the hipflask until I rediscovered them whilst clearing out his study after his death.

# Chapter 7

"These must be granddad's medals," commented Nigel. "I'd heard he'd won the DSO but I've never seen his medals before."

"They must be worth quite a bit and to think that they were just thrown into a drawer," replied Molly.

"I think that it is going to be very difficult for me to send these to auction," Nigel continued. "They are part of our family history after all."

Despite this they decided to place them on the auction pile. This made sense since it would be from this pile that he and Emma would eventually choose the things they were going to keep.

"What about the battered old hipflask?" asked Molly.

"Well it's hallmarked, so it's silver. I doubt if anyone will want to use it as a hipflask anymore, but it'll be worth quite a bit as scrap," and with that Nigel added it to the auction pile.

They carried on drawer by drawer sorting things out. One of the drawers contained a thick pile of papers, documents, old letters, Aunt Sarah's ballet certificates from when she'd been a young girl, notebooks containing homework, and a ticket for a school dance dated December 1944.

"Now I wonder why he kept this," said a bemused Nigel.

*******

In October 1944, my grandfather passed away, which meant that Father was now company Chairman as well as Managing Director. Granny moved in with us taking Rupert's old room and we sold their house in Spencer Street in order to pay the death duties.

Grandfather had been a fine Victorian gentleman born in 1865. He was the second generation of Goodyears to run the company, being the son of Benjamin Goodyear who had founded the brewery back in 1862.

I had never been that close to my grandfather. He was of that generation who believed that children should be seen and not heard. He was also of the opinion that the world started to go downhill with the invention of the internal combustion engine. In fact, our brewery was the last of the three in Chesterfield to introduce lorries thanks to his intransigence.

"The horse-drawn dray is the best way to distribute beer," he used to say. "The slow speed of the horse helps to preserve the flavour of the ale. It's far better than shaking it all to kingdom come on the back of a lorry travelling at speed. Also it helps keep beer local, since with a horse-drawn dray you can't deliver to any pubs that are more than ten miles from the brewery. Who knows where we'll get to by using lorries? We'll probably end up with the whole country getting their beer from one big brewery in Burton-upon-Trent."

In many ways Grandfather was eventually proven right. However, that didn't stop Father from introducing lorries as soon as he became Managing Director in 1930.

A month before he died my grandfather asked if he could see me. It was a surprise as the two of us had never had a conversation in private before. He was suffering from lung cancer and must have realised that he didn't have long to live.

"Miles," he said to me, "I've almost run my race."

"Don't be silly, Grandfather," I replied. "You've got years left yet."

"If only that were true," he continued with tears in his eyes. "I know you were the spare rather than the heir. But with Rupert's death, the future of the company is now in your hands and I wanted to tell you that I have total confidence in you. Do you know why?"

I shook my head.

"It's because you're a Goodyear. It doesn't matter that you weren't the first-born or that you were never destined to run the company. You are my grandson and you have the Goodyear will to succeed. When my father founded the company everybody said that he'd be bankrupt within a year. After all, when he bought the brewery it had already gone into liquidation on two previous occasions. My father had absolutely no experience of brewing. He was a carpenter by trade and he kept his carpentry tools just in case he ever needed to go back to his old profession. Later on though they served to remind him of his humble beginnings and of the life he'd left behind, the life he never wanted to go back to again. He presented them to me on my 21st birthday and now I want to give them to you. I'd originally planned to give them to your father, but I've spoken to him and he's happy for me to pass them on to you. Think of it as a symbol of my confidence in you, Miles."

With that he presented me with the fitted case full of my great-grandfather's tools.

"Look after them, Miles, and promise me that you will pass them on to your son or grandson in due course."

I promised him that I would do just that and took the case full of tools back to my room where I stored them under my bed. It was the last time I ever saw the old man alive.

I was a lot closer to my grandmother than I ever was to my grandfather, even though she was a little batty. She used to call me Yards when I was little, saying that she wouldn't call me Miles because I wasn't big enough yet. She used to buy me Old Fashioned Humbugs and Pear Drops from the local sweet shop and then eat most of them herself.

I liked Granny, but that still didn't stop me from resenting her when she moved into Rupert's room. I knew that he was never going to come home again, but that was no excuse for not keeping his room just as it had been before he went to war. The wallpaper he had chosen, the one with racing cars on it, was replaced with paper with pink roses on it, and all his toys, including his Hornby train set, were put in the attic.

However, family matters were the last things on my mind as I was about to start sixth form. I was far more concerned whether my friend Sprout would be allowed to continue at the Grammar School or not. It wouldn't be the same if there were just Herman and I from now on.

I was fearing the worst, but my fears proved to be unfounded as all three of us returned to the upper school in September 1944.

I liked being a sixth former. You got to wear a sixth form tie rather than a house tie and you didn't have to go outside during break time. Instead we patrolled the corridors wearing our house prefects' badges looking for any members of the lower school trying to escape from the cold outside. They were unceremoniously thrown out whenever we caught them.

Of course, our newfound powers meant that we no longer had time to climb onto the roof of the bike shed in order to grab a fleeting glance at the high school girls in their gym kits. But we didn't mind because now we were allowed to mix with the girls, albeit only at organised social occasions and even then only when teachers were present. The first of these events was the joint grammar schools' Christmas dance in December 1944.

Sprout, Herman and I were looking forward to this major social occasion although none of us knew how to dance. I was so keen to learn that I even let my sister give me a few lessons. Under normal circumstances I wouldn't have let her teach me anything. But she was quite good at dancing, having been to dance classes in the Market Hall. I needed to impress the girls and stand out from the other boys. So I thought, what the heck, and let her have a go at teaching me.

As it turned out my sister was not a very good teacher. The classes in the Market Hall didn't have many boys in them and as a consequence she had always danced the male role. This meant that whilst she was excellent at dancing with other girls she was absolutely useless at dancing with boys.

Still it didn't really matter as the school had arranged for a dance practice to take place on the Thursday before the ball. This was great news for us boys as it meant that we now had two opportunities to grope members of the opposite sex rather than just the one.

The night of the practice was a terrifying affair for those of us who'd never been to a dance before. We all huddled together in one corner of the school hall, nervously cracking jokes and wondering which girls we would get to dance with.

Finally the girls arrived, accompanied by three teachers who were there to protect them from any inappropriate touching.

Most of the girls knew how to dance and were under instructions to teach the boys. None of us had a clue what to do, including myself, despite my sister's best intentions.

"Right everybody," said one of the mistresses from St Helena's who I later discovered was called Miss Goodwin.

She looked like a real dragon, dressed in a tweed twinset and a pair of horn-rimmed spectacles, which hung from a chain around her neck.

"God," I whispered under my breath, "and I thought Ratty Owen, the chemistry master was scary, but he looks like a pussy cat compared to her."

"The first thing you need to know about a dance," she continued, "is that you gentlemen, and I use that expression loosely, have to ask a lady to dance. Do not merely hang around in groups discussing the latest cricket scores otherwise nothing will happen. Please remember that you have to ask them. They will not ask you."

I wanted to tell her that we were unlikely to be discussing cricket in the first week of December. But I had no desire to feel the wrath of her tongue and so I decided to keep quiet about it. However, I had taken her point on board.

"Well get on with it then," she shouted at us.

With that we all began to saunter over towards the girls who were standing on the other side of the hall. I'd already spotted Sarah and was determined to ask her to dance. It was three years since the unfortunate incident with the beret and although I'd seen her a few times since, I'd been too embarrassed to talk to her.

Tonight was the night this was going to change. I made my way over to her, eagerly anticipating holding her close, her heaving bosom pressed tightly to my chest.

"Faint heart never won fair maiden," I said to myself as I approached her. "After all she's probably forgotten all about my clumsy actions when I was fourteen."

"Please may I have the pleasure of this dance?" I asked her.

It was a line I'd been practicing since I'd seen Greer

Garson and Laurence Olivier in *Pride and Prejudice* at the Regal. Her reply was brief and to the point.

"No," she said.

It wasn't the reply I'd been expecting and I was dumbfounded. To make matters worse, Sprout unceremoniously pushed me aside and asked her to dance.

She looked at me, shrugged and said to Sprout, "Okay, then! Why not?"

It wasn't fair! I'd been looking forward to dancing with Sarah for weeks.

The problem was that I had no alternative plan.

As there were more boys than girls it was soon clear that I would be left without a partner; not even a fat girl or a girl with acne, or even a fat girl with acne.

To make matters worse Miss Goodwin came up to me and asked, "Haven't you got a partner, boy? What? Are you too scared to ask? Never mind, you can dance with me."

I wanted to shout out, "Nooooooo!" But I knew that would do no good and so I just prepared myself to be humiliated.

The first dance was a waltz and we were dancing to a band drawn from the two schools. They obviously had never played together before as they kept on making mistakes, which didn't endear them to Miss Goodwin. She kept on shouting out one, two, three, whenever they lost the beat.

That wasn't all she shouted out as we waltzed across the dance floor.

"Boy, your hand is supposed to be just below her shoulder blade not on her backside," was one of many comments she made as we stumbled across the floor. She was far more interested in spotting the transgressions of others than she was in teaching me to dance.

My friends all thought that it was highly amusing and I could see them laughing at me over Miss Goodwin's shoulder. Sprout and Sarah thought it was particularly funny and I could see them giggling every time we danced passed them.

At the end of the first waltz, Miss Goodwin announced that we should keep the same partners for the rest of the night being as though this was only a practice. I was absolutely horrified but in no position to object.

We danced the quickstep and the foxtrot and although I say it myself I was beginning to get the hang of it. My sister's efforts had not been in vain after all. That was not the case for Sprout though who kept on treading on Sarah's feet. You could see she was getting more and more annoyed with him as the night went on.

Finally, after what seemed like an eternity, the night was over and we headed for home.

"I didn't know it was grab a granny night," said Sprout as we walked down Glumangate. "Have you arranged to see her again? It's a match made in heaven, she won't even need to change her initials when the two of you get married."

"Bugger off," I replied still annoyed with the events of that evening.

I was virtually home by that stage and as a result my suffering for that day was nearly at an end. However, it came as no surprise that the micky-taking by my classmates was to continue unabated right until the Christmas break.

When the night of the actual dance came around it was a grand affair. We were wearing suits rather than school uniforms. Some of us were even wearing dinner suits. All the girls were wearing their best evening dresses. They looked so grown up, totally unrecognisable from the girls in school uniforms of the previous week.

The hall was decorated ready for Christmas and the school had even rented a glitter ball for the night.

Unlike at the practice, we now had the opportunity to ask as many girls for a dance as we wanted and I was determined to make the most of it. That said I had no desire to be the first on the floor and so I held back to see what the others did.

Everybody else had the same idea, but fortunately the teachers had a plan in order to counter such an eventuality. Froggy Philips and Miss Goodwin were the first on the floor, closely followed by some of the other teachers. The effect was similar to a cork being let out of a bottle, as pretty soon the dance floor was full.

I wanted to join in, but there was no way that I was going to ask Sarah again so I asked Margaret Bishop, a girl with mousy hair, glasses and a tooth brace. There was absolutely no chance that Margaret would refuse to dance with me as two days earlier her friend Olivia had approached me outside the school gate and had said to me, "Miles Goodyear, this is your lucky day because my mate fancies you."

At the time I was quite flattered until I saw what her mate looked like. Still, beggars can't be choosers and the two of us were soon doing the quickstep together. She didn't even mind that my right hand had slipped down and was grabbing her arse. Well, that was until Miss Goodwin danced past us and slapped my wrist without even breaking stride.

Looking around I noticed that Sprout looked crestfallen as it had been his turn to be rejected by Sarah this time. It seemed that she had no desire to have her feet trampled on again.

However, he quickly put his disappointment behind him as he found himself another partner in Georgina Nicholls, a plain girl with lank ginger hair. Meanwhile Herman was dancing with the Amazonian girl with the big tits that he had spotted three years earlier from the roof of the bike shed.

"Bloody hell," I thought to myself, "He must fancy her after all. I assumed he was only joking when he said he was going to marry her."

At the end of the first dance, I thanked Margaret and decided to sit the next one out. She was obviously disappointed, hoping that we might have continued and perhaps even gone on to become boyfriend and girlfriend. But I wasn't interested and I went and stood by myself watching Sprout and Herman.

Suddenly, I felt a tap on my shoulder.

"Would you like to dance?"

I turned around and to my amazement I saw Sarah was standing next to me.

"I thought that I was supposed to ask you," I replied.

"It's the 1940s not the 1840s," she replied. "We women can do whatever we like nowadays."

Then she whispered, "Don't tell anyone but we've even got the vote these days."

Not that Sarah had the vote, of course, she was only sixteen.

I took her hand and we set off on a foxtrot across the dance floor.

"So what's changed your mind since the dance practice?" I whispered in her ear.

"Oh, that was just to pay you back for pinching my beret," she replied.

"Bloody hell," I continued, "that was three years ago. Anyway I seem to remember that you more than paid me back that same day."

She merely smiled before saying, "I'd forgotten about that. I do hope that everything is still in working order."

I was in seventh heaven and the evening went past in a whirl. Even the band seemed a lot better, although to be fair they had improved quite a lot since the dance practice.

I didn't dance with anybody else that night and when it was all over we wandered outside together. Sprout and Georgina were standing against the bike shed and Sprout looked as though he was enjoying himself as Georgina was eating his face.

"Shall I walk you home?" I asked.

"No, my dad will be waiting for me," Sarah replied. "He said he'd come and get me as I'm not normally allowed out this late and he wanted to make sure I got home all right."

Naturally I was disappointed but undeterred I said, "Would you like to go to the pictures with me tomorrow evening?"

"Sure," she replied. "What's on?"

I told her that I didn't care what the film was and suggested that we meet at the Odeon at half past six. She told me that was okay, after which she kissed me on the lips before disappearing out of the school gates where her father was waiting for her. I was the happiest man alive although strictly speaking at seventeen years of age I wasn't really a man yet.

On the way home Sprout, Herman and I compared notes.

"She's got the sweetest kiss in the whole world," I told them.

"Well, Georgina's taught me what a French kiss is," said Sprout.

Both Herman and I looked at him speechless. Neither of us wanted to admit that we didn't know what a French kiss was.

Eventually Herman, who was very keen to find out, asked, "Is it something to do with a French letter?"

Sprout and I both started laughing.

"No, you idiot," said Sprout. "It's when you kiss with open mouths and touch tongues."

"Oh," said Herman. "Anyway I can do better than that as June let me feel her jugs."

I presumed that June was the name of the Amazonian girl that Herman had been dancing with all night.

"I'm surprised you could reach them," joked Sprout, referring to the fact that she was at least two inches taller than Herman. "Anyway I bet you didn't feel her jugs, I bet you didn't even kiss her."

"I did so and they were lovely and firm just like a pair of melons."

"Okay," said Sprout. "Did you feel them inside or outside her bra?"

"Outside of course. It was only a first date. But we've agreed to go on another. We're going for a walk through Walton Woods on Sunday."

"Oooh," said Sprout and I in unison.

"Anyway what about you two?" asked Herman. "Are you seeing your girls again?"

"We're going to the pictures on Saturday," I replied.

It turned out that Sprout had been in so much of a daze that he had forgotten to ask Georgina for a date. But fortunately he knew where she lived, so he said he was going to go around to see her as soon as Saturday morning classes had finished.

"I'll ask her if she wants to go to the cinema as well," he said before adding. "Hey perhaps we can make up a foursome?"

"No way," I replied. "I want to be with Sarah by myself. If you want to go to the cinema you can go to the Regal. I don't want to see you grinning at me."

"I don't think I'll have much time for that," said Sprout with a wink.

With that the three of us split up and went our separate ways.

Back in my bedroom I emptied my pockets and hung up my dinner jacket. As well as my hanky and some loose change there was the ticket for that night's dance. I went to throw it in the bin but then had second thoughts. It had been the best day of my life so far. Sarah had kissed me and I was going on a date with her tomorrow. Today was a day that I would always remember, but just in case I ever forgot, I decided to keep the ticket as a memento.

So I opened one of my drawers and put the ticket safely inside. I went to bed with a smile on my face and only one thing on my mind and that was Sarah.

# Chapter 8

"It was probably of great sentimental value to him," said Molly. "But it doesn't mean anything to us. It will have to go in the bin liner I'm afraid."

Nigel looked at the ticket for a few seconds before placing it with all the other rubbish.

"Cup of tea?" asked Molly.

"Yes please," replied Nigel and whilst Molly went downstairs to put the kettle on he continued to look through the drawers.

When she came back up again she found Nigel holding a large bunch of keys.

"Look what I've found," he announced. "The keys to Goodyear's Brewery."

"They'd be really useful if it wasn't for the fact that the brewery was demolished in 1968," she replied. "Still, I'm sure that we'll discover plenty more old brewery stuff when we look downstairs. You'd better put them on the auction pile."

*******

The film we went to see was a love story starring Margaret Lockwood and Stewart Grainger. Normally I wouldn't even have given it a second glance, as it was a real tear-jerker. Sarah seemed to like it though, well the bits she saw of it in between bouts of snogging.

This time I did walk her home and we kissed again in the gennel between her house and their next-door neighbours before we parted. It was now official, Sarah was my girlfriend.

I'd agreed to meet Sprout after saying goodbye to Sarah so that we could compare notes. It seemed that he didn't even know the name of the film they'd been to see. They'd sat in the back row in the double seats and spent the whole time playing tonsil hockey, apart from during the intermission when they'd shared an ice cream tub.

The Odeon didn't have double seats and so I made a mental note to take Sarah to the Regal next time.

Then our conversation turned to Herman.

"Do you really think he felt her breasts?" I asked.

"Do I buggery," replied Sprout.

We decided that the only way we were going to resolve this issue was to confront him with it the next day. Which is why at lunchtime on Sunday, Sprout and I were sitting on the wall opposite Herman's house.

We didn't have long to wait before Herman appeared, looking very smart in his Sunday best.

"Hey Herman," shouted Sprout. "Are you going to feel some more titty this afternoon?"

We then started singing 'Thanks for the Memory,' a 1938 hit sung by Bob Hope, except that we changed the words and sang 'Thanks for the Mammary' instead.

"Ho ho, very funny," said Herman as he walked across the street to us.

"So, where are you going to take her?" asked Sprout.

"You know full well that we are going to go for a walk through Walton Woods," he replied.

"And after that?" asked Sprout.

"Well, I thought I might take her to see my dad's allotment."

Sprout and I couldn't contain ourselves.

"You old romantic, Herman. You certainly know how to make a girl swoon. Are you going to show her your dad's turnips?"

"That's not why I'm taking her there," said Herman. "Very few people go to the allotments in winter and I've taken the key to my dad's shed."

"So it's romance amongst the potato sacks then?" I added.

Herman just ignored me and headed off for his date.

"Why don't we hide out on the allotments?" suggested Sprout. "After all, we can then prove one way or another whether he's been able to feel her breasts."

I wasn't so sure if it was a good idea or not, but decided to go along with it anyway.

Shortly after three o'clock, Herman and June appeared arm in arm and disappeared into the shed. Sprout and I were hiding behind a nearby water-butt giggling like silly little schoolgirls.

We gave them a quarter of an hour and then wandered over to look through the window. To our surprise, Herman wasn't just fondling June's breasts. He was fondling her naked beasts having removed her jumper and bra. This was no mean feat considering that the temperature that day was barely above freezing. She must have been really cold without her top on.

"Fair play to old Herman," said Sprout. "I will never doubt him again. Look at her nipples sticking out. They're just like the wheel nuts on my dad's Bedford truck."

"Her breasts are absolutely magnificent," I added. "They remind me of a dead heat in a Zeppelin race."

The two of us started giggling again, which caused June to look up and notice our two faces looking through the window. She let out an almighty scream and, realising we'd been rumbled, the two of us decided to leg it.

Of course she'd recognised us and knew we were Herman's friends. As a result poor old Herman got the blame. It was the end of a short but passionate affair, as she didn't want anything to do with him after that.

Herman quite rightly blamed the two of us for ending his relationship with June and he refused to speak to us throughout the whole of the last week of term. Fortunately, by the time we went back in January, he'd forgiven us and we were able to reconvene again as the Three Musketeers. But things weren't quite the same as they'd been before. Sprout and I both had girlfriends whereas Herman did not.

It was now 1945, which turned out to be a major year in my young life. Most importantly, the war ended, which was greeted with wild celebrations throughout the land. In addition, it was the year I turned eighteen.

Victory in the war against Hitler did not mean that everything returned to pre-war normality. Far from it. Some things would never be the same. For a start, my parents never replaced Evans. From now on the only help my mother received was from Mrs Charlesworth, our new cleaning lady, who came in three days a week.

Chesterfield had emerged virtually unscathed from the war, unlike Sheffield twelve miles to the north. However, rationing was still in force and would be for several years to come. Also, many of the servicemen who'd been called up were yet to return home. Times were hard and the brewery, which had been starved of investment during the war years, was struggling to make a profit.

At least by turning eighteen I could now do my bit to help our beer sales, as I could finally buy a drink in a pub. Of course, many of my friends had already been served whilst under age, but this was where being the son of a local brewery owner was a major disadvantage. I was known in all the Goodyear's pubs and Father would have killed me if I'd set foot in one of our competitors' outlets.

Therefore, it came as a blessed relief to reach the age of eighteen. Who cared that I still couldn't vote for another three years? It was far more important that I could now enjoy a pint of Goodyear's Pride in the Market Tavern.

On the day of my birthday, Father took me on a pub crawl around town. We didn't get very far though. By the time I was halfway through my fourth pint, I had to rush into the toilet to throw up. Father promptly took me home and I was fast asleep in bed by half past eight. I woke up at five o'clock the following morning with a throbbing head and the room spinning around.

"Why do people drink when it makes them feel like this?" I asked myself.

It was my first ever hangover, the first of many in the years that followed.

It was also on my eighteenth birthday that Father presented me with a set of keys to the brewery. I wasn't allowed to have a key to the house until I was 21, but I was considered mature enough to be given keys to the family business at the tender age of eighteen.

It was more out of pragmatism than anything else. For by that stage I was working in the brewhouse during the holidays. This involved getting in early to help Mr Jones, the head brewer, start the brew off. The title 'head brewer' was an interesting one since Mr Jones was the only brewer, except for one pupil brewer and myself.

The Holiday Pay Act of 1938 had made all employers provide paid holidays for their employees. As a result, there was just Mr Jones and myself doing the brewing at the end of August, because Stuart Datcheler, the pupil brewer, was enjoying a week's holiday at Butlin's in Skegness.

Everybody used to drink at work back in those days. It was one of the perks of being a brewery worker. Some used to drink more than others and Mr Jones used to drink more than anybody else. He saw it as his duty to consume large quantities of the beer he brewed. It was his way of giving it his seal of approval.

Unfortunately, on one particular day, he'd consumed even more than usual and failed to get up the following morning in order to start the brew off.

I arrived at the brewery only to find that I'd been locked out. By eight o'clock other employees had started to arrive and they couldn't get in either. So I went to the phone box across the road and phoned Father, who turned up a few minutes later looking absolutely furious.

Mr Jones was reprimanded but not sacked. After all, qualified brewers were not easy to find back in 1945. But that incident was behind Father's decision to give me a set of keys. Of course, once school started again, I was back to working Wednesday and Saturday afternoons, so I wouldn't have the opportunity to use them until the Christmas break. But giving me the keys was a major act of faith by my father and I appreciated the confidence that he was showing in me.

By now I'd been going out with Sarah for ten months and we saw each other often. We went to the cinema and the Victoria ballroom together and for walks in the countryside around Chesterfield. Sometimes we'd make up a foursome with Sprout and Georgina. Georgina's nickname was Carrot on account of her red hair, which I thought was highly amusing being as though she was going out with Sprout.

"All you need is roast beef, Yorkshire pudding, potatoes and gravy and you've got a full Sunday lunch," I said to him, but he didn't find it funny.

Herman, of course, didn't have a girlfriend following the

incident at the allotments. But sometimes he would make up the group along with Lydia, Sarah's friend who'd been with her when she'd hit me in the balls. Lydia had short hair, glasses and a flat chest. She looked like a man in a skirt, not Herman's type at all and it was obvious that he wasn't hers either. Still it meant that neither of them were left out.

The trouble with being a teenager in the 1940s was that there was nowhere to do our courting. Okay, Sarah and I could have a snog in the cinema and in the darkness of the gennel alongside her parents' house. Mind you, we ran the risk of being interrupted by Mrs Lock, her next-door neighbour. But there wasn't anywhere where we could be alone in private. I'd passed my driving test the previous May, but that proved to be a false dawn. Father wouldn't let me drive the Alvis, his pride and joy, unless he sat next to me.

Sprout was far more fortunate as he and Carrot had access to the storeroom at the back of one of his father's shops. The rumour around the school was that they had been the first couple to actually do it. I confronted Sprout about this and he flatly denied it. However, he was given away by the fact that he was now getting his hair cut once a week, which Herman and I both thought was a bit excessive. A few days later I happened to be in the barbers at the same time as Sprout and I witnessed the barber asking him if he wanted something for the weekend. It seemed the reason he was getting his hair cut so often was so that he could buy packs of French letters.

"Bloody hell," I said to him. "I thought when the barber asked if you wanted anything for the weekend he was just trying to sell you some Brylcreem."

Sprout made me swear not to tell anybody and I didn't, except for Herman. As a result, the story was all over both schools by the end of the following week. Of course,

Sprout's reputation was greatly enhanced, whereas Carrot's reputation was shot to bits. Women may have got the vote but they still had a long way to go in the sexual equality stakes back in 1945.

Now that I had the keys to the brewery, we had the opportunity to emulate Sprout and Carrot. Sarah and I finally had somewhere where we could be alone together.

The first time we snuck in was after watching a play at the Civic Theatre. I let us in using the keys I'd been given and we made our way to the hop store. I had already worked out that it was the best place for some late night canoodling. It was warm and the hopsacks provided an ideal makeshift bed for us to lie on.

We immediately got down to some serious snogging. I'd progressed before to feeling Sarah's breasts over her jumper. On one occasion, I'd even got my hand inside her blouse until Mrs Lock interrupted us whilst putting out her dustbin.

This time there was to be no interruption and I undid her blouse. Then I decided to push my luck and put my hand inside her bra and was amazed that she actually let me.

"Can I take it off?" I asked as I felt her nipple stiffening.

She nodded and I didn't need a second invitation as I removed her blouse and went around her back and tried to unfasten her bra. I couldn't get it undone though and in the end she had to undo it for me.

"If my life ends now I will die a happy man," I thought to myself as I looked at her perfectly formed breasts and her pink nipples.

"Why stop there?" I thought as I put my hand up her skirt.

"No you don't," came the firm response as she grabbed my hand and removed it.

"But Sprout and Carrot have gone all the way," I pleaded.

Before I could finish Sarah cut in.

"I'm not Carrot," she said. "I don't believe in sex before marriage."

I thought that was going to be it for the day, but pretty soon we were snogging again and I was fondling her breasts.

She could tell I was disappointed but soon all my disappointment vanished as she reached down and unzipped my fly. I already had an erection and was extremely grateful that she'd released my dick from its confinement.

We continued for several minutes, passionately snogging. I stroked her breasts and she rubbed my cock. Then something happened. Suddenly my cock began to shudder and I immediately grabbed hold of Sarah's hand in order to stop her from rubbing it. To my amazement it was all wet and sticky.

"Don't worry," she said. "You've only ejaculated."

"Ewhatulated?" I asked in horror.

Sarah started laughing.

"My poor little innocent," she said.

Sarah and I returned to the hop store many times over the coming months. It was fantastic, although she never let me get inside her knickers.

Nevertheless, it was another step on my journey towards manhood. They say you never forget the first time you have sex. Well, it wasn't actual intercourse that we had that night, but I will never forget it all the same.

# Chapter 9

"I don't think we will finish clearing out the house today," said Molly.

They had been working for two hours and were still nowhere near finished emptying the second bedroom. The problem was that there was just so much to sort out. Okay, most of it was junk, but they still had to examine everything just in case they missed something of value.

Just as in the main bedroom, the second bedroom contained two chests of drawers. The difference was that none of the drawers in the second bedroom contained clothes or bedding. Instead, they all contained a variety of papers and objects that Uncle Miles had accumulated over his long lifetime.

Not only that, but there was a wardrobe that was also filled with similar items. The wardrobe had the letters M and S carved on the front.

"That must stand for Miles and Sarah," commented Nigel. "From its style it looks like it was made in the 1950s. I wouldn't be surprised if it was a wedding present."

With that the two of them went back to the task of sorting through their uncle's things.

It was when Nigel and Molly were halfway through clearing out the second chest of drawers that Nigel discovered an RAF cap badge.

"Do you think this is worth anything?" he asked, holding it up to the light.

"Probably not," came the reply, "although we might find more militaria later."

\*\*\*\*\*\*\*

It was June 1946 and the three of us had just finished school after taking our higher national certificates. Under normal circumstances, Sprout and Herman would have gone to work for their fathers and I would have spent all summer in the brewery before heading off to university.

But these were not normal times. World War ll had only ended twelve months previously and all eighteen year olds were expected to do their National Service.

I could have gotten out of it if I'd decided to go and work down the pit, but I had no desire to do that. Alternatively, I could have trained to become a doctor, but I hated the sight of blood. I briefly considered pretending to be mad before eventually bowing to the inevitable. After all, how bad could it be? Britain wasn't at war anymore so it wasn't as if I was likely to get killed.

Father said that he could have a word with his old regiment and get me a commission, but I told him that I had no desire to make a career out of the army. I merely wanted to serve my eighteen months and then get out, which is why I signed up for the RAF.

This was quite normal for boys who'd been to the Grammar School. The RAF attracted a better class of recruit than the army, which was full of rough sorts from council estates. In fact, it turned out that most of my class had enrolled in the air force, including Sprout and Herman.

I knew the odds were stacked against me being stationed at the same base as anybody I knew. So imagine my surprise when both Sprout and I were posted to RAF Spitalgate in Lincolnshire. Herman wasn't so lucky though as he was sent to RAF St Mawgan in Cornwall. It was a nice place if you were on holiday, but not if you were doing your National Service, especially since it was an eight-hour train journey from Chesterfield.

Herman looked pretty dejected as the three of us met for a drink on the Saturday before we were due to start our RAF training.

"You know Sarah said something really odd to me the other day," I announced whilst supping my pint of Goodyear's Pride. "She said that being apart was a real test of our relationship. She also added that she would wait for me, but if I wanted to sow some wild oats whilst I was away, then it was okay. Just as long as I kept quiet about it and returned to her once my National Service was complete."

"Bloody hell," said Sprout. "Carrot would cut my balls off if I messed around with another woman." Then he added, "What about you and Lydia, Herman?"

It was just a wind up since Herman was not at all romantically involved with Lydia. It had the desired effect though as Herman told us in no uncertain terms that he and Lydia were not an item.

We reflected on the fact that the girls were far luckier than us since female conscription had ended with the war. Carrot had a job as a trainee with a firm of chartered accountants on Saltergate. Lydia had joined the police as a WPC, which Herman said made her even scarier once she'd put on her uniform. Sarah, meanwhile, had enrolled at the new teacher training college in Matlock, which she went to every day on the bus.

It wasn't as if we'd never be allowed home whilst doing our military service. But despite this, we couldn't help thinking that we were starting an eighteen month prison sentence.

As a result it was with heavy hearts that Sprout and I caught the train to Grantham the following Monday morning.

Any ideas we may have had about learning to fly were soon dispelled when we arrived at the barracks. It appeared that we were going to spend the next year and a half scrubbing floors, cleaning toilets and learning how to march.

The worst thing about National Service was that no one had any privacy. There were sixteen of us all bunked down together in one large dormitory and even the showers weren't private. In fact, the only place where we could be alone was on the toilet and that was questionable due to badly fitting doors.

Many of my fellow recruits had come from other grammar schools around the country and Sprout and I soon became friends with Frank Johnson from Guildford and Richard Wells from Stockport. At least, there were four of us looking out for each other.

We were all under the watchful eye of Sergeant Dyke, or Dastardly Dyke as we christened him. He liked nothing more than to torment us ex-grammar school boys. He'd obviously been to a secondary modern himself and he was now able to get his revenge.

The first day we were there he shouted out,

"Right you bunch of namby-pamby grammar school boys. Your mummies aren't here to wipe your arses for you any more. There will be no one to tuck you into bed at night and read you a bedtime story. I am your mother now and, believe me, Snow White's wicked stepmother was an angel compared to me. Do I make myself clear?"

"Yes sergeant," we all replied in unison.

"Right," he said. "I am now going to inspect your beds."

One of the first things we had been told to do upon arrival was to make our beds and put our personal possessions into our bedside cabinets.

"That's not good enough aircraftman," said the sergeant as he ripped the bedding off the first recruit's bed. "I want to see square corners. What do I want to see?"

"Square corners, sir," came the reply from the serviceman who was visibly shaking.

"You do not refer to me as sir, aircraftman. I am not an officer. You refer to me as sergeant. Do I look as though I have too much Brylcreem in my hair? Do I have a plum in my mouth?"

"No sergeant," answered the terrified recruit.

"Well, there can be no mistaking me for an officer then, can there?"

The sergeant was barking all of this into the face of the frightened aircraftman who was only a few inches away. You could see the spittle flying into his eyes.

Sprout was next.

"That's a better effort," said Sergeant Dyke.

Sprout thought he was going to avoid a tongue-lashing from the sergeant, but his optimism was short-lived.

"Is that bum fluff I can see on your chin, aircraftman?"

Sprout didn't know what to say in reply, as he had no idea what bum fluff was. Fortunately he didn't have to wonder for long.

"I'm asking you aircraftman, if you've shaved this morning."

"No sergeant," replied Sprout.

"Well, you're in the RAF now lad," said Sergeant Dyke, "and in the RAF we shave in the morning not in the evening. Is that clear?"

"Yes sergeant," answered Sprout.

With that Sergeant Dyke moved on to the next recruit much to Sprout's relief. He didn't want to admit that he'd never shaved in his entire life until that point.

Soon it was my turn.

"What on earth is that, aircraftman?" said the sergeant who was pointing to Edward who was lying on my bed.

"It's my teddy bear, sergeant," I replied.

"And have you brought your dolls with you as well?" he asked. "Perhaps we could have a tea party for them later?"

"No sergeant, just Edward here. I've slept with him ever since I was little."

"Really?" replied sergeant Dyke. "Now let me tell you this, you little nancy boy. Sleeping with small furry animals may be normal where you come from, but it is not normal in the Royal Air Force. Get rid of it and report to me at six o'clock tomorrow morning for toilet cleaning duties."

"Yes sergeant," I replied and hurriedly placed Edward in my bedside cabinet.

As it turned out I wasn't the only person told to report for toilet cleaning duties. In total there were five of us who assembled outside the toilet block at 6 o'clock the next morning waiting for further instructions. We waited and waited until eventually Sergeant Dyke showed up at half past seven and gave us all mops and buckets. It was a harsh introduction to life in the RAF. However, things were to get even worse, as Edward was missing when I got back to the dormitory.

"Which one of you bastards has taken him?" I shouted out.

"I think he's gone absent without leave," replied the chap from the next bed.

I wanted to punch him in his stupid face. But I had no desire to find myself on a charge and so I let it rest. After all, I was confident that whoever had taken him would return him to me eventually. It never crossed my mind that it would be another fifty years before I got him back again.

Life in the RAF didn't get any better over the forthcoming weeks and months. I felt like a prisoner just counting down the days until my release.

After spending a year in Lincolnshire, we were eventually transferred to RAF Altona in Germany. It didn't make any difference to us where in the world we were stationed, as one RAF base was pretty much the same as every other one.

The only thing that altered when we were in Germany was that it was no longer possible for Sprout and I to return to Chesterfield during our leave. So we usually went into some of the towns and villages close to Hamburg instead.

Hamburg had been badly destroyed by allied bombing during the war and we were there in 1947, only two years after the war had ended. At the time, Hamburg was still under British control and we Brits were not popular with the locals. That was especially true for those of us in the RAF, since they blamed us for destroying their city. Personally, I thought it was a little harsh. For a start, I hadn't been old enough to fight in the war and, if they wanted to blame anyone, they should blame Adolf Hitler not us.

Irrespective of this, the fact was that Hamburg was still largely a pile of rubble and, as a result, we usually went to nearby Lüneburg instead. Its medieval centre was totally unscathed and there were plenty of good Bier Kellers to choose from.

It was on one such visit that Sprout, Frank, Richard and I started talking about our favourite subjects, girls and sex.

"So, who's still a virgin then?" asked Sprout.

It was an unfair question, since I knew that Sprout wasn't, whereas the closest that I had come to going all the way was being tossed off in the hop store by Sarah. If only the beer drinkers of Chesterfield knew what was putting the froth on their pints they'd have thought twice about downing a glass of Goodyear's Pride.

Eventually, Frank and Richard admitted that they had never been with a girl either. This came as no surprise to anyone as they were both nice lads, but no one would ever describe them as 'men of the world'.

I was forced to admit that I had never had sex either, which came as a bit of a shock for Sprout.

"But you've been going out with Sarah for nearly three years now," he said aghast. "What on earth do you get up to in that hop store of yours?"

"If you think that I'm going to give you a detailed description of what we do in there then you've got another thing coming," I replied.

"It doesn't sound to me as if there's been anything happening that's worth telling us about anyway," replied Sprout before asking if Sarah and I had ever done *soixante-neuf.*

"What's that?" asked Frank.

"*Soixante-neuf,* top and tail," said Sprout only to be met with blank expressions. It was obvious that neither Richard, Frank nor I knew what the hell he was on about.

"Never mind," he said "Because today is your lucky day, as I am going to pay for all three of you to have a jump."

"A what?" said Richard.

"A jump, a shag, a fuck," said Sprout before explaining. "Some of the other recruits have told me about a house of ill repute called the Eros Centre, which is just around the corner from where we are now."

Five minutes later we were standing outside the entrance. You would never have guessed that it was a brothel. It looked more like a private members' club, and since it was the type of place where you could get your member out in private, I guess that was precisely what it was. I was pretty nervous as we entered the whorehouse. Was I betraying Sarah? Was I even still going out with Sarah?

I'd assumed that the Eros Centre would have girls behind windows with red lights in the background. I couldn't have been more wrong. Instead, it consisted of a large room full of scantily clad women. There were no red lights and no glass to separate the girls from the customers. Much to the concern of Frank and Richard they came up to us and stroked our manhoods before grabbing our hands and placing them on their breasts.

"How much?" Sprout asked one of the girls who was wearing next to nothing.

"Fifty Marks," came the reply.

Sprout did a calculation in his head.

"That's about four bob."

"Right," he said passing a Fifty Mark note to the girl and pointing to Frank, "Take him upstairs."

With that she led Frank to one of the bedrooms.

Sprout pushed Richard forward and summoned over a large Brunhilde type who was wearing an outfit made of leather and covered in zips. She was extremely frightening especially since she had a cat-o'-nine-tails in one hand and a pair of nipple clamps dangling from her belt.

"I hope you are going to satisfy me, leetle man, othervise I am going to have to punish you," she announced and at the same time cracked her whip.

Sprout gave her Fifty Marks and told her to take Richard upstairs. Richard looked absolutely terrified. He was five foot four inches tall and only weighed nine stone sopping wet.

"She will eat him alive," I said.

"If he's lucky," Sprout replied.

"Anyway, what about you?" I asked Sprout. "Are you going to have a jump?"

"Good god no," came the reply. "I'm in a serious relationship with Georgina and I've asked her to marry me as soon as I get demobbed."

I was shocked and said, "But you're only twenty. You've got your whole life ahead of you. Why would you want to buy a cow when you can get your milk for free?"

"Life isn't just about sex, you know," he replied. "Granted, it's important. But I've got the best of all worlds with

Georgina. She's funny, she's intelligent, she's my best friend and I bet she's better than any of this lot between the sheets. She's the only girl for me and I'm going to spend the rest of my life with her."

I could tell there was no point in arguing with him so I merely said, "And I thought I was your best friend, Sprout?"

"You are, Crapper," he replied. "You are the best friend out of all of those that I'm not sleeping with."

"Very funny," I continued. "Anyway, what's with calling her Georgina, I thought only her parents called her that?"

"Carrot was all right when we were kids. But we're grown up now so I'm going to call her by her proper name from now on."

With that he signalled to one of the girls to come over, gave her Fifty Marks and ordered her to take me upstairs.

One of the other girls had noticed what Sprout was doing and thought that he was some kind of pervert who got his rocks off by paying for other men to have sex. So, she brought a guy over who didn't have enough cash on him and told Sprout to give him Fifty Marks. She then started to get angry when he refused, which we all thought was highly amusing when he told us about it later.

The girl I was with was athletic, with blue eyes and blonde hair, the epitome of Hitler's master race. She had a faraway look and I couldn't help but wonder what had happened to her during the war. Lüneburg seemed a million miles away from Hamburg and yet you could only guess what horrors this girl had experienced.

When we'd finished, we all went back to the bar we'd been in before.

"So, how was it?" asked Sprout.

"It was disappointing," said Frank. "She only gave me a hand shandy. I could have done that myself and spent the Fifty Marks on beer."

That caused Sprout to choke on his stein of Moravia Pils.

Richard admitted that the same thing had happened to him, although his large lady had allowed him to play with her breasts by way of a bonus. I confirmed that it had been the same for me.

"Didn't you ask them about their price list?" asked Sprout.

"What price list?" I replied.

"I only paid for the basic service," said Sprout. "If you wanted anything more you should have asked them for their price list."

"Bloody hell, Sprout," I replied. "You make them sound like hairdressers rather than prostitutes."

"But they are just like hairdressers," replied Sprout. "Hairdressers charge one price for a basic cut, but it's extra if you want a blow-dry. It's the same with the prossies. One price for a basic wank, but you have to pay extra if you want a blow job."

"But I did ask her," Richard protested. "When she took me up to her room I asked her what would she say to a little fuck?"

"And what did she reply to that?" asked Sprout.

"Hello, little fuck," Richard replied, which caused everyone to fall about in fits of laughter.

We didn't visit the Eros Centre again and a couple of months later we were back in the UK, our National Service over.

We had to hand our uniforms back, but the RAF let us keep them for a couple of weeks so that Sprout could get married in his.

I was his best man and the two of us looked really smart as we stood side by side waiting for Carrot and her father.

The reception at the Station Hotel was a modest affair as rationing was still at its height. My speech went down well and I got a few laughs when I suggested that, in a few years' time, Sprout and Carrot would have children called Leek and Cauliflower.

Then the couple set off on their honeymoon, five nights in Ilfracombe, before returning to Chesterfield where Sprout was going to manage his father's new shop in Sheffield Road. The shop had a flat above, so Sprout and Carrot had somewhere to live as well. It was also convenient for Carrot's job as a chartered accountant, although she gave this up soon afterwards as Sprout's father now had four shops and wanted her to work for him as his bookkeeper.

Shortly after the wedding, I gave my uniform back. National Service hadn't been the best eighteen months of my life and I had no desire to be reminded of it. In fact the only thing I kept was my cap badge, which I retained as my one souvenir from those days.

# Chapter 10

Nigel's phone started to ring. It was Emma wanting to know how the house clearance was coming along.

"It's a slow job, far more difficult than I imagined," admitted Nigel.

Emma explained that she and Ralph were thinking about coming up for the weekend in order to give the two of them a hand with the house clearance. Nigel said they didn't have to, explaining that he and Molly should be finished by then anyway.

"But on second thoughts, it's not a bad idea after all," Nigel continued. "Molly and I are sorting out a load of stuff to sell at auction. However, if there is something you want for yourself, you'd need to choose it before we send anything to the auction house. Molly and I have decided to take one item to remind us of Uncle Miles, but we haven't decided what it's going to be yet."

"Fair enough," replied Emma. "I'd also like something to remind me of the old bugger, and I would like to see the house one last time."

After their mother passed away in 2006, Emma and Nigel had cleared out and sold the house on Chatsworth Road where they grew up. A lifetime of memories were swept away in a matter of days so that they could sell the property with vacant possession. Visiting her uncle's house would be nowhere near as painful for Emma as that had been. After all, she wasn't particularly close to either her uncle or his house.

So after saying that she and Ralph would arrive at approximately seven o'clock on Friday evening, Emma said goodbye. It was then that Nigel and Molly returned to their mammoth task of emptying the house.

The two of them had soon cleared out the two chests of drawers, which only left the wardrobe to go. They had hoped that this would be an easier task, but were disappointed to discover three suitcases inside. All three of them were full to the brim with items that needed sorting.

The first contained various papers including their uncle's birth certificate and his school reports. It also contained his degree certificate, which was still in its frame from the days when it used to hang on his office wall.

"I hate the thought of throwing these away," said Nigel. "But I guess they're no use to anyone anymore."

*******

It was spring 1948 and I was back working at the brewery. The war had completely messed up my plan for life. By now I should have been in my second year at university and Rupert should have taken up his role as Tied Trade Director. But Rupert was dead and I'd just completed my eighteen months' National Service.

I'd been accepted at Oxford, but I knew that the family business needed me. So I went to see my father and told him that I wasn't going to take up my place at St John's College.

I'd expected him to be pleased, but for my father it was like telling him that the family was going downhill fast. He told me that his grandfather Benjamin Goodyear, who'd founded the brewery, had only been semi-literate. I knew that he'd been a carpenter, but I didn't know that he'd never had a proper education. Because of this, Benjamin had been determined that his son would get a better education than he'd had, and therefore paid for him to go to the Grammar School. However, money was tight, so Grandfather left when he was sixteen in order to join the family firm.

The family were far wealthier by the time my father was born. As a result he was able to complete his education and at the age of eighteen went to St John's College, Oxford. Father was adamant that if I didn't follow in his footsteps, it would be like admitting that our fortunes were on the wane.

Consequently, I was going to St John's College whether I liked it or not and that was the end of the matter. Until then, I was to continue to learn the ropes in the brewery, this time as a drayman.

Working on the drays had its advantages and disadvantages. On the plus side, it got me out of the brewery and into the Derbyshire countryside. The brewery had 35 tied pubs and ten off-licences. There were also about fifty free trade customers, which were mainly small sports clubs and a few working men's clubs, where we supplied one of the beers on their bar. This was usually alongside those of our competitors.

The brewery had two drays and between them they delivered about 500 barrels a week to our 95 customers. That equated to fifty barrels per day per lorry, which was an awful lot of beer.

One of the commonest mistakes that people from outside of the brewing industry make is to think that a barrel is a wooden container made by a cooper. It is, but only if it contains 36 gallons, because a barrel is actually an Imperial unit of volume. Four nine-gallon firkins equate to one barrel, as do 48 dozen half-pint bottles. In fact, the largest container that the brewery supplied was a hogshead, which contained a barrel and a half or 54 gallons.

Whatever the container size though, the job was physical and tiring, but that was not why I say it had its disadvantages. No, the main disadvantage was down to the sheer volume of beer we had to consume whilst making our deliveries.

We used to deliver to about ten outlets every weekday. We would start at 7.30 in the morning and load the lorry with beer for our first run. Depending on how far we had to drive we would usually arrive at our first drop at about 8.30. After delivering the beer, it was customary for the landlord to give the driver and his helper a pint of bitter. If we were lucky he would also give us breakfast.

This was only the start of it though, as we would continue drinking in every outlet we visited. When our first run was complete, we would return to the brewery to pick up the beer for our second trip and the whole process would start again.

By the end of the day, we would have consumed at least ten pints. Well that's what Sid the driver would have consumed. I physically could not drink that volume of beer and as a result I usually only drank halves.

Of course it was extremely dangerous to drink so much alcohol whilst at work. In fact, the only reason I was doing the job was because Sid's former mate had forgotten to close the cellar flaps after making a delivery to a pub in Bolsover. It was the last drop of the day and it was dark by the time they went back to the lorry after finishing their beers. Unfortunately, Sid's mate didn't notice his mistake and fell into the cellar, fracturing his arm in the process.

It wasn't just the volume of beer I was expected to consume that concerned me. All this drinking added hours onto our working day. Quite often, we would not get back until seven o'clock in the evening and then Sid would head straight for the brewery cellars, where he'd have a few more pints. As if that wasn't enough, he'd always go for a final pint in the Spa Vaults across the road before eventually going home.

Much to Sid's annoyance I wouldn't accompany him to the brewery cellars or to the Spa Vaults. It was bad enough getting back as late as we did. It was playing havoc with my love life.

That said things were going pretty well between Sarah and I. Okay, she still wouldn't let me have sex with her, but at least the uncertainty caused by my time in the RAF was now at an end.

She'd been true to her word. She had waited for me and if being apart had tested our relationship, then we had both passed that particular test with flying colours. Of course, I was due to go away again in October. But at least with university, I would only be in Oxford for thirty weeks of the year. The other 22 I'd be back in Chesterfield with her, unless of course, I was in hospital with liver failure.

By now she'd started teaching at a local junior school, although she wasn't really enjoying her new job.

Fortunately, we no longer had to rely on the hop store for our courting, which was just as well as the last time we'd been there we were shocked to discover Mr Jones. He was fast asleep and snoring after consuming his own body weight in Goodyear's Pride.

Father had bought me a second-hand Austin 10 soon after I'd returned from National Service. It had been his idea as he still didn't like the thought of letting me loose with his beloved Alvis. Having a car of my own opened up a whole new world of things for Sarah and I to do. We would go for walks on the Chatsworth Estate, have afternoon tea at the Rutland Arms in Bakewell, visit well dressings and village fêtes. We even went down Peak Cavern in Castleton and I bought her a Blue John broach afterwards.

But the best thing about having a car was that Sarah and I could do our courting in it. The Austin was already ten years old when Father bought it for me and it wasn't the most reliable starter in the world. Consequently, I always parked the car on a hill, so that if the worst came to the worst I could bump-start it after we had finished. This I achieved by putting the car into second gear, depressing the clutch, then releasing the handbrake and letting the car build up speed before gently lifting my left foot. Fortunately, it always worked as the last thing I wanted was for the two of us to get stuck after dark in the middle of nowhere.

My favourite spot was in a layby near Striding Hall. It was just outside Chesterfield on a road that hardly anybody used after dark. We'd park up and get in the back. It wasn't as comfortable as the hop store but at least we didn't have to put up with pissed up head brewers.

Eventually however, the time came for me to start at university. I'd decided to study Latin and it was a four-year Master's Degree course. Latin was never going to help me in my career after university, but that wasn't the point. Hugh Janus had been a great teacher and I had really enjoyed the subject. It was also the one subject in which I was quite proficient and consequently, I decided that it was my best chance of getting a good final grade.

College life was a doddle compared with life in the RAF. It was even good when compared to life at home. I was 21 when I started, an adult with the vote and the key to the door. My parents had thrown a large party to mark my coming of age before I left. I loved them both dearly, but I was growing restless and wanted to fly the nest. In that respect, university answered most of my prayers. I had my own room in college and a cleaner. So I could be as untidy as I liked and then, as if by magic, it was as neat as a pin again by the time I got back from lectures.

Of course there were some disadvantages to living in college. Firstly there were no girls as St John's was an all-male college. Secondly we had to be back in our rooms by ten o'clock at night, as that was the time the porter locked the front gate. If you got back after that time it was tough luck. You'd be left with the choice of trying to find a bed for the night or dossing down with the crusties on a park bench.

Of course it was fine if you were the son of a duke, just out of Eton or Harrow as they could afford a room at the Randolph Hotel. In fact, Bertie Applethwaite, the son of the Duke of Cumberland, had missed the curfew on so many occasions that the rumour in college was that the hotel kept a room free just for him.

My family weren't poor, but they definitely didn't have money to waste on things like that. Consequently, I made sure I never missed the ten o'clock curfew. Well, that was until I made friends with Howard Morcom who had a room down the corridor from me.

Howard was two years my senior and had previously held a commission in the Royal Tank Regiment before coming to Oxford. Prior to that he'd been at a minor public school in Lincolnshire. Howard was different to most of the others in my corridor, as he didn't want to spend all his time studying. He wanted to get out and enjoy life and as a result the two of us became firm friends.

One day, the two of us were enjoying our sixth pint of the night whilst sitting in the Eagle and Child across the road from the college. The conversation was flowing and I had lost all track of time when I happened to look up at the clock and noticed that it was five to ten.

Howard had only just returned from the bar where he had bought another round.

"We'll have to down these in one," I said to him pointing to the clock above the bar.

He told me not to worry about it as he had a backdoor key to the college.

"How the hell did you get that?" I asked him. But all he did was to tap his nose.

An hour later, we let ourselves in through the rear gate usually reserved for deliveries to the college's kitchen. We both crept back to our rooms trying not to disturb any of our fellow students. However, we failed in that respect when I collided with one of the fire extinguishers and knocked it off the wall. All the time I was wondering how on earth Howard had managed to obtain a key.

A few days later I discovered the answer when I was woken up by the sound of a woman screaming in a room nearby. It was unusual because it was half past eleven at night and women weren't allowed in college after the curfew. It was then that I realised they weren't screams of pain I could hear. They were screams of pleasure and they were coming from Howard's room. When I challenged him about the noise the following morning he admitted that it was one of the college cooks. It also solved the mystery of who had appropriated the backdoor key for him.

Despite her nickname, Gorgeous Gail was not a particularly attractive woman. In fact, she had a flat face, which made her look as if her head had been run over by a steamroller. But she had other attributes, two of them to be precise, which Howard used to refer to as the Hindenburg twins. She was eight years older than Howard and a widow. Her husband had been killed when a German torpedo had hit the merchant ship he was serving on.

Howard told me that she might not be the most attractive woman in the world but that she was fantastic in bed. She was a real screamer. Given the choice between her and his right hand he would choose her any day of the week and indeed he did choose her on most days. Also, being part of the college catering team, meant that she had access to the keys that unlocked the back door and this was how she'd been able to get a duplicate cut for Howard.

This was a real bonus and I wondered if Howard had started their affair purely to get hold of that key. However, this particular question was answered after we graduated, as Howard never missed a college summer reunion for the next twenty years. He didn't give a toss about the college of course; it was Gorgeous Gail that he wanted to be reunited with. She may have had a face that looked like a shovel, but Howard was obviously telling the truth when he said that she was a devil between the sheets.

Plain she may have been, but by the end of four years she had become the most beautiful woman in the world and as a result I was extremely jealous of Howard. It was not that she'd got any prettier. It was just that she was the only woman I saw on a regular basis. That was as long as you discounted Mrs Gibb, my cleaning lady who was 55. Mind you after four years even she was starting to look desirable as she bent over to empty my wastepaper basket.

Once the holidays arrived it was back to a bit of tonsil hockey, breast fondling and being tossed off in the back of the Austin by Sarah. But as soon as the holidays were over, it was back to my life of celibacy again.

Sarah never came to visit me whilst I was in Oxford. There wouldn't have been much point. However, just before I graduated, she finally came down for the May Ball and stayed in a local guesthouse.

A week later, my time at university was over and I returned home to Chesterfield. I'd had a great time in Oxford. Howard and I had enjoyed many adventures together, like the time we broke into Somerville Hall, one of the girls' colleges, and placed a huge boulder in the fountain in the centre of the quadrangle. It was a miracle how we ever managed to pick it up, let alone how we got away with it.

Or the time when we were returning to college one night after a drinking session and found an abandoned handbag in the street. In our drunken state, we decided to hang it from the statue of William Herbert outside the Bodleian Library. We then put Howard's university scarf on his head so that it looked like he was wearing a headscarf.

We thought that it was highly amusing. However, the university authorities didn't share our sense of humour and tried to discover who had done it. Fortunately, it had been the early hours of the morning and nobody had seen us. It was also fortunate that we had chosen Howard's scarf as Mother had sewn my name into mine, which would rather have given the game away.

In July 1952, I returned to Oxford to get my degree. I'd passed with a 2:2, which was a little disappointing. I'd probably have gotten a 2:1 if I'd never met Howard but that's how it goes.

Both my parents were as proud as punch as they sat in the audience at the Sheldonian Theatre watching the university's Vice Chancellor present me with my degree. My mother was not at all well, but she still insisted on coming. It was the last event she ever attended.

"You must get it framed and put it on your office wall," she said to me after the ceremony.

I had already started as Tied Trade Director at the brewery by then and so that was precisely what I did.

# Chapter 11

"That's one case done," said Nigel as the last document was removed from the first case.

All the paperwork from the case had been put into a black bag destined for the recycling centre, which included their uncle's degree certificate. Nigel and Molly had a brief discussion about whether the frame was worth keeping before it too was unceremoniously placed in the bin liner.

"Let's break for a cup of tea before we continue," said Molly.

Nigel didn't need asking twice and the two of them went downstairs to the kitchen.

"You know, I can't help feeling guilty about all of this," said Nigel as he dunked his digestive biscuit into his tea. "Uncle Miles must have studied really hard for four years to get his degree and we've just thrown his certificate into the bin like yesterday's newspaper."

"I've said it before, but I'll say it again. We just haven't got the space for all your uncle's stuff. If we took that degree certificate home with us, all we would do is to put it into a drawer and it would never see the light of day again until we died. At which point Jacob and Flo would throw it away. I know it might seem harsh, but your uncle is dead now. Having a degree certificate isn't going to help him anymore."

Nigel knew she was right, but it didn't help him to feel any less guilty about the whole situation.

It was now nearly twelve noon and they wanted to try and finish the second bedroom before lunch. So the two of them drank their tea before heading back upstairs again.

"I wonder what we'll find in the second suitcase?" asked Nigel as he pulled it out of the wardrobe.

He didn't have to wait long before he found out. The case contained all manner of things from their uncle and aunt's wedding. There were photos, cards, telegrams and even a piece of wedding cake.

*******

Mother died three months after I graduated and three weeks after my 25th birthday. She'd been suffering from stomach cancer and there was nothing the doctors could do for her.

She was only 51. I'd thought that she would always be there for me, but suddenly she was no more. Father was devastated. He'd nursed her by himself through her final weeks at home.

"She looked after me back in 1918 and now it's my turn to do the same for her," he told me. "She needs me and I will never let her down."

Because Father had to stay at home to look after my mother, the day-to-day running of the brewery was down to me. I had only just started as Tied Trade Director, but now I found myself doing the Managing Director and Chairman's roles as well. It was a tough introduction to my new working life, but one that I was happy to take on as it freed up Father to look after my mother.

Truth be told, the brewery virtually ran itself. Most of our employees had been with the firm for years and were usually the sons and grandsons of former employees. None of them had to be told what to do and they just kept on doing their jobs without the need to be supervised, consuming vast volumes of beer at the same time.

I also had Rebecca to help me as she had decided not to go to university and had started working in the brewery offices when she left school in 1949. It seemed that Father had a different set of standards when it came to girls.

She was a quick learner and by 1952 she had progressed to the role of Office Manager. Being the boss's daughter may have played a small part in her promotion. Still I was a fine one to talk after going straight into the business as Tied Trade Director, with my only previous experience being my holiday jobs.

Mother's funeral took place at Old Brampton church, the same church where her father had been the vicar during the First World War. It was only a small church and there were so many people that a great number of them had to stand in the rain outside and listen to the service. As well as her friends and family most of the brewery employees were in attendance including Bill Jones, who'd sobered up as a mark of respect for her. Also present was Joseph Maynard along with his wife and daughter. The Maynards owned Brimington Brewery, our biggest competitor, and were distant relations of ours.

Her coffin was brought to the church on the back of a horse-drawn dray. The undertakers had arranged it specially, using two of their horses and one of our old drays that had been taken out of service in 1930. Since then it had been standing in the reception area of our offices, where it served as a constant reminder of our long history.

It was a nice touch, as was the fact that Father and I were two of the pallbearers. I'd promised myself that I wouldn't cry, but I couldn't stop the tears from running down my face as I entered the church. Then I looked over and saw Father brushing one away as well.

The service itself was very fitting. It was not a solemn affair, as the vicar made it a celebration of her life by telling a few light-hearted stories from her past. When it was over we laid her to rest in the churchyard, alongside her mother and father, within sight of the vicarage where she grew up.

And that was it, apart from the wake. We used the Station Hotel because none of our pubs were big enough to cater for all the people who wanted to pay their respects. My wonderful mother was gone forever, which left my grandmother, my father, my sister and myself as the only remaining members of the Goodyear family. In the space of eight years, our number had been reduced from seven down to four.

A week later, Father asked me if I was going to marry Sarah, as I'd been going out with her for seven years by then and we weren't even engaged. I told him that I'd been waiting for the right moment, as I wasn't going to ask her whilst I was doing my National Service or whilst I was at university. Even now that I'd started in a proper job I wanted to concentrate on learning the ropes, rather than have my mind distracted by thoughts of getting married.

Father looked at me and said, "Miles, you need to have a long hard think about the type of girl you want to marry. There are plenty more fish in the sea, you know. Perhaps Sarah isn't the right one for you."

He told me that he'd been talking to Joe Maynard after the funeral. His daughter, Elizabeth, was an only child and eventually she would inherit the brewery and its 47 tied houses. He then went on to say that things would only get tougher for small brewers like us. But that combined with Brimington we would have 82 pubs, making us a much greater force in the local beer market. Also we could close one of the breweries, which would make us more efficient and therefore more profitable.

"Let me get this right, Father," I said to him. "You want me to marry Elizabeth Maynard just so that our two businesses can be combined? This is England not India. We don't do arranged marriages here."

"Believe that and you will believe anything," Father replied. "The Royal family have been doing it for centuries for a start. Anyway, you could do far worse, she has good childbearing hips and would make a fine mother. I'm sure you'd have many sons together, sons who could carry on the family business."

With neither Rebecca nor myself married or even engaged, Father was clearly quite worried about the future of both the family and the brewery.

"Good childbearing hips," I replied. "What you really mean is that she's got a fat arse. Anyway, she looks like a horse."

'You don't look at the mantelpiece whilst you're stoking the fire, son,' was his reply.

This really shocked me, as we'd never had a conversation like this before. It certainly wouldn't have happened if my mother had still been alive.

"All I'm saying is give it some thought," Father continued. "If you want I can set up a date for you. You can come back here if you like. I'll make sure that Granny and I go out for the evening. It'll be far more comfortable than the hop store or the back of your car."

I didn't know what shocked me the most. The fact that my father was trying to arrange for me to have sex with Elizabeth Maynard, or the fact that he knew where Sarah and I did our courting.

"Don't look so surprised," he continued. "It never fails to amaze me how each generation thinks they invented sex. Where do you think your mother and I did our courting? Also Bill Jones wasn't always so pissed that he couldn't stay awake, and you've forgotten that Derek Middleton from Striding Hall and I go shooting together."

For a second, I pictured a drunken Bill Jones spying on Sarah and I as we rolled around in the hop store, she topless and me with my trousers around my ankles. It wasn't a pleasant thought and I soon shook it out of my head.

"Sarah is my girlfriend," I replied. "She's the one I'm going to marry and that's the end of the matter."

With that I left the room, although if I'm truthful I did give the matter a fleeting thought. After all, even though Elizabeth wasn't the prettiest girl in town, her father did own Brimington Brewery. Perhaps she'd turn out to be every red-blooded male's fantasy, a girl whose father owned a brewery and who shagged on the first date.

It was only a brief thought though, probably brought on because I was still a virgin aged nearly 25. However, it did help to crystallise my thoughts and two days later I asked Sarah to marry me.

It was in the front room of her parents' house and I got down on one knee just like the old romantic that I was. She didn't reply straight away and for a brief moment I was reminded of when I'd asked her to dance at the dance practice back in December 1944.

Finally she said, "Of course I will Miles," much to my relief. Then I had to go and ask her father's permission, which was pretty nerve-wracking even though he was one of the nicest, mildest mannered men I'd ever met.

My father was obviously disappointed, but congratulated us both nonetheless. My sister seemed to be even more excited than the two of us. Sarah had said that she could be one of the bridesmaids and she was keen to find out what dress she would be wearing.

The following day I met up with Sarah and both of us went to see Herman to choose our engagement ring. It was a foregone conclusion that we were going to buy it from his shop as he was my friend. Besides which he had promised me mates' rates, which meant a 10% discount.

The ring that Sarah chose was very expensive, far more expensive than I had anticipated.

"There's no point in buying a cheap ring," she said to me, as we were looking through Herman's stock. "It would send out all the wrong messages about how well we were doing and our place in society."

I'd never taken Sarah for a snob before, but then again we'd never discussed anything as important as getting married and spending the rest of our lives together. She came from a good middle-class family. Her father was the manager of Williams Deacon's Bank in the centre of town. They lived on New Queen Street. Okay, it was a terraced house, but it was a large terraced house in a good part of town. The people who lived there were all professionals. In fact, Mr Lock who lived next door was a director of Eyres, the furniture store in the centre of town.

However, it was becoming increasingly obvious to me that Sarah realised she would get a leg-up socially by marrying me. After all, my family were business owners rather than managers. We lived in a large detached Georgian house with servants' quarters, even though nowadays we didn't have any servants living in them. To be perfectly honest, I didn't care whether Sarah was a social climber or not. She was beautiful and I loved her. That was all I cared about.

I was planning on spending about a month's salary on the ring but in the end it cost me nearly three times that amount, even with the discount. It was a two-carat diamond solitaire and it did look spectacular. That said I was feeling decidedly impoverished by the time we left the shop.

Sarah's parents were overjoyed when Father offered to pay half the wedding costs and a date was set for April 18th the following year. The service was booked in the Crooked Spire with a reception in a marquee at the brewery.

The big debate was over where we were going to live once we were married. Sarah wanted us to buy a house, whereas I thought that we would be better off renting to start off. Father, however, had other ideas saying that it was ridiculous having a massive house in the centre of Chesterfield with just him, Granny and Rebecca living in it and that we ought to move in with him instead. He added that Granny was now in her eighties and probably wouldn't be around for much longer. Rebecca was 22 and would undoubtedly be getting married herself in the near future, which meant that he'd be there all by himself. This ignored the fact that Granny was as fit as a flea and Rebecca didn't have a boyfriend, even though there were plenty who would have liked to have taken on that role.

Needless to say, Sarah wasn't too keen on the idea of moving in with my relatives, but in the end we came to a compromise. Father offered to refurbish the entire top floor of the house, in order to create a separate one-bedroomed flat for us. This comprised Evans's old room, a bathroom and a storage room. However, this would only be a temporary solution, as Sarah and I would then start looking for a suitable plot on which we could build our dream property.

Sarah liked the idea of designing her own house and so she reluctantly agreed to this proposal.

It was raining on the day of the wedding, which should have told me something. As a result, all the photographs had to be taken in the brewery, apart from a couple that were taken in the porch of the Crooked Spire. Sprout was my best man and Herman was an usher. Many of my old friends were there including Frank and Richard, my old RAF buddies, and Howard from university. There were also a few of my old classmates from the Grammar School, including Frith, Bateman and Stanley Worthington, the lad who'd told Mr Duggins what his nickname was.

Altogether, it was a gathering of the great and the good or, more accurately, the debauched and the disreputable. Either way, they were all my friends and I was pleased that they had all accepted our invitation to join us on our happy day.

Rebecca and Lydia were Sarah's bridesmaids, with Lydia looking decidedly odd in a blue satin dress with white lilies embroidered around the neck. Rebecca looked far more at ease though and it was she who caught Sarah's bouquet when she threw it over her shoulder.

Sprout's speech went down well with the guests. He said that he hoped our marriage would be as happy as his and Georgina's was.

Marriage had been the best thing that had ever happened to Sprout and he loved being a father. Carrot had given birth to two sons, Richard now aged three and Gordon aged eighteen months. They were like two peas in a pod, which was pretty apt given their parent's nicknames.

Sprout went on to tell the tale of how, as naughty school-boys, we were standing on the roof of the school bike shed when I first caught sight of Sarah. Even at that early stage I'd said she was the girl I was going to marry. He recounted with mirth that my plan was nearly scuppered later that same day, when my first encounter with Sarah had resulted in her hitting me in the balls.

That line got the biggest laugh of the day. He also said that our first date had been at the school Christmas dance and that we'd been in love ever since.

For a moment I thought he was going to mention the visit to the Eros Centre in Lüneburg, but fortunately for me he didn't. He ended by saying that the only person who was more pleased about the wedding than the two of us was

Derek Middleton of Striding Hall. He was looking forward to being able to get out of his drive once more, as an Austin 10 with its windows misted up would no longer block it.

I could see that Sarah was starting to go extremely red by this stage but she was also laughing, so I knew that everything was okay. He then proposed a toast to the bridesmaids. Pretty soon after that the reception was over apart from a dance in the evening to which all our employees were invited. Father had arranged for two hogsheads of Goodyear's Pride to be put on stillage for them at the back of the marquee.

It was a hell of a lot of beer, 864 pints to be exact. However, he'd underestimated the capacity of his workforce and the beer was all gone by 9.30, so he had to bring in some emergency bottles in order to prevent a riot. I don't think that Sarah's mother and father could quite believe it. The most they ever got through at the bank's annual Christmas party was a single bottle of sherry.

Many of the guests had bought us gifts for the new flat. Father had bought us a TV and Sarah's parents had commissioned a wardrobe with our initials carved on the front. Sprout and Carrot had bought us a Charlotte Rhead jug, which Sprout had filled with French Letters. He said that I was going to need plenty of them from now on.

Herman had bought us a set of silver fish knives and forks, which I'd noticed had been in the sale when we'd been in his shop buying the wedding ring. We got a full canteen of cutlery from Granny. The brewery workers had all clubbed together and they'd asked the local Pearson's Pottery to make us a personalised vase. It said, 'Miles and Sarah April 18th 1953. From all the staff at Goodyear's Brewery.'

By eight o'clock, it was obvious that things were starting to get raucous. Sarah and I had long since performed our final duty by starting off the first dance. So we got in our car and quietly went home. Well, it was meant to be quietly except that Sprout and Herman had tied all manner of things to the rear bumper, including brass barrel rings, a stainless steel brewery bucket and a couple of empty beer crates. It took me another twenty minutes to untie them before we could finally set off.

It only took us five minutes to get home and I dutifully carried Sarah over the threshold and kissed her once we were safely inside. As soon as we were on the top floor I also carried her through the door to our new flat.

I took her straight to the bedroom where I was surprised to discover a hopsack laid out in the middle of the bed.

"Bloody Sprout and Herman," I said to her and we both started laughing. Then I kissed her again.

"You know that this is the moment I've been waiting for since we went to the hop store together when we were teenagers."

"I know," she replied. "I hope it will be worth the wait."

With that we both stripped off and climbed into bed luxuriating in our Egyptian cotton sheets.

Finally, I was about to lose my virginity.

How was it?

Well to be truthful, it was a bit of an anti-climax or to be more accurate a bit of a quick climax. It certainly was not as memorable as that first evening in the hop store. Personally I put it down to the stress of the day. Still at least I was no longer a virgin and I had the rest of my life to improve my technique starting with our honeymoon. Father had paid for us to spend four nights at the Hotel Bristol in Le Touquet and the two of us were off to France in the morning. It was to be the start of a long and happy life with Sarah. Or so I thought at the time.

# Chapter 12

"So what do you think we should do with all of these?" asked Nigel.

"I don't want to appear hard-hearted," Molly replied. "But you know what I'm going to say."

"Okay, okay. But it won't hurt if I just keep one photo. This one of the family has got mum, dad, granddad and great granny on it. I'm not going to throw that one away. Maybe Emma will want one as well."

It was at this point that Molly had second thoughts.

"All right why don't we take all the photos home so that Emma and Ralph can look through them with us at the weekend. We will probably still end up throwing the majority of them away, but it will be fun to go through them all together."

Nigel agreed and fetched a large cardboard box to put the photos in. However, the cards, telegrams and piece of wedding cake weren't given a similar stay of execution and they all went straight into one of the black bags.

Finally, they were down to the last case, which Nigel opened and was pleased to discover that this time it didn't contain anything personal. Instead it was filled with loads of old papers concerning the brewery's tied estate, including invoices, plans and drawings regarding proposed refurbishments. It also contained the original designs for the George Stephenson pub next door.

*******

Sarah had never been abroad before. She thought Le Touquet was wonderful, like a chic and sophisticated version of Skegness. The two of us loved walking along the seafront and visiting the array of small shops in the town centre. We'd driven to Le Touquet by car and Sarah was determined to fill it with as many goods as she possibly could. She mainly bought things for the flat like bed sheets, ornaments and saucepans.

The latter was a bit premature since we didn't have a kitchen of our own, but Sarah said she wanted to start storing things for when we got our new house. My wife was such a keen shopper. I was glad that customs restrictions had meant that we could only take £50 worth of traveller's cheques with us when we left the country.

The food in Le Touquet took a bit of getting used to, as it was very different to what we ate back in the UK. Personally, I was a meat and two veg man and the only sauces I usually had with my meals were made by HP or Heinz. Sarah said she liked the meals we had in France, but I wasn't keen on all those veloutés and béchamels. Even when I discovered that jus meant gravy and crème anglaise meant custard, they still didn't taste like they did back home.

In spite of the food we still had a wonderful honeymoon. But all too soon it was time to return to Chesterfield and go back to work.

By the summer of 1953 I'd been Tied Trade Director for a year and it was obvious to me that things had to change. We owned 35 pubs and the vast majority of these were male boozers. They were spit and sawdust pubs with outside toilets and no facilities for women. Some of them didn't even have a ladies' loo. They were dingy and decrepit and the newest of them was over fifty years old.

Of course the years immediately after the war had seen a major surge in house building in the UK and Chesterfield was no exception in this regard. Rows of Victorian terraces had been demolished and, at the same time, the town was expanding with lots of new estates being built.

As a consequence, many of our pubs were now in the wrong locations. Also, we were facing increased competition from the local working men's clubs. Whilst some of these were staunchly men only clubs, the more forward-thinking ones admitted women. Not only that but they had large concert rooms where they put on entertainment. Most of them had billiard rooms. Some even had sports facilities.

It was clear to me that the world was changing and that in future pubs would have to offer far more than just beer.

"We do offer more," said Father when we were having one of our arguments on the subject. "We offer darts, dominos and cribbage."

"But none of those things appeal to women," I replied. "So we are missing out on the opportunity posed by half the population."

"But women don't drink beer," he said, which was his stock response to my argument.

It was at this point that Rebecca came to my aid.

"All my friends drink beer, Father. They just don't drink it in our pubs. Not only that but there are loads of young men who go where we go and they all drink beer as well. It gives them Dutch courage."

After reconsidering for a few moments, Father asked me what I wanted to do. I told him that I wanted to close one of our worst performing pubs and transfer the license to a brand-new pub, which we would build close to one of the new housing estates. The main difference between this pub and the rest of our estate was that this outlet would have letting bedrooms and a restaurant. In that respect it would have more in common with an inn or a small hotel than with a traditional pub. There would be nothing for women to fear in this new type of pub and its large windows would make this plain for all to see. It would be the kind of pub that you would be proud to take your wife to.

Father gave it some thought before enquiring how I was proposing to pay for all of this and which pub I was recommending we closed down.

I told him that the pub I had in mind was the Travellers Rest in Cutthorpe as it was now only selling four barrels per week, the lowest volume of all our 35 pubs. Furthermore, it could easily be converted into a private house and it still left us with one other pub in the village.

Where funding was concerned I said that we'd probably get a decent price for the delicensed Travellers Rest and that we could borrow the rest from the bank.

"But I had my first ever pint in the Travellers Rest, and Frank Hargreaves, the tenant, has been with us for forty years," Father protested. "Surely there must be a better candidate for your proposal than that?"

"Frank Hargreaves is 72 years old and wants to retire," I replied. "In fact, he'd have retired years ago if we could find a new tenant to take over from him. But the pub is doing so little trade it is difficult for anyone to make a living out of it. Also, the private accommodation is awful and the roof leaks."

I could tell that Father wasn't completely convinced, but I left him to mull the whole thing over. Afterwards I thanked Rebecca for backing me up.

"That's the least I can do," she said. "Somebody has to drag this company into the twentieth century."

She then went rather quiet before adding. "Actually Miles, there's something I've been meaning to tell you. Dirk and I are going out together."

"So you've got a boyfriend, about time if you ask me. Do I know this Dirk fellow?"

"Of course you do, it's your friend Dirk Friedrich."

"What, Herman?" I replied.

To say that I was astonished by my sister's announcement was an understatement. I hadn't even realised that the two of them fancied each other. Also I'd called him Herman for so long that I had forgotten what his Christian name was. After all I'd never called him Dirk when we were at school or even after we'd left for that matter. He was Herman the German, always had been and always would be. Dildo Duggins had seen to that.

I didn't know whether to congratulate my sister or what to say to her. The fact that she and Herman were romantically involved had come as a complete surprise to me.

In the end I just joked by saying, "Hey, you mustn't let him take you to his dad's shed on the allotments."

With that she went crimson and I realised that I had well and truly put my foot in it.

"No, I'm really pleased for both of you," I said trying to avoid my sister's embarrassed look. "How long have you been going out with him? Is it serious?"

"We've been together since your wedding and it is pretty serious. He's asked me to marry him."

"Bloody hell, when are you going to tell Father?" I asked her.

"I was waiting for the right moment," she replied.

"Bloody hell," I said for a second time. "Still I guess you'll get a fantastic engagement ring, with him being a jeweller."

The following week two things happened. Firstly, Herman came around to ask my father for Rebecca's hand in marriage. Father could hardly object as she was 22 and Herman was an upstanding member of the Chesterfield Chamber of Commerce, having taken over the running of the shop from his father the previous May.

Secondly, Father approved my idea for the new pub. He made it clear to me that it was only a trial and said we would decide whether or not it was a success after the pub had been trading for a year.

We closed the Travellers Rest and Frank went to live in a local almshouse. I had several options for where the new pub was to be built, but eventually chose a site in Newbold. We sold the delicensed pub to a local builder who converted it into a detached house and we transferred the licence to the new pub.

I had already decided that it was going to be called the George Stephenson after one of Chesterfield's most famous former residents. So we leaked the news to the *Derbyshire Times*, which got us a bit of free publicity.

One of the reasons why I was so keen on the site in Newbold, apart from the fact that it was on a main road close to a new estate, was that the plot of land we had bought was bigger than we needed for the pub. As a result, we were also able to build a three-bedroomed detached house next door and got a good price for the job since we used the same builder as we used for the pub.

Sarah was overjoyed when I told her that we were going to live in a brand-new house. If she had to live under the same roof as my father for another year, she thought she might end up strangling him.

Of course we'd always planned to move into a new house. This was one of the promises I'd made to her when we were discussing getting married. Despite this, she was beginning to get restless and on one occasion she even accused me of going back on my word.

She'd never really liked living in the flat, as it was only two rooms and a bathroom on the top floor of my father's house. There was no kitchen, no dining room and we didn't have our own front door. Now at last we would have our own place, somewhere we could really call home, somewhere we could have some privacy.

The new house would have all the modern facilities such as a washing machine and a refrigerator. It would also have a parquet floor in the living room, a modern fitted bathroom and a garage for my company car, which Father had provided me with when I became a director.

The house was completed a few days before the pub and the two of us moved in at the start of May 1954. Two weeks later, the George Stephenson opened and its first function was to host Herman and my sister's wedding reception.

It was a happy time for all of us except for my father. Our family home, which had for so long been filled with shouts and laughter, had now gone quiet. My father and my grandmother were the only two occupants still living there.

The George Stephenson was a success and I was keen to build more pubs like it. Father, however, was less keen. Although the George Stephenson was trading well, much of the turnover came from food and from the letting bedrooms. If you judged it purely on beer turnover, it was less than double that of the Travellers Rest, after what had been a massive investment on our behalf.

Father's argument was that our main priority was to keep the mash tun at the brewery full, as we were a brewer first and foremost. He told me that he could have sold more beer just by buying an extra pub and it would have been a lot cheaper for us.

My argument was that we also made money from the sale of wines, spirits and soft drinks. In addition to this, we could charge a higher rent for a pub with a higher turnover.

But Father had made his decision. There would be no more pubs like the George Stephenson.

I felt that my father was wrong and that he couldn't see that the world was changing. However, he was the Managing Director as well as the company Chairman and so had the final say about everything. That wouldn't always be the case, of course, as he was now in his sixties and would soon be looking to take more of a back seat. Things would be different once I took over from him. So I decided to take the plans for the George Stephenson home with me. After all, they would be the blueprint for our new pub estate once I was in charge of the business.

# Chapter 13

"That's it," said Molly. "We've finally cracked it."

The second bedroom was now completely cleared out except for the furniture.

"What about the pictures?" asked Nigel. "We've also forgotten about the pictures on the walls of the first bedroom."

"I suppose that most of them will be prints," Molly replied. She wandered over and took one of the pictures off the wall revealing a load of cobwebs where it had been hanging. "Mind you this one looks as if it's oil on canvas and looks as if it's quite well painted."

"I'm no art expert, but I doubt if Uncle Miles's taste in pictures will fetch much at auction though," Nigel replied.

"You never know," continued Molly whilst still looking at the picture in her hands. "This one might be worth a few quid as it depicts the marketplace in Chesterfield. Somebody local might want it."

In total, there were three pictures in the second bedroom and four in the first. Nigel and Molly carefully removed them and took them downstairs before putting them on the auction pile.

*******

By 1955, Sarah and I had been married for two years. If I said that the marriage was going well I would be lying.

Firstly, our sex life wasn't the wonderful thing that I'd always thought it would be and secondly, Sarah was spending far too much money. I didn't mind so much the things she bought for the house, such as a top of the range black box record player and an expensive Persian rug. It was more the amount she spent on clothing and jewellery that concerned me.

We'd had fitted wardrobes built just to house all her purchases. She'd bought so many dresses that she could go for an entire month without wearing the same one twice. In fact, the number she now owned was only exceeded by the number of pairs of shoes she'd bought.

As for jewellery, I jokingly told her that only the Duchess of Windsor owned more than she did, which went down like a lead balloon.

It wasn't as if we went out that much. When we did, it was usually to trade related events such as the Chesterfield and District Licenced Victuallers annual dinner. In fact, she used to go out with her friend Lydia far more than she did with me.

The whole thing came to a head in October 1955 when she and Lydia went to see a play at the Civic Theatre.

"I remember the days when you and I used to go to the theatre together," I said to her.

"But we didn't really go to see the play," she replied. "That was back when we were courting. Things are different now. Besides which, you don't really like the theatre do you?"

"Too right things are different now," I replied. "And yes, I do like the theatre now that you come to mention it."

She didn't continue the argument, she merely picked up her handbag, one of several she now owned, and walked out.

When she returned two and a half hours later, she was carrying a large package under her arm. It was a picture she'd bought from the artist who was exhibiting in the bar of the theatre. I held it up to the light to look at it.

"It's not very good," I announced. "I think I did better paintings than this when I was at infant school. How much did it cost?"

"Fifty pounds, and you have no taste Miles. Derek the manager tells me that the artist is going to be the next big thing. He's only here in Chesterfield for a week and this is the only picture he's painted whilst he's been here."

"How much?" I shouted. I was totally flabbergasted. Fifty pounds was more than one of our draymen earned in a month. Mind you some of them would also drink more than fifty pounds worth of beer in addition to their wages.

"We aren't made of money," I went on. "You are going to have to stop your spending, or at the very least, limit it to what you are earning as a teacher."

"We are one of the wealthiest families in Chesterfield," she replied. "Not only that but we've got two wages coming in. Okay, my salary isn't much but you're a director of your family's business. You make it sound as if we can't afford anything. I never realised you were so tight-fisted."

I wanted to tell her that we might have been asset rich, but we were definitely cash poor. In fact, we were getting poorer by the day thanks to her extravagant habits. Things at the brewery had improved since the war had ended, but we were barely making enough money to cover the repair bills to our pubs. But there was no point in continuing the argument. As far as Sarah was concerned, we may as well sell the brewery and spend the money on ourselves, without any concern for what might happen to our employees.

I decided to confide in Sprout and talk to him about the problems I was having with my marriage. He was my best friend and he had never been happier since he'd married Carrot. If I were honest I'd always been closer to Sprout than I had been to Herman. In fact, Herman and I had drifted apart slightly since he'd married my sister. I still considered him to be my friend, but it was as if his relationship with Rebecca had built a barrier between us. This meant that neither of us could be as open with each other as we'd once been.

Sprout and I didn't go for as many nights out as we once did. It wasn't really surprising when you consider that we both had businesses to run. Well to be completely accurate, it was Sprout who was running a business. His father had retired and had passed the running of the chain of fruit and veg shops over to him and Carrot. In contrast I was still playing second fiddle to my father.

Sprout's father had founded the company that Sprout now ran when he'd lost his job as a welder during the Great Depression. He'd started with a fruit and veg stall on Chesterfield market before renting his first shop in 1938. By the early 1950s he owned six successful shops and both Sprout and Carrot were working in the business.

Sprout's father knew the value of a good education and he also knew when the right time had arrived to pass the business over to his son and daughter-in-law. He had been the person who'd paid for Sprout to go to the Grammar School and had agreed that he stay on until he was eighteen. He was also the person who had insisted that Carrot join the business as its bookkeeper. He might have been poor at choosing Christian names, but he was quick to spot that Sprout and Carrot would take the business further than he could. As a result, he stepped down from managing the business in 1953, taking early retirement aged only 58.

The decision proved to be a good one as the number of shops in the chain increased to eleven over the next two years. They now stretched from South Yorkshire to North Nottinghamshire, as well as the six shops in North Derbyshire.

Unfortunately, my father didn't have the same level of confidence in me and, despite being 62, was still showing no signs of retiring. As a consequence, I was the only one out of the three of us who wasn't in charge of the family business by the time I was 28.

Sprout and Carrot now lived in the suburb of Walton and it was for this reason that we decided to meet in the Blue Stoops, one of our better pubs and close to Sprout's house.

"Sprout, you're a man of the world," I started off by saying.

"I don't know why you say that," he replied, before taking a large gulp of his pint of Goodyear's Pride.

"For a start, you were the first person in our class to have sex."

"Ah, but I cannot claim to have had sex with lots of women. I was lucky, you see. I knew right from the start that Georgina was the right one for me. I was never like Prince Charming looking for the person who would fit Cinderella's slipper. I managed to find the person who was the perfect fit for my nob at the first attempt."

A man who was sitting at the next table started choking on his beer. I was embarrassed that he had overheard our conversation and so I continued in a hushed voice.

"You're joking, aren't you?" I said.

"Of course I'm joking," Sprout replied. "Believe me there's nothing straightforward when it comes to the opposite sex. However, I'll admit that I was lucky to find Georgina at my first attempt."

I lowered my voice even more. "Well, you know that I've known Sarah for as long as you've known Carrot."

Sprout gave me a disapproving look.

"Sorry Sprout," I said. "But I've been calling her Carrot for over ten years now. It's difficult for me to get used to calling her by her proper name.

"Anyway I've known Sarah for as long as you've known Georgina, longer in fact if you go back to when we first saw her over the school wall. But unlike you two, we didn't have sex until we were married. It was the single thing that I wanted to do more than anything else in life. It was eight long years between our first date and getting married. Believe me, for eight years there wasn't a day that went by when I didn't envisage what sex with her was going to be like. Then when it finally happened, well it was a big disappointment."

"That's probably because you waited for eight years," replied Sprout. "During that time you'd built up your hopes so high that reality could never live up to it."

"Maybe you're right. But what about you and Georgina? You've been in a serious relationship for nearly eleven years. You've been married for eight years. You have two kids. Surely your sex life must have gone downhill?"

"Not in the slightest. It's just as good as the first time we made love. But believe me, a relationship is not just about sex. It's about conversation and having things in common as much as it is about games of hide the sausage. That's why it's good that we also work together. Georgina would hate it if she were just sitting at home all day looking after the kids. It worked out really well for us when she trained as an accountant. It meant she could do the bookkeeping from home whilst the children were little. However, now that both of them are at school she's able to get into the office far more often than she used to.

"It's great. We both have our individual interests, I like football and she likes singing in the local choir. We can both pursue our individual hobbies. But what we do have in

126

common is the business and as a result there is always plenty for us to talk about."

"But don't you ever fall out?" I asked.

"Of course we do, about all sorts of things, especially with regards to work. I'm the one who's always having new ideas about how to take the business forward. She's the accountant who has to curb some of my excesses. She's the main reason why our profits have consistently improved for the past five years. But don't you dare tell her that I said that. Anyway, the arguments never last that long and they usually finish with some of the best sex we ever have. You know, sometimes I think that it's worth starting an argument with her just for the sex at the end."

"Sarah and I don't have much in common," I told him. "She likes shopping and I like my work. She's got her teaching job, of course, but she's never shown any desire to join the family firm."

"Okay, so what about children then?" asked Sprout. "The other thing that Georgina and I spend hours talking about are the kids. Have you and Sarah ever talked about having children?"

"Well yes, although I told her that I wanted to wait until I was thirty before we started trying for one. After all, my father was 31 before he and my mother had Rupert."

"And Sarah was happy with that decision, was she?" asked Sprout.

"Yes, of course she was. At least, I think she was."

"Ah, women are such complex creatures," Sprout continued. "I think you will discover that when she said that she was happy, what she really meant was that she was not happy at all.

"You know I think that I have discovered the root cause of all your problems. If I were you I'd go home and tell her that you've had second thoughts about waiting until you are thirty and you want to start trying for a baby straight away. If nothing else, it means you'll be able to have sex without using a French Letter. You know what they say, having sex with a condom on is a bit like taking a bath in a Macintosh."

I looked a little apprehensive about Sprout's idea, but he either didn't notice or chose to ignore it. After all, he was in full flow by now so he continued with his advice.

"If I may ask, what position do you and Sarah usually adopt when making love?"

The conversation had been difficult as it was. But this new question from Sprout took my embarrassment to a whole new level.

"The missionary position, of course," I replied trying not to go red.

"There you have it," said Sprout. "The missing piece of the jigsaw. That's your other problem. There are far more positions for you to try and you will find that they can really spice up your sex life. I've got a book that can help you there. I'll drop it off tomorrow."

I thanked Sprout and with that both of us finished off our beers. The next day Sprout dropped a parcel wrapped in plain brown paper at my office. I unwrapped it to discover that it contained a much-thumbed copy of the *Kama Sutra*.

"Bloody hell," I thought as I looked through the book. "I don't think I could ever persuade Sarah to do that. As for that one, how on earth did they ever manage to get into that position? They must both be contortionists."

# Chapter 14

"What are we having for lunch today?" Nigel asked Molly as she put the kettle on.

"I've just got us a Cornish pasty each. It'll be a few minutes yet as I want to heat them up in the oven. It would have been a lot easier if your uncle had owned a microwave, but he never really did embrace the modern age, did he?"

"So what's the plan for rest of the day?" she continued.

"Hopefully, we can finish clearing the rooms upstairs this afternoon. We only have the third bedroom and the bathroom left and neither have anywhere near as much stuff in them as the first two rooms. It's a good job really, since we are going to have to make more than one trip to the recycling centre when we've finished. Also I want to find out more about what the hospice shop will take. Obviously, we will have to come back tomorrow to clear downstairs and probably on Thursday as well. After everything we've discovered so far I'm not convinced that we will be able to clear out the rest of it tomorrow. We still have to empty the attic, the shed, the living room, and the dining room, as well as the study."

"You know that I can't come back on Friday if we haven't finished by then," said Molly. "Don't forget I've got a dentist appointment at ten o'clock."

"I know," replied Nigel. "Even with the amount of junk that my uncle's accumulated over the years we should be finished by then. Mind you, I say that, but we haven't even looked in the attic yet. God only knows how much rubbish we will find up there."

The pasties were now ready so Nigel and Molly tucked in. After a second cup of tea they returned upstairs to finish clearing the remaining bedroom and bathroom.

The third bedroom was far smaller than the other two and unlike them was virtually empty, with just a chest of drawers and a cot.

"That's a surprise," said Nigel. "Aunty Sarah and Uncle Miles never had any children. So I wonder why there's a cot in here?"

*******

I decided not to broach the subject of different positions to Sarah. I didn't know how she would take to the idea. The *Kama Sutra* may have been all well and good for Indian contortionists, but not for a middle-class couple from Chesterfield. However, I did raise the subject of children with her and she seemed genuinely pleased by the idea.

That night we made love for the first time without a condom and it was a better experience, just as Sprout had promised it would be. It still wasn't earth shattering though and I began to wonder if I'd been right to forgo mentioning the *Kama Sutra*. After all Sprout had told me that the lack of variety was the other reason why our sex life wasn't right. Perhaps if we tried the wheelbarrow position that might all change.

A couple of months later Sarah seemed very excited. She told me that she had missed her period the previous month and that she thought she was pregnant. Only it proved to be a false alarm.

Ian Walker

Three months after that though she was definitely pregnant. Our doctor had confirmed it. But two weeks later she had a miscarriage.

Sarah was inconsolable.

"Never mind," I said to her. "We'll just have to keep on trying."

"Never mind. What the hell do you mean, never mind," she screamed back at me.

"It isn't you who's lost the child. It's me."

I didn't know what to say to her or how to comfort her. I remembered what Sprout had told me, how making love to Carrot was best after they had had a row. But I soon put these thoughts out of my mind and it was another six weeks before we had sex again.

By then it was the summer of 1956 and we had agreed that she would give up her teaching job whilst we continued to try for a child.

A few weeks later, Sarah announced that she was pregnant again. She was extremely nervous and so was I. Neither of us wanted to get our hopes up too high in case she had another miscarriage.

The two of us didn't speak that much over the coming months as her stomach got larger and larger. Looking back on it I guess we were both worried about jinxing the pregnancy.

When she got to six months, we both started to relax a bit and the situation improved further when she got to seven months. After all, the baby could survive if it was born prematurely at that stage of the pregnancy.

Sarah was far happier than I'd seen her in a long time and we agreed to go out shopping to buy things for the new baby. We bought a new top of the range cot for the nursery and lots of baby clothes. Most of these were in green or yellow as we had no way of knowing whether we were going to have a boy or a girl.

Everything was going perfectly and the baby was due on March 27th 1957. Then four weeks before the due date, Sarah came to me with her eyes full of tears.

"I can't feel the baby move anymore," she sobbed.

"Perhaps he's asleep," I replied hopefully.

"You don't understand," she said. "I haven't felt the baby move for three days now."

I rushed her to the maternity unit at Scarsdale Hospital where they confirmed our worst fears. The baby had died in her womb.

The next 24 hours were a blur. Both of us were heartbroken and Sarah was in floods of tears. I will always remember going to her bedside after she had given birth. She was fast asleep and she looked so lovely and peaceful lying there. I had forgotten what attracted her to me all those years ago and I started crying.

"How have we ever ended up like this?" I pleaded.

That was when the doctor came into the room and broke the really bad news to me. They had to give Sarah an emergency hysterectomy. The two of us were destined never to have children and neither of us was even thirty years old yet.

"What sex was the baby?" I asked the doctor whilst trying to hold back the tears.

"It was a baby boy," he replied.

If he'd lived, he would have been the next Goodyear to run the family business. But now there would never be a next generation of Goodyears. The family name was destined to die with me.

This time there was no screaming or tears from Sarah. She took the whole thing far better than I did. At least I thought she did. But a few days later, she had emptied the chest of drawers in the nursery and burnt all the clothes we had bought in the back garden. She probably would have burnt the cot as well if it hadn't been too heavy for her to move by herself.

That night Sarah moved into the spare room. Her excuse was that my snoring was keeping her awake, but in reality it was because she no longer wanted to have sex with me if she couldn't have a child.

"Where do we go from here?" I thought as I got into bed by myself for the first time in four years.

# Chapter 15

"Well that's the first piece of good luck that we've had since we started clearing this house," said Nigel as he discovered that the chest of drawers was completely empty.

The second bedroom may have taken all morning to clear, but the fact that the third bedroom contained only a cot and an empty chest of drawers meant that he and Molly could progress straight on to clearing out the bathroom.

"Perhaps I was a little bit pessimistic," commented Molly as the two of them made a start on the bathroom cabinet. "We'll probably be able to clear out one of the downstairs rooms this afternoon after all."

"As long as we crack on," added Nigel.

Miles may have been a hoarder as well as a little untidy, but he was extremely well organised where his toiletries were concerned. He had a spare one of everything: spare toothpaste, spare soap, spare razors and shaving foam, spare shampoo and conditioner, as well as spare bathroom cleaner and numerous spare toilet rolls. In fact, he could have been snowed in for weeks without ever running out of deodorant or aftershave. It was quite sad really as he would never use any of the items he had bought.

"We can use most of these," said Molly as she put some of the toiletries into a box.

All the rest of the stuff went into a black bag destined for the recycling centre except for some of the towels, which Nigel and Molly considered good enough to take to the hospice shop.

Pretty soon the bathroom was cleared out. After taking down the pictures on the landing and a series of Royal Doulton plates from the walls of the staircase, Nigel and Molly moved downstairs to the dining room.

It was a room dominated by a large oak table and chairs.

"I think mum told me that this was originally in my grandparents' house," said Nigel, "and now we have a decision to make. Do we take it to auction or do we give it to charity?"

Until that point, the things they'd decided to take to the auction house were all relatively small items. These would all fit into the car. But a dining table and a set of chairs would have to be collected by the auction house.

"Well, if it's any help, the antiques programmes on TV say that brown furniture isn't selling at the moment," added Molly.

After a brief discussion, Molly said, "Let's think about it overnight and we can make the final decision tomorrow."

As well as the table and chairs, the room also contained a sideboard. There were several items on top of it, including a Moorcroft fruit bowl, matching candlesticks and an ornate clock. The clock had an inscription on it, which Nigel had never noticed before.

He picked it up and read the inscription out loud. It said 'To Major Goodyear on the occasion of his retirement, September 5th 1958. From all your employees and tenants at Goodyear's Brewery Chesterfield.'

*******

Father knew that Sarah and I could never have children. He also knew that we were both devastated by this. He never talked about it, but I knew that he was worried about the future of the brewery and, in particular, who in the family would take over the business from me.

Eventually his prayers were answered when Rebecca gave birth to a baby boy in March 1958. He was a bonny little chap with fair hair and rosy cheeks. He was the spitting image of his father. Sprout suggested they call him Frederick, as he said it was cool to have the same name twice, even cooler if his Christian name was English and his surname was German. However, my sister was not impressed, so she and Herman decided to call him Nigel instead.

My father had been waiting for some kind of sign like this, especially since he was about to turn 65. So he finally decided to step down as Managing Director, although he kept his Chairman's role. But since that role only involved him attending board meetings once per quarter, he effectively handed over the day-to-day running of the company to me.

We worked side by side for a few months before he eventually retired in September 1958. On his last day, we held a farewell party for him in the brewery cellars. I will always remember him standing there, pint in hand, laughing and joking with his employees. The staff presented him with a clock as a retirement gift before consuming even more beer than they did at our wedding. It was a fitting tribute to the man who'd been Managing Director of the brewery for the past 28 years.

I asked him what he was going to do in his retirement and he told me that he intended to enjoy the rest of his life. He said he wanted to travel and see a bit of the world. The first place he wanted to go to was Italy, where he planned to visit Rupert's grave. It had been fifteen years since Rupert was killed in action and Father was finally able to face the prospect of seeing where his eldest son was buried.

Unfortunately, my father was destined never to visit Italy or to have a long and happy retirement, as four months later he was knocked down and killed whilst crossing the road outside his house. I later discovered his false teeth in the gutter. They'd been knocked out by the impact.

His funeral was one of the largest Chesterfield had ever seen with all the brewery employees and tenants attending the service. It had to be held in the Crooked Spire, as it was the only church large enough to accommodate all the people who wanted to attend. There were representatives from both of Chesterfield's other two breweries and from various suppliers, as well as family and friends. And my father had many friends.

His coffin was taken from the Crooked Spire on the back of the same horse-drawn dray that had been used at my mother's funeral. He was buried in the graveyard of St Peter and St Paul Church in Old Brampton, in the same grave as my mother. It had been his dying wish.

The contrast between the burial and the service at the Crooked Spire could not have been greater, as the only people at his burial were the undertakers and the six members of his immediate family.

I'd learnt so much from my father and as I stood alongside his grave watching his coffin being lowered, I couldn't help shed a tear as I remembered my happy childhood with him. In particular, I reflected on him sitting in front of the radio listening to the BBC whilst smoking his pipe, looking happy and content with his lot in life.

In his final months, my father may have retired from the business, but he still acted as a sounding board, giving me advice about running the brewery whenever I needed it. Now he was gone. I was all alone at work especially since Rebecca had left when she became pregnant with Nigel.

The brewery may have been a family business, but right at that particular moment in time the family consisted of just myself. I was alone at work and as good as alone at home. It was not a happy time for me. This was made even worse as our beer sales had started to decline.

The late 1950s had seen many changes. No longer did sons merely follow in the footsteps of their fathers. Rock 'n roll had been thrust on an unsuspecting world when Bill Haley released 'Rock Around the Clock' in 1955. The same year saw James Dean portraying a disaffected teenager in *Rebel Without a Cause*. Elvis Presley released his first single in 1956 and in 1957, the Russians launched Sputnik 1, the first artificial satellite to orbit the earth. I was in my late twenties by then and I began to think that I no longer understood the world.

The British brewing industry was not immune to these changes as witnessed by the fact that a new type of beer was sweeping the UK. It was a different beer to all those that had gone before and was the drink of choice of the young generation. It was called keg and we didn't make it. The reason for this was simple: we didn't have the equipment. To make keg beer you needed to be able to pasteurise, chill and filter the beer and, most importantly, you needed a supply of kegs and a keg-racking machine in order to fill them. In total, the cost would have been several thousand pounds, which was money we just didn't have.

Our tenants, of course, were demanding the new type of beer, as they didn't want to see their customers going elsewhere. The Ashgate Brewery demonstrated one possible solution, when it introduced Flowers keg alongside its own beers. Overall sales in their pubs increased, but this proved to be a false dawn, as sales of their own beers fell dramatically. As a consequence of this, they sold out to Mansfield Brewery in 1959.

In his will my father had split everything between Rebecca and I. If it had been just down to me, we would have sold his house and invested the money in the company. Rebecca, however, wanted to spend her share on buying a larger house for her family to live in. She said that they needed the space as she and Herman were planning to have more children in future. In the end, we agreed that if I invested my inheritance in the business and Rebecca did not, I would increase my shareholding to 55% with Rebecca's share dropping to 45%.

There was also the little matter of what to do with our grandmother before we put the house on the market. She was 92 by then and was incapable of looking after herself. Father had done his best, but even he was thinking about putting her in a home just before his death. Rebecca and I both agreed that with his passing this was now the best course of action. So in February 1959, we arranged for her to take a room at the Riverside Old Folks home just outside Chesterfield.

It was very nice, but Granny didn't like it. She said it smelt of cabbages and they wouldn't let her drink sherry before her evening meal or have a brandy at bedtime. She died only three months after moving in. I did feel guilty about this, but what choice did I have? She couldn't continue to live by herself and she couldn't move in with Rebecca and Herman and their young son. As for moving in with Sarah and me, well I wouldn't have wished that on anybody.

In June 1959, we sold the house where my sister and I had both grown up to a firm of solicitors who wanted it for their offices. It was a great location for them right in the centre of Chesterfield, but it meant that it was destined never to be a family home ever again. Rebecca took most of the furniture in order to furnish the new four-bedroomed house that she and Herman had bought on Chatsworth Road.

I took the oak dining table, chairs and the sideboard. Sarah was not at all happy as she claimed that they were too old-fashioned for our house. However, by this stage I was past caring about what she thought. I took my father's radio even though it was 25 years old, as well as the clock he was given when he retired. One other thing that I kept was the art deco nude from his desk.

Mind you, the saddest part of the whole process for me was when I discovered his medals and the hipflask, which he'd given to Rupert when he'd gone off to fight in Italy. He'd thrown them in the bottom drawer of his desk where they had remained for the past fifteen years. There was no way that I was going to throw them away and so I took them home with me as well.

I went up into the attic to clear it out and discovered many of Rupert's old toys. These included the Hornby O gauge train set he had received as a Christmas present back in 1933. It had always been his favourite, but despite this he'd always let me play with it. There were also loads of old family photos including a framed picture that my father had told me was the earliest photo ever taken of our family.

It was taken in 1871 just nine years after Goodyear's Brewery had been founded. It featured a seated Benjamin Goodyear with his walrus moustache, flat cap and Albert chain, his wife Mavis with their youngest son Alfred, who was then only six months old, on her knee. Also in the photo was my grandfather, who was five years old alongside his sisters Ruth, aged seven and Felicity, aged three. The final person in the photo was Benjamin's mother Rose, my great-great-grandmother who must have been 72 at the time the photo was taken, since she had been born in 1799.

It was an odd feeling looking at her dressed in her long

skirt. She had a stern expression on her face and her hair was scraped back into a central parting. She had been born in the eighteenth century, long before the invention of photography. It was also before Waterloo and Trafalgar and 38 years before Queen Victoria came to the throne, at a time when slavery was still legal in Britain.

I wondered why the photo had been kept in the attic and could only think that it was because of the subsequent family feud. In 1897, Alfred had fallen out with his father after declaring his love for Cassandra Maynard, the youngest daughter of Ernest Maynard who owned our great rivals, Brimington Brewery.

Alfred subsequently married Cassandra and went to work alongside her brother at their brewery in Brimington. It was said that he and my grandfather never spoke again. I guess it was not surprising then that the photo of them as children should end up in a chest in the attic.

Funny to think that fifty years later my own father had actually wanted me to marry the granddaughter of Cassandra's brother.

We didn't have space for the items I'd discovered in my father's attic, so I merely transferred them to my own attic. I meant to find a more permanent home for them at some point, but I never did and so they are still there to this day.

# Chapter 16

Nigel and Molly took the clock, the Moorcroft fruit bowl and the candlesticks into the living room. They put them with the growing collection of items that were going to be sold at auction.

Returning back to the dining room, they discovered that the sideboard contained a canteen of silver cutlery, which they added to the auction pile. Some of the drawers contained several tablecloths and a set of place mats, which they opted to give to charity. One of the cabinets in the sideboard housed a collection of glasses, whilst the other contained various bottles of spirits, most of them half full.

The spirit bottles looked extremely old so Nigel and Molly decided to tip their contents down the sink and put the bottles into the bottle bank. The glasses were nothing special so they opted to take them to the charity shop.

One of the drawers in the sideboard contained several tins full of old coins, which Nigel and Molly added to the coins they had discovered in the first bedroom.

Finally, they took down the pictures and a large copper charger from the walls and carefully placed them amongst the other items destined for the auction house. They had finished the dining room and it had only taken them a little over an hour.

It was now half past three so they decided to call it a day, as they still had to fit in several visits to the recycling centre and the hospice shop.

In the end, it took them three visits to the recycling centre before they were finally able to go to the hospice shop.

Whilst they were there, they wanted to arrange for some-body to pick up the larger items of furniture.

The manager explained that they would only take items that they were confident would sell. Anything that was either stained or worn out, or that didn't comply with the latest safety legislation wouldn't be acceptable to them.

Nigel and Molly thanked him and after agreeing that the furniture would be collected at 9 o'clock on Thursday morning, they set off back to Ashbourne.

"We'd better think of an alternative plan," said Nigel once the two of them were sitting in the car. "I just assumed that they would take the lot. It now looks as if that won't be the case and so we'll need to get someone else to collect anything they don't want."

"I think the council will collect bulky items," said Molly. "I'll check on the internet to see how much they charge. But I'll do it tomorrow as the first thing I want to do when we get home is to put my feet up and have a glass of wine."

"Good idea," said Nigel as he started the car and set off for home.

The following day they arrived at their uncle's house even earlier than they had the day before. It was day three of the great clear out. They still had their uncle's study, living room, attic, shed and the garage to go through and they wanted to get as much of it done as possible that day.

It was the turn of their uncle's study next. This was only a small room, but they were disappointed to discover that once again it was packed full of junk. The fact that both the dining room and the third bedroom had contained relatively few things had lulled them into a false sense of optimism. It was clear that they had underestimated how long the process was going to take.

The study was more like the second bedroom, however. It contained numerous papers and documents, which had to be examined before being thrown away. It would just be their luck to bin the whole lot only to miss a valuable share certificate.

As well as being a study, it had also been their uncle's den and it contained many objects that must have been of great sentimental value to him.

Molly went to make tea for the two of them whilst Nigel removed the art deco nude from their uncle's desk. It was obviously quite valuable and would make a good lot for the auction house.

Also on the desk was a plastic beer cowl with 'Goodyear's Sparkling Bitter' written on it.

"I'd forgotten that the brewery also made keg beer," Nigel thought to himself as he picked it up.

*******

Father's house sold for £8,350 and once the estate agent and solicitor's fees were paid, my half share meant I had a little over £4,000 to invest in the business.

However, I had a dilemma. I'd always wanted to build a second pub to the same design as the George Stephenson. But now I had an alternative way in which to spend the money, namely on a keg-racking machine and all the rest of the equipment needed to produce keg beer.

It was a tough choice, but in the end I decided that we needed to produce keg beer. What swayed me was the feeling that buying another pub would only delay the inevitable, that ultimately it wouldn't stop the decline in our beer sales. We needed to embrace the new world we were living in, a new world that wanted keg.

I decided to base our new brand on Bottoms Up Bitter. With an original gravity of 1035 it was our weakest bitter, and sales had been going backwards for many years, as most people preferred the stronger Goodyear's Pride.

Bottoms Up Bitter was to be relaunched as a keg beer called Goodyear's Sparkling Bitter with an advertising strapline that read, 'Add sparkle to your life with Goodyear's Sparkling Bitter'. I devised it myself and thought it was quite catchy. Of course, it was never going to be advertised on TV like Mackeson Stout or Davenport's. But it was on several billboards around Chesterfield, as well as on drip mats in our pubs.

Despite the fact that the launch of the new beer was relatively low-key, the whole exercise proved to be very expensive. It wasn't just the cost of all the equipment we needed for the production of keg beer, there was also the outlay for all the dispense equipment. It cost me £1,500 to buy 300 steel kegs and even the cost for designing the new cowl came to over £300. Mind you, I was very happy with the pre-production model and decided to keep it as a souvenir. In the end, the total expenditure came to £8,000 and I had to increase our mortgage with the bank in order to make up the funding gap.

However, the new beer was a success and sales began to soar, albeit mainly at the expense of our other beers. So in April 1960 I took the decision to make our cooper redundant. Sales of cask ale were declining and I had decided to introduce steel casks alongside the kegs, as they cost far less to maintain than ones made of oak. He was 66 at the time so we didn't have to make any redundancy payment to him, although I did feel sorry for his apprentice who had to retrain as a fitter working on the new keg beer.

I felt less sorry for the Maynards at Brimington Brewery, who couldn't afford to change over to the new keg beer and therefore sold out to Whitbread's in May of 1960. The first thing Whitbread's did was to close the brewery down.

For nearly one hundred years there had been three breweries in Chesterfield. But with the closure of Brimington Brewery we were now the only one left. Consequently, I was now even more alone than ever.

# Chapter 17

"Do you think this cowl is worth anything?" asked Nigel as Molly returned to the study carrying two mugs of tea.

"I doubt it," she replied. "Although there is a market for old brewery items, I'm not at all sure that it extends to old keg cowls. Mind you, they can always make it part of a job lot."

Which was how the cowl ended up amongst the items being taken to auction.

Nigel pulled out the top drawer of the desk and saw that it was full of papers. He found another copy of Uncle Miles's will and various folders containing the gas, electricity and numerous other bills relating to the house. Once again, it appeared that their uncle never threw anything away as some of the bills dated back to when the house was built in the 1950s.

"This lot all has to go," said Nigel who was looking despairingly at over thirty years' worth of council tax and water rate bills.

"Bloody hell," he added as he pulled out a file containing all their uncle's old TV licenses.

It appeared he had continued to pay his annual license fee even though it should have been free for the past seventeen years. Either he hadn't realised what the situation was or just hadn't bothered to inform the TV licensing authority that he was over 75.

"Perhaps we could get some money back," said Molly hopefully.

"I very much doubt it," Nigel replied.

An hour later Molly and Nigel had cleared out half the drawers in the desk and had filled four black bin liners with rubbish.

"You know, I never would have believed that so much rubbish could hide in one desk," said Nigel, "and to think that the only useful thing we've found is one book of stamps."

Nigel was just about to make a start on another drawer when he turned to Molly and said, "You know, I've seen this type of desk before on TV and sometimes they have a secret drawer."

With that he started to feel under a small shelf, which was about two inches below the top of the desk. Suddenly, they both heard a click.

"Got it," said Nigel. Then looking at Molly, he continued, "See I told you so! I wonder if there's anything in it."

The secret drawer was only about an inch deep, but it was big enough to contain a bundle of letters tied together with a bow.

"The dirty old bugger," exclaimed Nigel as he undid the bow and started to read the first letter. "He was a dark horse. They're love letters. Uncle Miles had a lover."

*******

I wasn't looking to start an affair. Far from it. My life was complicated enough at the start of 1960. My father had died only twelve months earlier and I was frantically trying to persuade the bank to lend me the money necessary to launch our new keg beer.

At home? Well, my marriage wasn't a marriage anymore, which was probably why I was such an easy target for Jane Carghill.

Jane had joined us as a clerk the previous year. She was 27 years old, five years my junior and although not a classic beauty, she was a pretty enough girl. She was married to a purser on a P&O cruise liner who was away from home for months on end.

She certainly knew how to make the most of her attributes as she often came to work in a low-cut top. This made her both popular with the male staff members and unpopular with the female ones in equal measures.

Mind you, she was good at her job. This was why I asked her to stay behind one day in order to help me pull the projections together and to work on the presentation I was due to make to the bank.

The projections were particularly difficult to do and I was extremely grateful for her help. By the time we had finished, it was nearly 9 o'clock and I asked her if she wanted a drink before she left.

"Sure thing," she said. "Do you have any Scotch?"

Of course I did, I had a whole pallet of it in our wine and spirits store. Still, there was no need for me to go there as I also had a decanter full of whisky in my office. I turned my back on her and went to pour us both a glass.

"So do you miss your husband whilst he's away?" I asked her.

"Not really," she replied as I turned around, only to discover that she had undone her blouse revealing her white bra underneath. I said nothing as the blouse dropped to the floor.

She smiled at me before putting her hands behind her back and removing her bra. By this time, my eyes were as big as saucers as she removed her skirt and then very slowly took her knickers off. She was standing there stark naked in my office as bold as brass; naked that was, apart from her stockings and suspenders.

I was shocked, but at the same time I was enthralled as I looked at her beautiful round breasts and her dark pubic hair.

I walked over to her and put the whisky glass in her hand.

"Do you want any water with that?" I asked her.

"I think I'm moist enough as it is," she replied taking my hand and placing it between her legs.

She wasn't joking; she was very wet. I tried to remember if I'd ever made Sarah as wet as that and decided I hadn't.

"Aren't you a bit overdressed?" she asked me, as she looked me up and down.

I wanted her more than anything at that moment. It had been two years since I'd last had sex and I wasn't going to turn down an open invitation. So I hurriedly removed my suit, shirt, tie and pants. Normally I was meticulous about hanging them on a hanger in my wardrobe or folding them on a chair, but on this occasion I just threw them on the floor as Jane and I kissed each other passionately.

"I don't have any condoms," I whispered in her ear.

"Don't worry, I've got some," she replied reaching for her handbag before giving me a wink and asking, "Do you think three will be enough?"

"Three," I thought to myself. "Sarah and I had never made love more than once in an evening let alone three times."

She took the condoms out of her bag and I suggested that we go to the hop store. It had been fifteen years since Sarah and I had first gone there for a bit a teenage fumbling. Now I was just as excited as I had been that first day with Sarah.

The two of us ran hand in hand through the brewhouse. Both of us were completely naked except for her stockings and my socks. As soon as we got there we started kissing again before Jane broke off and took out one of the condoms, which she gently put on my erect penis.

Then we started making love, and not just in the missionary position. Jane preferred to be on top, controlling the motion and I was happy to let her do so. Finally, I was having the type of sex that I had always dreamed of. Not only that, but Jane was enjoying it as much as I was. She was sticking her nails into my back and moaning when suddenly her whole body started to tremble.

"Bloody hell," I thought to myself. "So that's what an orgasm is."

# Chapter 18

"You shouldn't really be reading those," said Molly. "They are personal."

But Nigel couldn't help it, he was intrigued. The uncle he remembered was an old man without any female friends. He was astonished to discover that he'd had a sex life when he was younger and had embarked on an illicit affair.

"So that's what Beaky meant when he said that Uncle Miles's dick had got him into all kinds of trouble over the years," announced Nigel. "I wonder what happened?"

In total, there were six letters dating between February 1960 and March 1961.

"I think Aunty Sarah died in April 1961," said Nigel. "Perhaps the two things are connected?"

*******

We used all three condoms. I was never in any doubt that we would.

"That was unbelievably good," I said to her once we'd finally finished.

"You weren't too bad yourself," she replied. "A definite nine out of ten. If you want to do it again, I can go and get another condom from my bag."

"I don't think I'd be capable of doing it a fourth time," I replied. "Anyway, what do you mean nine out of ten? I was fantastic."

"You weren't bad," she said. "Good enough to qualify for a repeat performance if you like. But you still have quite a way to go to match my best ever lover. He managed it six times in one night."

"Good grief, how many lovers have you had?" I asked her.

She didn't even have to think about it. She replied straightaway, "You're my 105th."

"Christ almighty," I cried. "You're only my second."

"Well, you'd better make up for lost time," she replied, "and you won't find a better teacher than me. I've taught most of the lads at the local rugby club. If any of them are still virgins by the time they reach eighteen then I'm the one who breaks them in. It's a bit like breaking in a horse, which is ironic as some of them are hung like stallions."

The more she told me about herself, the more she shocked me. But, to be honest, I was also keen to find out more.

Jane leant over and kissed me.

"Are you absolutely sure that you don't want me to go back for another condom?" she said.

"No, I'd better be getting home," I replied. "What about tomorrow?"

"Steady on tiger," she joked. "Mind you, why not? You can come to my house after work."

With that the two of us walked back to my office where we both got dressed.

The next day I couldn't wait for work to end. I could see Jane through my office door and was amazed at how calm she was. She had a large bruise at the top of her arm where I had grabbed hold of her. What if people realised we'd had sex the previous night? Or was I just being paranoid?

Fortunately for me nobody could see the marks on my back where she had dug in her nails whilst having an orgasm.

Was anybody suspicious? I guessed not.

Jane left bang on five o'clock and I waited another half an hour before I set off for her house on Park Road. It was a two-bedroomed mid-terraced property and I wondered what the neighbours would think when they saw my car parked outside.

Jane didn't seem concerned though as she grabbed me as soon as I went through the door.

"I want you inside of me," she whispered in my ear, which caused me to get a hard-on straight away.

She took me upstairs to her bedroom where we made love just as passionately as we'd done the previous night. This time I could only manage it twice and when we had finished we decided to take a bath together.

"Does your husband have any idea what you get up to when he's not here?" I asked her as she laid on top of me in the bath.

"He doesn't have a clue," she replied. "You know, sometimes I think I've got the perfect life. My husband goes away for months at a time and is absolutely gagging for it when he gets back. Meanwhile whilst he's away, I'm free to have sex with anybody I want."

"You know, I've never met a woman like you before," I replied. "You're a real nymphomaniac."

"I wouldn't call myself that. I just like sex, and I'm bloody good at it. It's my hobby in the same way that other women like knitting."

I didn't like a lot of the things that Jane said, but I was absolutely besotted with her. Was I in love or was it just the sex? I was totally confused and only time would tell.

The following day the bank approved a £4,000 loan and Jane's husband returned for two weeks of shore leave. She wouldn't have sex with me whilst her husband was at home, not even in the hop store. She ignored me at work and I was beginning to think that our affair was at an end, until I received a note from her ten days later. She told me that her husband was going back to sea the following Tuesday. This would be when her harbour would be looking for the return of my pocket battleship.

The following week we resumed our affair as if nothing had happened. She told me that she would write to me each time her husband left to go to sea, inviting me back into her bed.

I thought it was a strange way to carry on, but I had little choice other than to go along with it.

# Chapter 19

After reading the first letter, Nigel decided that he'd read enough. He threw all of them into the nearest black bin liner.

"Well I never! I didn't know my uncle had an interest in anybody other than my aunt," he said to Molly. "Now it appears that he was carrying on an affair at the same time as he was married to her. I wonder why the affair ended?"

Nigel didn't have to wait long to find out. Whilst they were clearing out the next drawer in the desk, they discovered another letter from Jane. It was very short and merely said:

April 20th, 1961

Dear Miles,

We've had a lot of fun, but all good things must come to an end. Deep down you must have realised that it wasn't going to last. You've started to ask too much of me and as a result I have decided to end our affair. Since we have to continue working together I hope you will behave like an adult towards me.

Yours truly,

Jane

The reason why this letter was not in the secret drawer soon became apparent. For immediately below it was a cutting from the *Derbyshire Times*, which was also dated, April 20th, 1961. It was Aunt Sarah's obituary. Her death meant that Uncle Miles no longer had to hide any details about his affair from his wife.

******

The affair with Jane continued for several months. I thought nobody realised what was going on, but I was wrong. Eventually, Mark Stephens, our Finance Director, asked if he could have a word with me.

"Look Miles," he said, "I don't want you to find out from anybody else, but it's all over the office that you and Jane Carghill are having an affair."

I was completely flabbergasted.

"Shit," I said. "How the hell did they find out about us?"

"Miles, she's bloody well told everyone," he replied. "That woman is bloody dangerous. If I were you I would drop her like a stone."

It couldn't have been easy for him to have this conversation with me. After all, I was his boss, but I realised that he had done it for my benefit and I thanked him for his honesty.

Later that evening I went around to Jane's house as previously agreed and we had a blazing row about it.

"How could you be so stupid as to tell everybody about us?" I shouted at her.

"As if they hadn't guessed anyway," she replied. "I was only confirming what had been going around the rumour mill for the past four months. Anyway none of them would hold it against you. They all know your wife is a lesbian."

"What?" I could barely contain myself.

"Well, she's either a lesbian or she's frigid, based on what you've told me, possibly both. And anyway, one of the other girls spotted her going into the Mucky Duck with that dyke policewoman friend of hers.

The Mucky Duck was the nickname for the White Swan, a pub of ours not far from the brewery. Throughout the early 1960s, it was a popular meeting place for homosexuals of both sexes. And whilst Queen Victoria may have ensured that it wasn't against the law to be a lesbian, that wasn't the case if you were a homosexual man. As a consequence, the pub had been raided on several occasions. But each time it had happened nothing illegal was found to be taking place there. Clearly, Lydia had been tipping the licensee off before each raid.

I was shocked but not really surprised. Things hadn't been right between Sarah and I even before she'd lost the baby.

Jane and I made up by making love and I was able to confirm that Sprout's theory was absolutely correct. Sex after an argument was the best sex of all. Jane promised not to discuss our relationship in the office any more, but in reality the genie was now well and truly out of the bottle. Deep down I realised she'd only done it to become untouchable at work. After all I was her boss. To be strictly accurate, I was her boss's boss. Barry Matthews, the office manager who'd taken over from my sister, was her actual boss. How the hell would he ever be able to take her to task whilst she was shagging the Managing Director?

If I thought I had problems, then things were about to get a whole lot worse. Sarah had been feeling unwell over the Christmas holiday and in early January she went to see the doctor.

At first he thought she was anaemic and recommended that she drink a pint of Guinness a day. However, when this had no effect she went back and had some blood tests in February.

The results were not good. They revealed that she was suffering from kidney disease and unless she received treatment it would eventually prove fatal.

Treatment would involve dialysis, but the problem was that Chesterfield Royal Hospital didn't have a dialysis machine back then. Her only hope was that we would be able to buy one ourselves. But at a cost of over a thousand pounds, we just didn't have the money.

"But we are one of the wealthiest families in Chesterfield," she shouted at me. "We must have the money. If you hadn't wasted your bloody inheritance on that fucking brewery, then we would have been able to buy one tomorrow."

I had never heard her swear before and I was quite shocked. She was correct, of course, but I couldn't put the clock back. Installation of the keg racking line had used up all my money and had also increased our loan with the bank.

I told her I had read in the paper of someone who'd been in a similar position to her. On that occasion, the man's family had raised the money through things like sponsored walks.

"Miles, I've only got weeks to live. How are we going to raise a thousand pounds through sponsored walks in that time? Why would anybody sponsor us anyway? Everybody knows how wealthy we are.

Why can't we borrow the money?"

"Because it has only been six months since we increased our mortgage with the bank," I replied.

"Well, why can't we go to another bank then?" she asked me.

We were with the Westminster Bank and her father, although now retired, still had contacts at Williams Deacon's. But that was immaterial. The truth was we didn't have any security left.

In the end I told her that the only thing we could do was to sell off one of our pubs. We'd have to pay part of our bank loan back, because they had a charge over our entire estate. But hopefully, we would still have enough money left over to pay for a dialysis machine.

She was not happy, although at least we now had a plan. Of course, in previous years, I'd have just phoned up Joe Maynard and he would have bought one of our pubs from us. He may have been our competitor, but when all was said and done, he was related to us. He probably wouldn't even have tried to knock the price down. But Joe Maynard had sold out to Whitbread's for a knockdown price and was now a broken man.

Breweries up and down the country were being taken over every day of the week. Nobody wanted to buy a single pub anymore, not when you could buy a hundred pubs for less than you would have paid ten years ago.

In the end, my plan to sell a pub came too late. Sarah went downhill so fast that she eventually went into a coma and passed away on April 11th, 1961. It was a week before our eighth wedding anniversary.

Part of me was devastated but part of me was relieved. On the one hand, there were all the happy memories. She was my first love and my only love for many years, before things had started to go wrong between us. On the other hand, the marriage had failed and her death had now freed me to start again. Anyway, it was probably for the best that she had died. After all, would she really have wanted to be hooked up to a machine three times a week for the next forty years?

I knew what I wanted or rather I knew who I wanted.

Jane's husband was home on leave at the time and so I asked her to stay behind after work so that we could talk things over. I told her that she was the only woman for me and she should get a divorce so that we could get married. I said that it would be wonderful not having to pretend anymore and eventually the two of us could start a family together.

Her response shocked me. She said that she had absolutely no desire to have children and that the current situation suited her down to the ground. She also pointed out that my wife wasn't even buried yet. She felt that, at the very least, I should have waited until a suitable period of time had elapsed. But then she added that it wouldn't matter anyway as she wouldn't change her mind. A few days later I received a letter from her ending our affair.

Sarah was cremated at the end of April and I fulfilled my role as the grieving husband. It was the least I could do for her. I didn't cry. By comparison, Lydia was in floods of tears. We had a wake for Sarah at the George Stephenson and all my friends and family attended. There was also a good turnout from amongst the brewery employees. But there were only a handful of people including Lydia and Sarah's mum and dad who had known her from the time before we got married. It made me realise how few friends and relatives she actually had.

A week after the funeral I decided to pay an unexpected visit to Jane's house. Her husband had returned to his ship by then and I wanted to confront her face to face.

I pulled into her road and immediately recognised the car parked outside her house. It was Barry Matthews's Hillman Minx. As I drove past, I saw him coming out of her house. He had a smug look on his face and his jumper was inside out. No prizes for guessing what he'd been up to. He may as well have had number 106 tattooed on his forehead.

I was furious. She'd humiliated me with one of my managers and the next day I sacked them both. Of course everybody knew why I'd done it, but I didn't care. I got a few black looks from people in the office over the coming months, but eventually they got over it and everything returned to normal.

# Chapter 20

The final item in the drawer was a large expandable folder containing receipts. Most of these were really old and Nigel considered just throwing them out with the other rubbish. But after discussing it with Molly, they decided to take the folder home with them. Molly had volunteered to sort through it, pointing out that if there were receipts for any of the items they were taking to auction, it might increase their value.

"That's the desk emptied," she announced before adding, "and I think it's high time that you go and make us some tea this time for a change."

Nigel went to the kitchen whilst Molly continued clearing out the office. As well as the desk there were several shelves, many of them full of files containing business records and wage slips. Since the records were at least fifty years old and the wage slips dated back more than 25 years, Molly didn't really have to go through them in much detail. They were all destined for the recycling centre so she merely transferred them to the cardboard boxes she had brought with her.

She had just finished when Nigel returned with the tea.

"Well, that's the bulk of the paperwork sorted," she said to him. "Now let's start on everything else."

Facing their uncle's desk was another set of shelves, only these were crammed full of all manner of things. Nigel leant over and picked up a silver tankard. It was inscribed with the words, "R and G Supermarket grand opening March 14th, 1962."

"I wonder why he's got this and what its relevance is?" said Nigel

"I remember R and G, they used to be huge in the eighties and nineties," replied Molly. "Don't you remember them? They were the first company to open a supermarket in Ashbourne. You know, the one that's now Sainsbury's?"

\*\*\*\*\*\*\*

I was pretty depressed after Sarah died. Mind you, it could also have been because Jane had dumped me. Odd expression 'dumped me' as it's usually associated more with teenagers than it is with men in their thirties.

Anyway, no matter what the reason was for my depression I was pretty miserable and so I should be, as I had a guilty secret. In January 1961 Sheffield Brewery had approached me about buying the business. I wasn't looking to sell, but it was a time when many small breweries were being taken over. So I guess it was only a matter of time before somebody made me an offer.

I was astonished by the amount that Sheffield Brewery was prepared to pay. It was £350,000 or £10,000 per pub, which was far more than I thought the business was worth. I say £10,000 per pub because, of course, it was the pubs they really wanted. They would almost certainly have sold the off-licenses and closed the brewery down.

It was a tempting offer, as even after paying off our loan this still would have left about £150,000 and 55% of this would have come to me. The thing was that I was only 33 years old and I liked running my own company. What would I do if I sold up?

Besides which, for the first time in years, things were going well. We had launched Goodyear's Sparkling Bitter the previous year and our sales were increasing. If I held out for another year or so, the price would almost certainly go up, or so I thought at the time. Also, the bid from Sheffield was unsolicited. What if another brewery was prepared to offer even more?

As a result, I rejected the offer from Sheffield out of hand. In fact, I didn't even discuss it with my sister, which I should have done as she owned 45% of the company.

All of this took place only three weeks before Sarah was diagnosed with kidney failure. At this time I should have picked up the phone to Andrew Walsh, the Chairman of Sheffield Brewery, and told him that I'd changed my mind. This would have meant that Sarah could have bought her dialysis machine immediately. But I didn't.

I tried telling myself that the reason I didn't contact Andrew Walsh was because I knew all our employees would lose their jobs, and I am sure that this is partly true. But was there a much darker reason? Did I really want shot of Sarah or was it because I feared that Andrew would sniff out my desperation and reduce his offer?

These were the thoughts that kept going through my head during 1961. It even got to the point where my guilty conscience was worrying me so much that I went to the doctor for some sleeping tablets.

Sprout and Herman could see that things weren't right. They presumed it was because Sarah had died. They had no idea that I could have saved her but didn't.

The two of them really wanted to cheer me up and so they decided to invite me out for a few beers around town one evening.

It had been ages since I had gone for a drink with my friends and I was really looking forward to meeting up with them again. This was despite the fact that I couldn't help comparing their lives with my own.

Herman still ran the family jewellery shop. He only had the one outlet and had no desire to expand as he valued his work–life balance. He liked nothing better than curling up with his newspaper in front of the fire, whilst my sister read a book. He was quite content with his lot in life and he proudly announced that he and my sister were expecting another child the following spring.

Sprout was far more ambitious than Herman. He was the type of person who relished a challenge. He loved taking risks and was not a man for resting on his laurels. That said, there was one part of his life he never wanted to make any changes to and that was his marriage. It was obvious that he was as much in love with Carrot as he had ever been and as a result I was massively envious of him. They'd had their two sons early in their marriage and Richard, the eldest, was about to start at the Grammar School in September, having passed his eleven-plus. The days when you had to pay to go to the Grammar School were only a distant memory now.

"Of course, he's going to be in Heathcote House the same as I was," said Sprout as the three of us sat down with our drinks in the Market Tavern.

Since taking over the business when Sprout's father had retired, Sprout and Carrot had concentrated on building up the chain of fruit and veg stores. By 1961, they had no fewer than 35 of them across the North Midlands and Yorkshire.

I asked Sprout what he was going to do next and wondered if one day he wanted to have shops throughout the whole of the UK.

"Funny you should ask me that," replied Sprout. "Because

Georgina and I are flying to Chicago next week to look at a new concept in retailing."

"Really?" I replied not wanting to show him how envious I was. After all, the only time I'd been in a plane was in the back of an RAF transport plane to and from Hamburg.

"So what's this new concept called?" I continued.

"It's called a supermarket," he said. "You may have heard of them as there are some in this country, mainly around London. But the Yanks have really perfected the concept. They have massive supermarkets, some of them in out of town malls. That's what we're going to look at as Georgina and I are planning to build one in Chesterfield. In fact, we've already acquired a suitable site on Sheffield Road."

"Are you really sure that Chesterfield is quite ready for an American-style store?" asked Herman. "After all, you must realise how set in our ways we all are in this town."

"Well, we'll see. I know it's a big risk, but the opportunity is massive. Did you know, for example, that an average supermarket sells ten times as much per square foot as an average retail shop?

Ten times as much," he repeated just in case I hadn't heard him the first time. "It's absolutely mind-blowing."

Sprout was almost evangelical in his belief in supermarkets, so I asked him what Carrot thought about it. I remembered what he'd once told me about her reigning in some of his excesses.

"Oh, she was sceptical at first," he admitted. "That was until I showed her the figures and then she was converted. One day, fruit and veg shops will be a thing of the past. We have to embrace this new opportunity or eventually we will whither and die."

"Well, all I can say is that I'm thankful for the fact that we will never have to open a jewellery supermarket," said Herman. "Could you imagine it, everybody helping themselves to rings and watches. We'd be bankrupt inside a week."

True to his word Sprout did open his first supermarket on Sheffield Road. He decided to call the new venture R and G Supermarkets in order to differentiate it from his chain of greengrocers, which was called Russell and son. Of course, the R stood for Russell and the G for Georgina. Sprout later told me that originally he'd wanted to call the new venture RR Supermarkets using his own initials. But he had worried about possible legal action from Rolls Royce. In reality though, I think it was because Carrot had threatened to withdraw his conjugal rights if he didn't include her in the name.

Herman and I were both invited to the supermarket's opening and were given a silver tankard to mark the event. The truth was that both of us had done rather well out of Sprout's new supermarket. Herman had supplied the engraved tankards whereas I supplied the new store with three types of bottled beer.

"I'll put them at eye level," said Sprout whilst we were discussing our trading arrangement. "Because eye level is buy level."

This just went to show that he'd already picked up all the jargon, a fact that was confirmed when he also offered me the opportunity to promote the beers with a BOGOF deal. In which case, he told me, he could offer me a gondola end.

I explained that I had no idea what a BOGOF deal was and that a gondola end might as well be a bell end for all I knew.

Sprout told me that BOGOF stood for 'buy one get one free' and that 'gondola ends' were what they called the display areas at the end of each aisle. He went on to say that suppliers would pay a fortune to have their goods promoted there.

"Your suppliers pay for promotions?" I said in utter amazement. "I thought it was you who had to pay."

"Good Lord no," he replied. "The world is changing, Miles. Our suppliers pay for everything. It's their merchandisers who ensure that our shelves are fully stocked and make certain that all their advertising material is prominently displayed."

"So you don't even have to restock your own store?" I added incredulously.

"On the whole we don't," he replied.

"So what does your staff do?" I asked.

"Oh they have the most important job of all," he continued. "They take the customer's money."

In the end I turned down Sprout's offer of a gondola end. For if we'd sold our beer on a buy one get one free basis then we'd have sold it for a loss, which was a sure fire way of going bankrupt.

"But it wouldn't be permanent," added Sprout. "It would just be for a week or two in order to promote your brands. It's what we call a loss leader."

However, I was not convinced. I did want to make some profit after all.

Mind you, we never made that much out of supplying Sprout's supermarket, as we had to get the beer bottled by a firm of contract bottlers in Nottingham. It seemed that the new world order had no place in it for returnable bottles and our old bottling line couldn't cope with the new non-returnable type.

On the day the new store opened I was absolutely amazed by the number of people waiting outside for the ribbon to be cut.

"Bloody hell," I said to Herman as we waited for the official opening in the sunshine of a beautiful June day. "I was sceptical about this whole venture, but it looks like

Sprout's on to a surefire winner with this new supermarket of his."

"I think the jury's still out," Herman replied. "This crowd aren't really here to see the opening of a new shop. They're here to see the person who's opening it."

With that a buxom lady dressed in a sequinned dress appeared and cut the tape, declaring the supermarket open, before disappearing beneath a sea of people brandishing autograph books.

"Who's she?" I asked him.

"That's Pat Phoenix," replied Herman. Recognising the blank expression on my face, he continued. "You know, she plays Elsie Tanner in *Coronation Street*."

However, there was still a blank look on my face.

"Really Miles, you need to get yourself a life, old man," he added before the two of us went inside to have a look around.

# Chapter 21

"There's a hallmark on it so the tankard must be made of silver," said Molly, before taking it through to the living room and placing it on the ever-growing pile of items destined for the auction house.

Returning to the study, they continued to empty the shelves. There was an old Goodyear's bar towel, as well as a whole pack of drip mats advertising Goodyear's Pride and a complete collection of Goodyear's bottled beers from the 1960s.

One of the bottles caught Nigel's eye and he picked it up in order to examine it more closely.

"I never realised that we produced lager," he said whilst reading the bottle label. It said Gutjahrbrau Lager, brewed by Goodyear's Brewery Chesterfield, "It must have been pretty short-lived as I don't remember it at all."

*******

Herman and Rebecca's second child, a baby girl they christened Emma, was born on April 4th, 1962. She was a delightful child, always smiling. She looked adorable with her blue eyes and curly blonde hair. You could tell even at that age that she was going to be a real stunner when she grew up, probably breaking more than one man's heart.

Her birth only served to remind me how unlikely it was that I would ever have children myself. In order to take my mind off my predicament, I immersed myself in my work.

If I had thought that the 1950s were a time of great change, they were nothing compared to the 1960s with Beatle mania, the space race and the start of colour TV. People's aspirations and habits started to change as well. They no longer wanted to spend their holidays dodging rain showers in Blackpool. Now they wanted the guaranteed sun that a package tour to Spain would give them.

Closer to home, the early success of Sparkling Bitter was short-lived. People were starting to demand the new national brands that they saw advertised on TV. Beers such as Double Diamond, Whitbread Tankard and Watney's Red Barrel were putting the squeeze on small regional products such as Goodyear's Sparkling Bitter.

Overall, our sales were declining again and so were our profits. I slashed the repair budget for our pubs and soon I had tenants complaining about holes in their roofs. Of course the condition of our pub estate only served to hasten the decline in our beer sales. It wasn't as if our current competitors had the same issues as we had. This was because we were no longer competing with our fellow Chesterfield brewers. Instead, we were now competing with much larger companies, firms that had much deeper pockets than we did, and breweries that could afford to keep their pubs in good repair. Consequently it wasn't long before we were trading at a loss again and the losses were getting bigger every month.

Our bottling line was particularly badly affected. People were no longer drinking as many bottled beers as they once did. One of the reasons for this decline was that keg beer was now replacing cask ale and landlords couldn't adulterate keg. With cask ale they would water the beer down and put the contents of the drip trays back via a filter. In the past, people had drunk bottled beer because they knew that it would be a product that hadn't been interfered with. Sometimes, they added a bottle to a half pint of draught in order to liven it up. Sometimes, they would just drink bottled beer. Either way, they no longer needed to do this now that there was keg. By the mid-1960s, keg was king.

As if this wasn't bad enough, there was also the increased use of non-returnable bottles, something our old-fashioned bottling plant couldn't cope with. The obvious thing to do would be to close the plant down. But that would involve eight people losing their jobs. Many of them I had known since I was a boy, people like Marge, even though she still called me Little Dick.

It was whilst I was wrestling with these problems that I went out for a drink with Sprout one evening in spring 1965. I asked him how things were going even though I knew the answer to my question. Things were going extremely well for his business, and he had already opened two more supermarkets, one in Sheffield and one in Mansfield.

After exchanging some pleasantries, it was inevitable that our conversation would turn to business. Sprout told me that they were planning on opening another fifty stores over the next five years. I looked at him in absolute astonishment.

"How on earth are you going to fund an investment of that size?" I asked him.

"Easy," he replied. "The bank really likes what we've done so far and have offered to fund the whole thing."

"I don't know how much it's going to cost and I really don't want to know," I continued. "But if it's anywhere near as much as I think it will be, the interest payments must be absolutely crippling."

"There won't be any interest payments," Sprout replied. "The bank is going to take a 45% equity stake in the company. Georgina has already arranged it with them."

I couldn't help but be impressed. It was yet another example of Sprout and Carrot's perfect partnership. He had come up with the original idea for the supermarket. But it was Carrot who had come up with the way of turning that idea into reality. I was really envious of them both. Not only that but they were still having sex on a regular basis, which was something I could only dream of.

"How does the bank make its money?" I asked, interested to discover more about this financing package.

"That's the clever bit," he replied. "In five years' time when we have over fifty supermarkets, we will list the company on the stock exchange and the bank will sell its shares for a healthy profit. Our own shares should also be worth a lot of money by then and, by being listed, it will give us access to new ways of raising finance, which we can use to continue expanding."

"You make it sound so easy," I said. "What could go wrong?"

"Well, other than something like Britain going to war again, I think there's very little that can go wrong," he replied. "After all, supermarkets are the future of grocery shopping. Nothing can stop that. We were one of the first to recognise the opportunity. We've had a head start over most of our competitors and now we have the funding. Everything tells me that we are going to be successful."

It was great to see his optimism about his business, which contrasted markedly with my own pessimism. The conversation then moved on to my company and I explained the problems I had and how there was no easy solution to them.

"What you need is to spot the next big opportunity and get in quick," Sprout said, "and because you're my best friend I'm going to tell you what that opportunity is. It's lager. You may think that keg bitter is the future. But mark my words, lager will overtake it in a few years' time."

"Lager," I scoffed. "You do know that lager only accounts for 3% of the UK beer market, don't you?"

Sprout was undeterred by my argument and continued.

"When we opened our first R and G store, supermarkets only accounted for 2% of Britain's grocery sales. That figure has already gone up to 11% and the latest forecast is that in ten years' time over half of all groceries will be purchased through stores like ours."

I could see why he was so optimistic. Yet, I was far from convinced about lager, so I asked Sprout to explain why he thought it was the future.

"Do you know what the age profile of the people who shop in our supermarkets is?" he asked.

I admitted I didn't.

"Well, it's far younger than the people who shop in our fruit and veg shops," he continued. "Our typical supermarket customers are young professionals aged under thirty. They want the latest gadgets in their homes like washing machines and freezers. They set the trends that others follow and we accommodate them by stocking the type of things they want to buy."

I was intrigued by what he was saying and begged him to continue.

"Well, all I'm saying is that when we opened the first R and G outlet three years ago, we only stocked one line of bottled lager. Now we are up to eight. You might not notice the trend because your pubs are all full of middle-aged men. But you can bet your bottom dollar that what we are noticing today will affect you tomorrow."

I thanked him and told him that he had given me something to think about. But it wasn't just what he'd had to say about lager that had interested me. It was also Sprout's comments regarding bank funding that had captured my attention.

I had an appointment with the bank manager the following week at which I decided to ask him about the possibility of the bank converting its loan into equity in the company. I was disappointed though, as it was not the type of thing the Westminster Bank was interested in. However, the manager did offer me one crumb of comfort as he provided me with a contact in a merchant bank called WRD. He told me that equity sharing was the type of thing that WRD specialised in, whilst at the same time leaving the day-to-day banking still in the hands of a high street bank like the Westminster. However, he warned me that WRD was only interested in companies with ambitious expansion plans and a clear vision of the future. I thanked him and decided to go back and do more research about lager.

The more I looked into it, the more I became convinced that Sprout was correct and that lager was the future. For a start, more and more Brits were taking their holidays abroad and were acquiring a taste for lager in the same way that they were acquiring a taste for foreign foods such as pizza and pasta. Lager was also seen as a more sophisticated drink than bitter and as a result even people who had never set foot outside of the UK wanted to drink it. In addition, lager was different. In an era when young people were rebelling against everything that their parents had sworn by, lager stood out from the bitters, milds and brown ales their fathers drank. In short, it was the perfect product to be of interest to venture capitalists.

I spent the next three months doing more research and pulling together a business plan. One of the downsides of producing lager was that it is a bottom fermenting beer. By contrast, the ales that we produced were all top fermenting and for this reason we would need to buy a new type of fermenter. These were called cylindroconical fermenters and they were extremely expensive. We would also need a new yeast culture, but that was a relatively simple thing to acquire.

In order to boost my chances of success, I employed a firm of marketing consultants from Sheffield called Richardson and Bell. They assigned a girl called Amanda McDonald to my account. She was young, blonde and pretty. I wasn't old myself at 37 years of age, but she made me feel like my grandfather. She wore a miniskirt, whereas I wore a pin-striped suit. She was part of the new way of doing things, something that I clearly was not.

She suggested that we call the new lager Gutjahrbrau as it sounded foreign and sophisticated. In reality, it was Goodyear's brew directly translated into German, which I thought was quite clever. I was concerned that people wouldn't be able to pronounce it, but she convinced me that it would become a talking point that would certainly add to the intrigue and mystery of the new product.

Amanda also suggested that we go with a phased launch starting with the bottled product, in both returnable bottles for our pubs and off licences, and non-returnable bottles for supermarkets. The former would help to save our bottling line, but the latter would have to be contract bottled in Nottingham. If this proved to be a success then we would launch the draught version two years later, after which we would follow this up with a canned version.

Amanda designed a label for the new product, which had a German gentleman dressed in lederhosen holding a foaming stein of lager in his hand. I was a little concerned that he looked a bit like me, but Amanda told me that I was becoming paranoid.

Four months later, we had a sound proposal to put to WRD, which is why I found myself sitting in a room with Amanda, Mark Stephens, and four gentlemen from WRD who were all dressed in identical dark suits.

Our objective was simple. The company's loan from the Westminster Bank had risen to £225,000 and we required £25,000 to launch Gutjahrbrau and carry out repairs to our pubs. In other words, we wanted £250,000 from them and in return we were prepared to give them a 40% equity stake in the company.

The meeting started off well. They were clearly interested in our proposals. However, things took a turn for the worst when we started to discuss finance.

"So, Mr Goodyear," said one of the men in the dark suits. "We understand that the last offer you had for the business was £350,000. Therefore, simple maths tells us that our proposed investment of £250,000 should equate to 71.4% of the company rather than the 40% you are offering. And since we would require a safety net, I have to tell you that the minimum we would require would be 80%."

I was shocked. "But that was more than four years ago," I said. "The value of the company may well have increased since then and it will further increase once we've invested the money."

"But it may well have gone down rather than up," came the reply.

We carried on discussing the matter for what seemed like an eternity. Every time I came up with an argument, they came up with a counter-argument. In the end I was about to give up.

"Look gentleman," I said. "I am not prepared for my family to give up control of our company. Therefore, the maximum share I am prepared to offer you is 49%."

I expected the meeting to end there and then, but there was another twist. To my surprise, the men from WRD made another proposal. They offered us £250,000 of which £150,000 was to be for a stake of 49% of the company and £100,000 was to be a repayable loan. It also contained a clause guaranteeing WRD a minimum of 20% return on their investment, for which both Rebecca and I had to sign personal guarantees.

This was obviously their final offer and the three of us went away to consider it. I say the three of us, but in reality the decision had nothing to do with Amanda and Mark since they didn't own the company. Instead, that decision had to be made by my sister and I.

In the end we decided to accept. There were too many benefits for us not to. For a start, the interest on the loan was 1% less than we were paying to the Westminster Bank. In addition, it was repayable over a longer period of time and since it was a smaller loan, the net result was that our monthly repayments fell by two thirds.

Then there was the fact that we would now have the funds available both to launch our lager and to carry out all the necessary repairs to our pubs. How could we refuse?

Of course with WRD owning 49% of the shares in the brewery they wanted a seat on the board, but since Rebecca and I still owned the other 51% we knew that we could always outvote their representative.

We signed on the dotted line just before Christmas 1965. At last I had grounds for real optimism. The next year was going to be the start of a whole new chapter in the story of Goodyear's of Chesterfield.

# Chapter 22

"Add all the bottles to the auction pile," said Molly.

Once that had been done, the shelves were finally bare leaving only a trophy cabinet, which was filled with various cups and framed certificates. Some of these dated back to the nineteenth century.

Nigel pulled the first one out, which was a certificate for Best India Pale Ale at an exhibition held in Cape Town in 1892. There was also a trophy for best mild from a competition held in Burton-upon-Trent dated 1883 and other certificates that had been won from places as far afield as Berlin, Glasgow, Strasbourg, Bristol and Dublin. All of them were more than a hundred years old.

All of them that was apart from one, which was dated 1966. This was a framed certificate, which said:

Chesterfield Chamber of Commerce
Award for the Best Product Launch of 1966
Gutjahrbrau lager

******

The launch of Gutjahrbrau lager wasn't without its problems and yet, on the whole, it was a big success. Initially it sold well in both our off-licenses and in supermarkets, but less so in our pubs.

Lager needs to be served cold and in 1966 very few of our pubs had any form of refrigeration. Nobody wanted to drink a warm lager and as a result some of our customers renamed it Gut Rot Brew. We soon realised our mistake and made sure that each of our pubs was equipped with a cooling tray. Our tenants thought that this was a great idea as it meant they now had somewhere to keep their milk cold.

Mind you, they were even happier when we told them that we were going to carry out the long overdue repairs to their pubs.

Sales were increasing and due to our lower loan repayments our profits were increasing as well. In fact things were looking far better than they had for a long time.

In October 1966 the Chesterfield Chamber of Commerce informed me that we had won an award for Gutjahrbrau and that it would be presented to us at its annual dinner dance the following month at the Station Hotel.

Goodyear's Brewery always took a table of ten for this black-tie event, which was Chesterfield's premier social occasion of the year for businesses in the town. At our table were Herman and Rebecca along with Mark Stephens, Alf Parkes and both their wives. There was also Stuart Datcheler with his wife. He had finally taken over as head brewer after Bill Jones had retired the previous year. Amanda and I took up the final two places. I was really pleased she had accepted my invitation, partly because I would have been the only one without a partner otherwise, and partly because she looked absolutely stunning in her ball gown.

Sprout and Carrot were also there with their own table for what was certain to be a great night. The guest speaker was Freddie Laker who had founded Laker Airways earlier that year. The theme of his speech was 'seizing new opportunities', which was very uplifting.

At the end of his speech, Mr Laker presented the business awards for 1966, which included the one that we were to receive for best product launch.

I was as pleased as punch to have my photo taken with him presenting me with my certificate. The photo made the front page of the *Derbyshire Times* the following Thursday.

I returned to the table only to find that my colleagues had ordered a bucket with three bottles of champagne in it.

"Right, that's the serious part over with," I said. "Now let's start celebrating."

Mind you, nobody at the table needed an excuse to start consuming copious volumes of champagne. We worked for a brewery, so drinking large volumes of alcohol was the norm for us.

The one exception to this of course was Amanda. She'd never been to a brewery function before and her speech became more and more slurred as the evening went on. In the end, she dragged me to the dance floor not knowing that I wasn't at all comfortable with the new style of dancing. Give me a quickstep or a waltz and I'd show everybody what I could do, just as I had back in 1944. However, modern dances such as the twist or the type they did in the new style discotheques just left me cold. I'd never tried modern dancing before and when I did it took me quite some time to get the hang of it.

"You need to relax and let your hair down," said Amanda.

I realised what she meant, but instead I joked that I couldn't let my hair down as I'd had a short back and sides earlier that day.

"You ought to grow it a little. It would make you look like Mick Jagger," she replied. "I think it would suit you."

"What? A 39-year-old with a young man's haircut? I don't think so."

She brushed her hair back and started to laugh.

"Miles, you are still a young man," she said.

I hadn't enjoyed myself so much in years. Amanda was not only stunningly beautiful, she was also fantastic company and I was really enjoying dancing with her. The last time I'd danced with anybody had been with Sarah at the Licenced Victuallers ball back in 1954. This was a completely different experience though.

The band started playing a slow number and Amanda wrapped her arms around me and held me tight. I spotted Sprout and Carrot, who were also on the dance floor. Sprout was looking directly at me and gave me a knowing wink.

I was in seventh heaven. I was excited by the aroma of Amanda's perfume and the sound of her breathing in my ear. In fact I was a little too excited.

"Is that a gun in your pocket or are you just pleased to see me?" said Amanda doing an impersonation of Mae West.

I went red and started to apologise.

"There's no need to say you're sorry," she said. "I'll take it as a compliment. It would be rude and insensitive of me to ignore it and my parents taught me never to be rude." She laughed.

Then she whispered in my ear, "I'm staying in room 306. I'm going back to my room now. If you want to you can follow me up in ten minutes time."

I knew she was drunk and that she'd probably regret it the next morning. But I didn't care about that. I hadn't had sex for more than five years and there was no way that I was going to turn down an invitation from a beautiful woman so much younger than me.

We finished dancing and went back to the table.

"I'm absolutely knackered," said Amanda. "So if you don't mind, I'm going to go up to my room."

With that she winked at me as she got up and left. I prayed that nobody else noticed.

"You seemed to be getting on pretty well together," said Rebecca with a knowing look on her face.

"She's a nice girl," I replied. "But before you get the wrong idea, our relationship is purely professional. Besides which she's thirteen years my junior."

"When did that ever stop anyone?" she asked. "Look at Elvis."

She was referring to the fact that Elvis Presley was dating Priscilla Beaulieu who was more than ten years younger than him.

"He's a pop star," I replied. "They play by a different set of rules to the rest of us."

I didn't want this conversation to go on for too long and so I continued by saying, "If you don't mind, I think I'll call it a night myself. I've got a lot to get through tomorrow and I want a clear head, something I won't have if I stay here drinking all night."

"Don't change the subject Miles," Rebecca continued. "You need to find a nice girl. It's been over five years now since Sarah died. You've grieved for long enough. It's time you got on with your life."

The truth was that it was more guilt than grieving that I'd been going through. But that wasn't something I wanted to share with her.

Rebecca added, "Actually, we need to get back as well. We told the babysitter we'd be back before midnight. Why don't we share a taxi?"

"Shit," I thought to myself. I had to think quickly.

"If you don't mind, I'll walk" I said. "The exercise will do me good and there are a couple of things that I need to mull over. I find that walking gives me time to think."

"Whatever you say," Rebecca replied.

I wasn't sure she believed me. But the three of us got up from the table with me clutching my certificate and we went to get our coats. Once outside I was pleased to see that there was a row of waiting taxis. I kissed Rebecca on the cheek before I said goodbye to her and Herman. The two of them got into one of the taxis and as soon it was out of view I sneaked back into the hotel, a very relieved man. I headed straight up the main staircase hoping all the time that nobody spotted me.

Room 306 was on the third floor and my heart was beating so loudly as I mounted the stairs that I was surprised nobody could hear it. I was extremely nervous. What if she'd changed her mind or fallen asleep?

I knocked on the door, not too loud so that it would draw attention, but not too softly that she wouldn't hear.

The door was opened virtually immediately.

"I thought you weren't coming," she said. "I was just about to start by myself."

She looked absolutely gorgeous in a loose-fitting dressing gown. I closed the door behind me and we started to kiss. Her gown was undone at the front and I put my hand on her breast feeling her erect nipple.

She broke off our embrace and looked down before saying, "Are you going to burst out of those trousers, or are you going to take them off?"

I didn't need any encouragement and I took my clothes off as Amanda slipped out of the dressing gown and got into bed. I got in beside her and we started to kiss once more. However, before we went any further, I broke away from her.

"I don't have any condoms," I said.

"No need," she replied. "I'm on the pill."

They were the words I thought I'd never hear. The pill hadn't existed the last time I'd had sex. Its introduction had changed everything, giving women control over their own bodies and kickstarting the permissive society.

We made love passionately. It was absolutely wonderful,

reminding me of exactly what I'd been missing for the past five years.

I have to admit that we made quite a lot of noise whilst we were making love. This was due in part to a loose headboard, which kept banging against the bedroom wall. Amanda put her fingers to her lips, made a shushing noise and told me to quieten down a bit.

"You do know that Freddie Laker's in the next room," she whispered.

Then she started to giggle, "Do you think that qualifies us for the Mile High Club?"

That was really funny and I started to laugh uncontrollably before collapsing on top of her, both of us in stitches.

When we'd finished, I was in for another surprise as she took a large roll-up out of her bag, which she lit before inhaling and then passing it to me. I'd never been a heavy smoker, although I had smoked the odd Woodbine or two, especially whilst I was doing my National Service. However, I'd never smoked cannabis before and, to be honest, I never imagined I ever would.

It was at that point that Amanda leaned over and put her mouth to my ear.

"Welcome to the swinging sixties, Miles," she whispered before kissing me again.

The following morning I realised that I'd left my certificate on a shelf in the cloakroom, which resulted in an embarrassing moment when I had to go and retrieve it. I was still wearing my dinner jacket from the night before and so it was patently obvious to anybody watching that I'd got lucky the previous evening.

I was sure that the night with Amanda in the Station Hotel would be a one-night stand. But to my utter amazement she agreed to see me again and it was not long before I considered myself to be in a relationship with her.

She often spent the night at my house and I wanted her to move in with me, but she didn't want to give up her independence or her two-bedroomed flat in Sheffield. I knew it would take time to convince her, but I was prepared to wait.

I was overjoyed when she agreed to spend the Christmas holidays with me and decided that I would get her a really expensive present. Amanda had previously admired Sarah's jewellery and clothes, all of which were still in the house. So I asked her if she wanted something similar.

"You don't have to do that," she said. "You've got a massive collection of things that were your wife's. Just give me one of those."

"You can take the whole bloody lot," I replied. "I don't want them. They bring back too many memories."

In the end she chose a diamond necklace. It was a classy piece of jewellery, although I never knew precisely how much Sarah had paid for it. In fact, it was stunning, but not as stunning as the person who was now wearing it.

I had to go to the office between Christmas and New Year whereas Amanda had taken the whole week off. So I got a key cut for her so that she could let herself in and out. It was my way of saying, "You've got the key now, so why not make our relationship permanent?"

Christmas 1966 was the best I'd had since I was a child. The brewery was doing well and I was in a new relationship. Everything was right with the world.

I remembered the joke Rupert, Rebecca and I had shared about our parents only having sex at Christmas. Tonight it would be my turn, although I was now having sex every night rather than once a year.

# Chapter 23

Just as they finally finished clearing out the study, the door-bell rang. It was John from next door.

"I just popped around to see how you're getting on," he said. "I would have come earlier only I'd promised to visit my sister in Bolton."

"Come in John," said Molly who had answered the door. "The truth is that it's a far bigger job than we thought. Mind you, we've cleared out all the rooms except for the living room, although we've still got to sort out what to do with all the large pieces of furniture. We've got the people from the hospice shop coming around tomorrow, but I doubt if they'll take everything."

"The borough council will take things," he replied. "They charge a fee of course, but from memory it isn't a large sum."

"I thought so," said Molly. "I meant to look it up on the internet, but I haven't got around to it yet."

They sat down together in the kitchen and had a cup of tea. John told them that he'd known their uncle since 2002 when he and his wife Eleanor had downsized to the end of terrace house next door. Eleanor had died in 2005 and John explained that Miles had been of great support during those difficult times.

"Miles and I had always got on well together. But we

187

became firm friends after Eleanor died," John explained. "We'd go to the pub, talk over the fence and I'd take him to do his shopping. I was ten years younger than him and he was very conscious of the fact that all his old friends were dying off. He was grateful to have a younger friend who would help him. Your uncle gave up driving when he was eighty as he wasn't as confident as he'd once been. So the fact that I'd still got my own transport was really of great help to him. Mind you, talking of cars, have you been in the garage yet?"

"No," replied Nigel. "It was one of the last things we'd planned to do. Why? What's in there? I presumed that it was like everywhere else. Just full of old junk."

"Well, there's plenty of that in the garage," said John. "But there's something else that I think you'll like. Let me show you."

With that Nigel and Molly followed John around the side of the house to where the garage was. It had a pair of old-fashioned doors secured by a padlock rather than one of the more modern up and over types. Nigel took out the bunch of keys and quickly located the one that opened the lock.

He opened the doors only to discover a 1938 Austin 10 in original condition staring him in the face.

"Wow," said Nigel. "That's it, my search is now at an end. This is what I'm going to take to remind me of my uncle. I can still remember him driving it. I had absolutely no idea that he'd still got it."

"He last drove it twelve years ago," John explained. "But even before then I rarely saw him take it out. I believe he used to drive it to work until he retired. But after that he used it less and less, until one day he took the battery out and just left it in the garage."

"Well, I recently finished restoring a 1948 MG TC and

I was hoping to find another project. The Austin here is the answer to my prayers."

"I thought you'd like it," replied John. "Your uncle told me that you had an interest in classic cars."

Molly was less impressed. She'd hoped that Nigel would choose the Charlotte Rhead jug, or if he wanted something to remind him of the family business then the acid-etched mirror. However, as soon as she'd seen the car, she knew that there was no chance he would ever chose anything else.

Nigel asked John if there was anything he wanted to take from either the garage or the shed, as otherwise most of the stuff would end up in landfill.

John thanked him and said that if it was okay he wouldn't mind taking Miles's lawnmower since his had just broken down. Nigel told him that he would be doing them a favour by taking it, so John took the lawnmower and went back home with it.

Nigel and Molly returned to the job of clearing out the study, a task they had nearly finished before John had come to see them. In fact, the only thing left to do was to take down the items that were on the wall. These were all brewery-related including the acid-etched mirror and various old brewery adverts and pub signs.

"I remember when all these items were on the walls of Uncle Miles's office at the brewery," said Nigel. "He transferred them here when he sold the business."

*******

1967 had started well without the slightest hint of what was to come. Business was good and so was my sex life. In fact, I was getting on really well with Amanda and had got my fingers crossed that she would soon move in with me. She'd taken more of Sarah's old jewellery and clothes, which helped to alleviate my guilt. I knew that once she'd moved in, they would almost certainly come back with her, but somehow that didn't seem to worry me.

It was a pain in the arse having a representative of WRD on the board, but since he didn't attend board meetings that often it was nothing that I couldn't put up with.

His name was Hugo Ratcliffe and he lived in London. He was 27 years old and wore red braces, loud ties and white socks. In other words, he was a complete nob head and it wasn't long before he acquired the nickname 'Huge Ego'.

WRD stood for Withington, Ratcliffe and Dunne and Hugo was the eldest son of one of the partners. I disliked him intensely and never bothered to hide the fact.

By February 1967, he'd had a seat on the board for over a year and had only attended four board meetings. Therefore, it came as a surprise when he phoned me one day and told me that he was coming to Chesterfield the following Monday. He said he wanted to have a meeting with Rebecca and myself.

I immediately smelt a rat and asked him what he wanted to see us about. But he refused to tell me, saying that all would become clear on Monday.

I was definitely worried by this turn of events, but Rebecca told me not to be concerned because whatever he wanted to do, the two of us could always outvote him. However, that didn't stop me from worrying about it all weekend.

Hugo arrived at 10.30 on the Monday morning and the three of us went into the boardroom together.

"I'll not beat about the bush," said Hugo. "We've had another offer from Sheffield Brewery to buy the company and I think that we ought to give it serious consideration."

I was absolutely furious. "I'm the Managing Director of this company. Any approaches should be made to me not to you."

"Keep your hair on," he replied. "WRD have a long working relationship with Sheffield Brewery. It should not come as a surprise that they've spoken to us."

"Sorry, am I missing something?" asked Rebecca. "You said another offer. Have they made an offer before?"

"Didn't you know?" asked Hugo. "They last made an offer in 1961."

"And you didn't think to tell me," said Rebecca looking at me.

"We weren't going to sell. There was no need to tell you."

"I own a substantial part of this company," she snapped. "You had no right to keep it from me."

We both knew it was only by remaining united that the family would be able to resist any offer to buy the company. By revealing that Sheffield had made a previous offer for the brewery Hugo had managed to drive a wedge between Rebecca and I. Consequently, I was now very worried.

"How much have they offered?" asked Rebecca.

"£325,000," replied Hugo, "which is a very fair offer and one that the board of WRD wants us to accept."

"What?" I shouted. "But that's £25,000 less than they offered us six years ago and that was before we invested in the brewery and our pub estate. Furthermore, we are substantially more profitable than we were back in 1961."

I was completely flabbergasted by what Hugo had just said, so much so that I could barely speak. Finally, it was Rebecca who broke the silence.

"I think I speak for both my brother and myself when I say that the Sheffield Brewery offer is not acceptable to us. And since the two of us own 51% of the company, that is the end of the matter."

I realised that I had been wrong to doubt Rebecca. She may have been angry with me for not telling her about the earlier offer made by Sheffield Brewery, but when the chips were down she was always going to side with me against WRD.

"I thought you were going to say that," said Hugo without a trace of emotion in his voice. "Therefore I have to tell you that the board of WRD carried out a strategic review of our investment policy last week. As part of this review, we decided to make a complete withdrawal from the brewing sector. Consequently, I am instructed to inform you that if you do not accept the offer, we will call in our loan forcing the company into liquidation. I want to make it clear: accept it and you will walk away with some money; reject it and you will walk away with nothing. Possibly less than nothing, bearing in mind the personal guarantees you both signed."

"I thought you said that you'd got money invested in Sheffield Brewery. Are you really going to recall that as well?" I asked him whilst visibly shaking. I was so angry.

"What I actually said was that WRD had a long working relationship with Sheffield Brewery. I never said we had invested money in them."

With that he packed his briefcase and left, but not before he had told us that we had until Friday to make our decision.

After he had left, Rebecca and I discussed our options.

"If we accept the offer we will come out with less than £25,000," I told her. "That's because they invested £250,000 and their guaranteed minimum return of 20% takes them up to £300,000, minus the small amount that we've already repaid. Take that away from the offer of £325,000 and it will leave us with just over £25,000. However, we will have legal fees, outstanding suppliers' bills, excise duty and tax to pay out of that.

"If we go into receivership, then Sheffield Brewery could well buy everything from the receiver for less than the £325,000 they've offered. If they offer less than £300,000, then WRD will call in our personal guarantees in order to make up the difference. As a result, we could both lose our homes and end up bankrupt."

"These cannot be our only options," said Rebecca trying hard to hold back the tears. "Our family has built up this business over four generations. We've been going for over a hundred years. We can't see it disappear in the space of a week. There must be something we can do to save it."

"As far as I can tell, we have two other options," I replied. "Firstly, we could see if the bank is prepared to replace the WRD finance. They would only need to buy out the £100,000 loan, not their 49% equity share. WRD can threaten to recall their loan, but they can't do that with their shares in the company. They can only sell those to someone else. Our only other option is to find another buyer who will make us a higher offer."

I had four days in which to arrange either bank finance or to find another buyer and I began my search immediately.

My first port of call was the Westminster Bank but that drew a blank.

"Why won't you lend us the money?" I pleaded. "I'm only asking for £100,000. It was only a year ago that we had a £225,000 loan from you?"

The manager told me that he realised this, but unfortunately the Westminster Bank wasn't investing in breweries anymore

At least that part of Hugo's story seemed to be correct. Furthermore, numerous visits to various other banks confirmed that the entire banking sector had stopped investing in breweries. Too many of them had caught colds when they realised that the pubs they had taken as security weren't worth as much as they once were.

I was getting more and more worried and I was also getting extremely irritable. This didn't go down too well with Amanda, who started giving me the cold shoulder as a result. Her attitude did not concern me though as I had a far more pressing issue to sort out before I started worrying about my relationship with her.

My search for a 'white knight' also proved fruitless. It seemed that nobody wanted to buy a small provincial brewer any more, well at least not for a price that was higher than the Sheffield offer.

By the time Friday arrived, I had admitted defeat. Rebecca and I decided to accept the Sheffield Brewery offer as the lesser of two evils. I didn't want to tell Hugo, as I didn't want to give him that pleasure, so I phoned his father instead.

It was the worst day of my life so far. Little did I realise at the time that things were to get far worse before they got better.

I returned home that evening only to discover a note on my kitchen table. Sitting on top of it was my front door key. The note was from Amanda and just said, 'It's been fun whilst it lasted but now it's time to move on. Amanda x.'

Later I discovered that she'd cleared out the rest of Sarah's things, all her jewellery, her handbags, shoes and clothes. It was my fault for telling her that she could have the lot. But to tell you the truth, I was past caring by that point.

In fact, the only thing that she hadn't taken was Sarah's old school beret, the one that I had pinched all those years ago. It was the only thing that she didn't have any use for. I picked it up from the bed where she had left it and started sobbing uncontrollably.

# Chapter 24

Nigel started taking the brewery-related items off the wall and placing them on the ever-growing pile of articles to be taken to the auction house.

Meanwhile, Molly had gone into the kitchen to prepare some soup and a roll for each of them, as it was nearly time for lunch.

Nigel removed the acid-etched mirror first. It was very large and extremely heavy. It was at least a hundred years old, probably Edwardian.

The enamel advertising signs were next and fortunately these were quite light in comparison.

Finally, it was the turn of the three wooden pub signs. One of these was substantially larger than the other two and whilst he was taking it off the wall Nigel noticed that it wasn't a pub sign at all. It was, in fact, the sign that used to hang outside the brewery's sample room. It proudly announced 'Goodyear's Brewery Cellars' in gold letters on a green background.

Nigel turned the sign around and immediately spotted there were 35 names written on the back. Some of them Nigel recognised. There was Alf Parkes, Jim Stuart, and Eileen Greenbank, all of whom had been at the funeral. Also there was Bill Steadman who couldn't attend due to ill health.

"These must be the names of the employees who were working at the brewery when it closed," Nigel thought to himself as he looked at the old sign.

*******

The fact that we'd accepted the Sheffield Brewery offer didn't mean that we were taken over the next day. For a start, they had to complete due diligence and the legal side of the takeover.

Of course I had to tell the workforce that we were about to be taken over. It was another one of those jobs that I didn't relish and my worst fears were confirmed when poor old Marge burst into tears.

I said something bland like, "In the meantime it's business as usual."

It was the type of statement managers always make to their workforce just before something terrible happens. The problem was that everybody knew that Sheffield would close the brewery down and most of them would lose their jobs. As a result, the atmosphere in the brewery was pretty toxic during the three months it took to complete the sale.

Four weeks after the sale had been agreed, I received some terrible news, something that caught me completely by surprise.

It was whilst I was having a meeting with our solicitor that he turned to me and said, "Miles, you do realise that your house is included in the sale?"

I hadn't, of course, but after thinking about it I realised that my house and the George Stephenson next door were still on the same set of deeds. The two properties had both been built on one plot of land and we'd never asked the Land Registry to separate them. There had never been any need to do so since we owned both properties. Furthermore, we'd told the Inland Revenue that the house was built as staff accommodation, so we could offset the cost of building it against tax. Technically it wasn't a lie, being as though I was a brewery employee myself. However, thirteen years later that particular decision was about to become a major headache for me.

"Well, can't we just exclude it from the sale?" I asked.

"We could have done if you had told me about it earlier," came the reply. "But unfortunately it is on the list of company assets that has gone to Sheffield Brewery's solicitors. I very much doubt if they will agree to it being removed. After all, why should they? Even if they did they would almost certainly want to renegotiate the price and given your weak position I wouldn't recommend that at all."

"Shit, what can I do?" I pleaded. "I will be left homeless unless you can think of a solution."

"My advice would be to create a lease for yourself," he replied. "You can make the terms very favourable. I'd suggest a peppercorn rent and a clause saying that you have the right to remain in the house for as long as you are alive. In that way, they still get the freehold, but at least you would retain occupancy of the house for as long as you want to live there."

I thought about it for a couple of minutes before saying, "Do it."

The takeover was completed on May 22nd and the brewery closed down the same day. All our employees were made redundant except for a few who were transferred to jobs in Sheffield.

I didn't know whom I was most sorry for, myself or the workers who'd lost their jobs, many of whom were third or even fourth generation employees.

By the time we'd paid all the outstanding bills, I came out of the deal with a little over £3,000 whilst Rebecca got

£2,500, not really much for over one hundred years of ownership by the Goodyear family.

On the final day, I removed all the things from my office, my degree certificate, the mirror from the wall, the pub signs, advertising signs and all the awards we had won. Alf Parkes took them to my house in the back of one of the brewery vans.

Most of the other stuff we burnt in the backyard of the brewery, including the old horse-drawn dray that had last been used to carry my parents' coffins. Then it was all over. I'd arranged for the staff to have a final drink in the Spa Vaults across the road from our offices. It was the very least I could do. It was a sad affair as we all drank pints of Goodyear's Lament, a special final brew with an original gravity of 1056. It tasted good but it broke my heart to think that beer would never be brewed in the brewery ever again.

"It's the best thing I've drunk since I was on my mother's teat," announced Bill Steadman. This helped to lighten the atmosphere in the pub a little.

I was late arriving at the pub, as I wanted to take a last look around before I left. I wandered through the brewhouse where Bill Jones used to drink so much of the beer he brewed, providing of course that he turned up for work in the first place. I moved on to the fermentation room and the racking room before going into the bottling hall where the girls had stuck labels all over my bare backside. The men's locker room where I had first seen pictures of naked ladies was next, followed by the office where Jane used to work. I made a final visit to my own office, which of course had originally been my father's and before that my grandfather's.

Then I walked across the brewery yard, which had been the setting for my wedding reception and went over to the warehouse where we used to store all our full casks prior to delivery. I stood on the loading bank where the men used to load up our drays, before I moved on to our wine and spirits store. From there I wandered into the brewery cellars, the scene of so much drunken revelry over the years. Finally, I went into the one room that held the most vivid memories for me, the hop store. Like all the other rooms I'd visited it looked like a shadow of its former self with everything now removed from it.

Having completed my final tour I locked the front door for the last time with the keys my father had given me on my eighteenth birthday and went to join the workforce across the road. They had already consumed quite a few pints and the mood was far happier now than it had been when they'd started, fuelled as it was by extra strong beer.

I stayed for a couple of hours and enjoyed all the stories they were telling about their happy days spent working for Goodyear's.

Finally, as I was just about to leave, they presented me with the sign from the brewery cellars. They had all written their names on the back.

"So that you won't forget us," said Alf.

I thanked them all and asked Frank, the licensee of the Spa Vaults to look after it until I could collect it. With that I left.

The following day I drove back and collected the sign. I also took the opportunity to unscrew the brass plaque from the front of the brewery. It said:

Goodyear's of Chesterfield
Family Brewers since 1862.

Sheffield Brewery stripped all the equipment out of the brewery over the next few weeks and sold most of it as scrap. Only the keg racking line and the cylindroconical fermenting vessel were saved and they were sold off to other breweries.

The brewery was demolished the following year, but not the office block, which was allowed to fall into dereliction. It was a sad reminder of my family's former business and it upset me every time I had the misfortune to walk past it.

# Chapter 25

Molly had almost finished preparing lunch, but there was just enough time for Nigel to take down a couple of small pictures that hung in the hall. There was also a brewery clock, which Nigel carefully removed from the wall.

When he examined it, he was surprised to see that it wasn't a Goodyear's clock, but was from Sheffield Brewery.

Nigel took it through to the kitchen where Molly had just finished serving up the soup.

"Look at this," he said holding up the clock. "It's a Sheffield Brewery clock. I'm surprised Uncle Miles kept it, as it was Sheffield Brewery that took over Goodyear's in 1967. He always hated them."

"It's a good clock and if your uncle was anything, he was a pragmatist. Also he was a tight-fisted old bugger who wouldn't throw anything away if it meant he had to buy another one to replace it."

"Thinking about it," said Nigel. "I seem to remember that Uncle Miles actually worked for Sheffield Brewery after they'd taken us over."

******

I was down but I wasn't completely out. Yes, I'd lost my business, ownership of my house, most of my money and my girlfriend, but at least I still had a job. Sheffield Brewery had offered me a role as Regional Innkeeper Director for Derbyshire and Nottinghamshire.

In total, I was one of five people from Goodyear's who managed to get a job at Sheffield Brewery. The rest of my former employees were all made redundant, although the majority of those were close to or past their normal retirement date.

Sheffield Brewery had been expanding rapidly in recent years and as well as taking us over, they had also taken over Richardson's of Newark three months previously. Consequently, they were short of senior managers and since they wanted to have a smooth transition following our takeover, they appointed me to my new role. As a result, I started working for them at the beginning of June 1967.

Despite having the title 'Director' I did not have a seat on the board. That honour went to my boss, Phil Yates, the Tied Trade Director who had six Regional Innkeeper Directors reporting to him.

In reality I was a manager. I felt the only reason why I had the title of 'Director' was so that my boss could avoid any angry phone calls from tenants who called up demanding to speak to a director.

Sheffield Brewery was a far larger company with a completely different culture to the one we'd had at Goodyear's. For a start, the brewery itself was a dry site, with all drinking on the premises prohibited. Staff received vouchers for two dozen cans of beer per week, which they had to consume at home. In fact, it was a disciplinary matter if they drank them at the brewery.

Barbara Castle had brought in the Road Safety Act during 1967, which introduced the breathalyser for the first time. Sheffield Brewery announced that, if any of their staff were caught drinking and driving, they would face summary dismissal. It didn't matter what the circumstances were. If you got caught over the limit, you would be sacked, even if the offence had occurred during your own time.

I could see the sense in the new drink drive laws and I suppose that times were changing. But it still seemed strange to me to be working in a brewery where you couldn't even organise a piss up.

One other thing that was very different was the large variety of point of sale material that was available to support the Sheffield brands. At Goodyear's we only had drip mats and bar towels. At Sheffield, however, there were ashtrays, drinks trays, water jugs, key rings, lamps and even records with the company's advertising jingles on them. On my first day, I was given a brewery clock to take home. I didn't know if it was because they thought my timekeeping was suspect, but I accepted it nevertheless.

I had my own secretary and four business development managers reported to me. They, in turn, were responsible for 86 tenanted pubs, most of which had been Goodyear's pubs, or had been owned by Richardson's of Newark.

It didn't take me long to realise that I had a major problem on my hands. Despite the relative success of Sparkling Bitter, Goodyear's Pride had still been our best-selling beer accounting for 60% of all our sales. It was a cask ale and Sheffield Brewery didn't produce any cask ale. All their beer was sold either in keg form, or was delivered by road tanker into five-barrel cellar tanks. To make matters worse, Richardson's Brewery had never made any keg beer, they had only ever produced cask ale and Richardson's pubs accounted for over half of the tenancies I was responsible for. When you combined their former pubs with ours it came to 82 in total, leaving me with just four pubs that had always been tied to Sheffield Brewery.

If that wasn't bad enough, the problem was compounded by the name of the company's main product. It was Yorkshires Best. Now there were two ways in which you could interpret that name. The brewery, of course, meant that it was the best bitter in Yorkshire. In Derbyshire and Nottinghamshire, it was interpreted in another way. There, people took it to mean that we were telling them that Yorkshire was a better county than the one they lived in.

Sales in the pubs I looked after plummeted as a result of all these negative factors. People who'd been drinking in them for years, generations even, suddenly switched to other hostelries. I had publicans phoning me on a daily basis to complain that their drinkers didn't like Sheffield beers. Many of them handed the keys to their pubs back and left. Some of them were licensees that I'd known since I was a boy.

For the first time that I could remember, I was struggling to find new tenants and even when people did express an interest, they wanted to pay a much lower rent than the brewery were prepared to accept. Consequently by the autumn of 1967, I had temporary tenants in a third of all of my pubs, many of them paying minimal rent purely to keep the doors open.

My fellow Regional Directors, of course, didn't have anything like the number of problems I had. Their regions were all in Yorkshire where Yorkshires Best sold really well.

The region I was looking after was the worst performing in the brewery by a country mile. It was the worst performing no matter what you measured it by, volume, profit, or turnover of licensees.

Phil Yates was initially very understanding, but when he started to come under pressure from his boss, his understanding ended. At my appraisal in October, he graded me as 'poor' and warned me that, unless I turned everything around in the next three months, he would replace me by somebody who could.

I was not enjoying my new job at all. At Goodyear's the only person I'd ever had to answer to was my father. Now I was a small underperforming cog in a well-oiled machine. Well, it would have been well oiled if anybody had been allowed to have a drink.

If this wasn't bad enough the personnel director at Sheffield Brewery was Barry Matthews. This was the same Barry Matthews I'd sacked from Goodyear's following both our affairs with Jane Carghill. After leaving Goodyear's, he got a job as a personnel manager at Sheffield Brewery. He now had a fearsome reputation and had acquired the nickname of 'Barry the Hatchet' due to the number of people he'd sacked. He was just the type of person who did well at Sheffield Brewery and pretty soon he found himself promoted to head of department with a seat on the board, the same grade as my boss.

In reality, if it hadn't been for me, he'd probably still be an office manager in a small brewery in Chesterfield, but I guess he didn't see it that way. In fact, any suggestion that he was prepared to let bygones be bygones was quashed immediately during our first meeting.

"You're playing with the big boys now," he said to me. "So you'd better get your act together, otherwise you'll be out on your ear. Just remember that I will be watching your every move, Goodyear."

I didn't want to give him any excuse to reprimand me, but my situation wasn't helped by the poor performance of my region.

Then in November 1967, Phil called me in to give me a stage one written warning. He'd obviously had second thoughts about giving me three months to turn things around. It was either that or 'Barry the Hatchet' had persuaded him to speed matters up. In all probability it was the latter and my fears were confirmed when I discovered that he was sitting next to my boss as I entered the room.

Phil told me that he would give me another two months to improve my region's performance. If it didn't improve, they would have to give me a stage two written warning. One more warning after that would mean dismissal. I could tell that Barry absolutely loved it. For him it was the revenge he had long been waiting for.

I really hated work, everything about it, the people, the products and the culture. I considered resigning, but the only thing that stopped me was the thought that it would hand Barry victory on a plate.

Things didn't improve and by the middle of December 1967 I was already preparing myself for a second written warning the following month.

December 21st was the day of the office Christmas party. I wasn't looking forward to it especially since Barry was going to be there. But as a senior manager I was expected to attend.

The party itself was held off-site and therefore was one of the few work events at which we were allowed to drink, so naturally I took full advantage of this. All the staff were there along with their wives and girlfriends. Of course I didn't have either and so I went by myself. Janice, my secretary, was also there on her own and I made the mistake of making a drunken pass at her.

She was seventeen years younger than me with greasy long hair and glasses. She was not my type at all, but I had my beer goggles on and they clouded my judgement. I can't remember what I said to her, but I do remember her slapping me across the face and running out of the room.

"Shit," I thought to myself. "That was not a good idea."

I decided to leave and went to get my coat from the

206

cloakroom. While I was in there I heard the door closing and looked up to see a woman standing next to it. It was Brenda Matthews, Barry's wife, who I recognised from the annual staff trips and parties back at Goodyear's. Even in my drunken state I could tell that she was at least as inebriated as I was.

"Your secretary might not want to have a bit of fun, but that doesn't apply to everyone," she said to me.

Brenda had a bit of a reputation for getting drunk and propositioning men. If I'd been sober I'd have run a mile. But I wasn't, so I didn't. Pretty soon we were snogging in between the coats and jackets. To make matters worse I'd unbuttoned her blouse and my hand was inside her bra.

It was stupid of course. Anybody could have come into the room at any time. Eventually somebody did, and that somebody was Barry.

He stared at us for a few seconds as Brenda started to button up her blouse. Then the insults started.

"You pathetic excuse for a man. You never could control your drinking or keep your dick in your trousers, could you?"

"That's good coming from you," I replied. "I seem to remember that you were shagging one of the members of your staff whilst you were working for me."

It was a really cheap shot. I'd only said it so that Brenda would know what he'd been up to.

I could see the anger in his face. He stepped up to me and spat out the words,

"I'm not surprised your wife married you, I heard she liked cunt and there's no bigger cunt than you. No wonder everybody called you Little Dick."

If I'd been able to think about it, he was contradicting himself really badly. After all, I couldn't be both a cunt and a little dick. But I wasn't thinking, so that was the point at which I punched him. I'd never hit anybody before and was really surprised by the amount of blood that came out of his nose.

All this noise had drawn the attention of others and it was one of my team who came up to me and said, "I think you'd better go home, guv. Come on, I'll get you a cab." With that I left, whilst Brenda was trying to stem the bleeding from her husband's nose with his hanky.

When I woke up the next morning I knew straightaway my career with Sheffield Brewery was over. After thinking about it for a few minutes, I decided to go in and face the music rather than prolong the agony.

It didn't take long. Phil told me that I had two choices. Either I could resign and they would give me a reference or they would sack me, in which case they wouldn't. So I resigned. The only satisfaction I got was that Barry looked really rough, and he still had dried blood underneath his nose from where I'd punched him the night before.

Later I heard that he and Brenda had a massive row over Christmas and then an even bigger one three months later. They divorced shortly after that. It seemed that Barry had been having numerous affairs in addition to the one that I knew about. Mind you, his wife Brenda wasn't exactly faithful either, so in many ways they deserved each other.

Christmas 1967 was the worst I'd ever had, in complete contrast to that of the previous year and those of my childhood.

It was incredible to think that in the space of twelve months I'd gone from being a successful business owner with a beautiful girlfriend to an unemployed nobody with no prospects and no partner.

It was three days before Christmas, but it wasn't going to be celebrated in my house. I'd burnt the Christmas tree, all the decorations and my Christmas cards in the back garden.

I was all alone once more and I decided there and then never to celebrate Christmas again.

# Chapter 26

Nigel put the clock on the auction pile and returned to the kitchen for his lunch.

"This soup's good," he said to Molly in between mouthfuls.

"I'm glad you like it," she replied. "I made it from leftover chicken and vegetables."

"The roll's not bad either," he added.

When they'd finished Nigel turned to Molly and said, "Only one more room to go. Are you ready?"

Molly nodded and the two of them got up and went into the living room.

There was already a substantial pile of items in front of the fireplace waiting to be taken to the auction house. In addition, there were the old and new TVs, an old fashioned record player, a really old radio, a standard lamp and a Persian rug. Finally, there was the furniture, which comprised a three-piece suite, a coffee table, a magazine rack, a sideboard and a bookcase.

Nigel decided to tackle the bookcase first. Most of the books were in between being antique, which would be of interest to the auction house, and modern, which could be taken to the hospice shop. As a result, they weren't likely to be of interest to either of them.

That was why most of the books ended up in a black bin bag destined for the recycling centre. Some of them looked like old school books and Nigel took a couple down to have a look. One was titled *The Love Poems of Catullus*. The other one was *The Works of Pliny the Elder*. Nigel opened it and saw that it had a library sticker inside that said 'Ex Libris Chesterfield School'.

Nigel turned to Molly and said, "Hey, it looks as if my uncle nicked most of these books from the Grammar School library."

\*\*\*\*\*\*

I didn't do much at all during the next couple of years except to feel sorry for myself. It was pathetic really when you think about it. I thought that the world was against me, a feeling that got worse when I received the previous year's accounts for Sheffield Brewery. I shouldn't have been sent them as I had left the month before. But it seemed that nobody had told the person who distributed them.

In common with all the other breweries, the Sheffield Brewery year ran from October to September and it was their practice to send the accounts out to everyone at director level as soon as they were available. I was nominally a director, which was why I was sent a copy of the 1966–7 accounts early in January 1968.

A letter accompanied the accounts from the Chairman, Andrew Walsh, entitled 'Another great year for Sheffield Brewery'. I should have thrown them straight in the bin but something made me look at them, and there in the notes to the profit and loss accounts was a payment of £12,500 to WRD. The payment was down under 'consultancy fee', but I knew straightaway what it was. Sheffield Brewery and WRD had plotted against me. They had agreed to split the difference between the price that Sheffield had offered in 1961 and the price they had offered in 1967. WRD had only invested £250,000 in the brewery for twelve months and yet they had come away with £312,500. Contrast that with my family who had invested four generations of hard toil and yet only came away with five and half grand.

This was the final straw. I very rarely went out of the house except to buy food. I'd lost my company car when I'd lost my job, but I still had the old Austin 10. I'd kept it for Sarah to drive when I'd been given my first company car and since her death it had just remained in the garage.

It only needed a good service and a new battery, but I couldn't be bothered to take it to the local garage, so I just used to get the bus into town instead.

I was drinking too much and not keeping the house or myself as clean as I should have done.

Rebecca was getting more and more concerned about me, claiming that I wasn't eating as well as I should. So in early December 1969, she invited me to have Sunday lunch with her, Herman, Nigel and Emma.

I smartened myself up and even shaved especially for the occasion. The meal was good, the best I'd had that year and when we'd finished Rebecca turned to Herman and said to him, "Well, are you going to tell him or am I?"

"Tell me what?" I asked.

"Guess who I bumped into the other day?" said Herman.

"I've absolutely no idea," I replied.

"Philip Blatherwick," he went on.

"What old Blubber from school?"

"The very same, and guess what, he's back at the Grammar School again."

"Well, I knew he was thick, but I didn't think he'd still be a pupil aged 42."

"Very funny," replied Herman. "No, he's gone back as

head of languages. I bumped into him in town the other day. We talked about our school days and he asked after you. Anyway, eventually he told me that poor old Hugh Janus has had a stroke, which has forced him to retire. He's having great difficulty in finding a new Latin master and asked me if you would be interested."

I'd never considered a career in teaching and so what Herman was telling me came as a complete surprise.

"But I don't have a teaching qualification," I said.

"But you do have a Master's Degree in Latin from Oxford, so you're more than qualified. Besides which he's desperate, so will you think about it?"

I told him that I certainly would and he gave me Blubber's telephone number and told me to ring it.

If the truth were told, the prospect of me starting work again hadn't come a moment too soon. I knew I had to get my life in order. Furthermore, the money from the sale of the brewery had nearly run out.

I may have known Philip Blatherwick for over thirty years, but we'd never really been friends. That didn't stop me from being extremely nervous when I phoned him up. However, it turned out that I needn't have worried, as he was very pleased to hear from me.

He invited me for an interview later that week. At least I thought it was for an interview, but in reality he offered me the job as soon as I walked through the door. Herman was totally correct when he'd told me that he was desperate.

I agreed to start in January at the beginning of the new term. It was a two term contract to see if I liked it or not and also to discover how suitable I was. Little did I think at the time that I would still be there some 21 years later.

# Chapter 27

"There's not much call for books written in Latin these days," said Nigel.

"I don't think there's ever been much call for Latin textbooks," replied Molly, "and certainly not in charity shops."

Neither of them really liked throwing books away, but in reality they had very little choice.

"I think you were being a little harsh on your uncle by claiming that he'd pinched them from the school library. After all, he was a teacher at the school so they were probably given to him."

It didn't take them long to finish clearing the bookcase and afterwards they decided to tackle the sideboard. This contained yet more bottles of spirits.

"Your uncle was quite a drinker, wasn't he?" said Molly.

"Not really," replied Nigel. "Most of these bottles are very old and hardly anything has been drunk from them. If he'd really been a serious drinker then surely he would have finished them all off."

"Point taken," replied Molly.

*******

My New Year's resolution was to give up drinking, well to give up drinking spirits anyway. If I was going to make a success of my new teaching career, I couldn't turn up reeking of alcohol every morning. That said I still intended to allow myself the odd pint of bitter at the weekend and the occasional glass of wine with my meal. But whisky and brandy were definitely out from now on.

The Grammar School had changed substantially since I'd been a pupil there. Firstly, it was no longer officially called Chesterfield Grammar School. It was now simply known as Chesterfield School. Mind you that didn't stop everybody from still referring to it as the Grammar School.

Secondly, it had moved to a purpose-built modern campus on the outskirts of town three years previously. The old school had been close to the town centre and had been cramped and lacking in modern facilities. The new school was brimming with teaching aids and facilities such as a language laboratory, even though I never used it to teach Latin. It also had a state-of-the-art science block, a running track and an indoor swimming pool. Mind you, it still had links with its past as it had two courts for playing fives, an obscure game invented at Eton College back in 1877. There was also a memorial room, which contained the names of all the old boys who'd given their lives during both world wars. Rupert's name was on the World War II plaque, as was Mr Duggins's.

The new school had its drawbacks of course. For the boys, it was the fact that it was no longer next door to the girl's high school and for me, it was because it was no longer within walking distance of my house. As a result, I finally got the old Austin 10 going again.

It may have been thirty years old by then, but it still worked and made me stand out from all the other masters with their Ford Escorts and Vauxhall Vivas. I'd forgotten what a good car it was and was pleased to be reunited with it again. It seemed to be improving with age and was far better at starting now that it was kept in a garage.

The final thing that was different about the school was that all the staff had changed, which was only to be expected being as though over thirty years had elapsed since I first started there as a pupil. Well, I say all the staff, but the one exception was Ratty Owen who looked as if he was 105 but in reality was only in his sixties.

One thing that hadn't altered about the school, however, was that it was an all-male affair with 800 boys and 55 masters. Personally, it suited me that way as it meant there were no females to distract me. Well, not unless you included the school secretary and the dinner ladies, none of whom were likely to set my pulse racing. Furthermore, I'd decided that at 42 I no longer wanted a partner. I was perfectly satisfied with my bachelor life as it meant I could do what I wanted when I wanted. I was happy on my own, or at least that's what I told myself.

Many of the other masters at the school were single like myself. A group of us used to go to the pub on Fridays after school and five us would go abroad together during the summer holidays, visiting places like the Italian lakes, Salzburg and the Rhine Valley.

Of all the masters at the school, Brian King and Colin Potter became my closest friends. They were both ten years younger than me, but that didn't really matter. Neither did the fact that Colin was a homosexual. He never tried it on with me, so his sexuality was never an issue.

"It's legal now," joked Brian. "But I'll be buggered if I'm going to hang around once it becomes compulsory."

I took to teaching like a duck to water and nobody was more surprised by this than me. Finally I had discovered my true vocation in life and as a result I was relatively happy once more.

Keeping discipline was never an issue for me. To be fair, most of the boys came from good middle-class backgrounds and were intelligent. Furthermore, those who chose to study Latin were hardly likely to be troublemakers.

Shortly after I started, I overheard a group of them talking in the quadrangle. They hadn't noticed I was there.

"What have you got next?" asked one of the boys.

"Double Latin with old Crapper," came the reply. "Do you know what my mother told me about him? She said that he used to be a millionaire once upon a time. But that he blew all his fortune, which is why he now teaches here."

I immediately walked up to him and grabbed him by the ear.

"You refer to me either as Mr Goodyear or as sir. Do I make myself clear?" I said whilst twisting his ear and causing him to yelp in pain

"What's your name boy?" I asked.

"Hopkinson sir," said the terrified boy.

"Well Hopkinson," I replied. "You will write out fifty times 'I must always show respect to the masters in this school'."

It had taken me thirty years, but I'd finally turned into Mr Duggins. He must have been smiling down on me from above, not least because, thirty years on, pupils at the school were still calling me by the nickname he'd given me back in 1939.

As it turned out, Hopkinson was a good student coming top of the class in the final term's examination. I was very happy with his progress as I told his mother at the fourth form parents' evening in June of that year.

She was very pleased with my report, which I'd just about finished giving to her when she looked me in the eyes and said, "You don't remember me, do you?"

I'd thought there was something about her that I recognised, but I couldn't quite put my finger on it.

"It's Margaret," she said. "Margaret Bishop as was, Margaret Hopkinson now."

I was stunned. The girl I remembered from the school dance had glasses, mousey hair and a tooth brace. The well-dressed woman in front of me was sophisticated and beautiful with pearly white teeth, blonde hair and blue eyes. The ugly duckling had definitely turned into a swan, albeit with the help of contact lenses, hair dye and an orthodontist.

"Well I'll be damned," I said. "Margaret Bishop, I never would have guessed. You look absolutely fantastic. What have you been doing all these years?"

"If only you'd said that I looked fantastic 25 years ago, Miles," she replied. "Didn't you realise that I had a crush on you back then?"

"Well, I suspected that you liked me, especially after your friend Olivia told me that you fancied me. But back then I was completely dazzled by you know who, which turned out to be a big mistake on my behalf. But less of that, you still haven't told me what you've been doing."

"After school I went to Sheffield University where I studied Law. Following that I got a job working for a large firm of a solicitors in London, which is where I met my husband. We married in 1955 and Richard was born the following year. But my husband turned out to be a serial adulterer and we separated in 1962, which was when I decided to move back home to Chesterfield.

I now work for Skipton and Halesham in the town centre. Do you know them?"

"I certainly do," I replied. "Their offices are in what used to be my parents' house."

"Look, I'm holding you up. You've got other parents to see," Margaret continued. "Why don't we go out for a drink and we can catch up at our leisure? You can meet me at work and I can show you around."

"I'd like that," I replied. "I'm free most days. Not tomorrow though as I take Duke of Edinburgh Award sessions after school on Wednesdays. So how about Thursday?"

We agreed to meet at half past four and with that she smiled before going over to see Frank Kendal who taught her son maths. The boys affectionately knew him as Minty.

I was quite nervous when Thursday came around. Margaret was a successful solicitor with a high-powered job. Was it a date? If so, it was the first I'd been on for nearly four years. Also I was really apprehensive about what I might discover in my parents' old house. I had such happy recollections of my childhood there and part of me didn't want to disturb those memories. Another part of me was quite curious to see what Skipton and Halesham had done to the place.

From the outside the building had hardly changed at all. But inside it was a different matter. When we'd lived there the ground floor consisted of a large hallway with stairs going up to a galleried landing. To the left was our living room and to the right was my father's study. Then there was a dining room and the kitchen at the back of the house.

The first thing I noticed after going inside was that the wall between what had previously been the hallway and my father's study had been removed. Now the whole area served as the reception for the solicitors' practice.

I approached the receptionist and said, "Miles Goodyear. I'm here to see Mrs Hopkinson."

The receptionist told me to take a seat and offered me a coffee, which I politely declined. A few moments later Margaret appeared, kissed me on the cheek and asked me if I wanted to have a guided tour of the building. I told her that would be nice.

To be honest, there was very little to remind me of my boyhood home. The stairs and galleried landing were still exactly the same as I remembered them, but that was where it ended.

Our living room where we had spent so many happy Christmases in front of the fire, opening our presents before playing carpet bowls and Escalado was now a meeting room. The dining room where we'd tucked into Christmas dinner was now a solicitor's office. Most of the fittings had been removed from the kitchen with only the sink remaining. It now served as a staff common room with tea and coffee making facilities.

Margaret's office was on the first floor in what had once been Rupert's bedroom. The other four bedrooms had also been converted into offices and the bathroom now served as ladies and gents toilets. Finally, the top floor, which my father had lovingly converted into a flat for Sarah and I, now served as a storage area and was packed full of legal files.

I don't know what I'd been hoping to get out of looking around my former home. But it was clear to me that it had changed out of all recognition, just a mere shell of the fabulous Georgian home it had once been.

Once the tour was completed Margaret and I left and went for a couple of drinks in the Market Tavern. I didn't really like visiting our old pubs as they tended to bring back too many memories. But the Market Tavern was only a few yards away from where Margaret worked. Besides, it was one of the better pubs in Chesterfield town centre.

We chatted about our school days and our old friends. Margaret didn't know that Herman had married my sister, although she knew that Sprout and Carrot had wed and that they were now running a successful chain of supermarkets. That was because she specialised in corporate law and had done some work for R and G.

I was thoroughly enjoying myself and didn't want the

evening to end, which it did far too soon as Margaret had to get home to make Richard's supper. She told me that she had enjoyed herself and that we really ought to do it again sometime. She gave me her telephone number and asked me to give her a call before she picked up her handbag and left.

I never phoned her. Perhaps it was because I was too set in my ways by then or perhaps it was for Richard's sake. After all, he would have been teased mercilessly if it were known that I was going out with his mother. It was bad enough for poor Nigel and I was only his uncle. But the main reason was because I couldn't help but feel that it was never meant to be. If it had been, then I would have gone out with her 1944 instead of going out with Sarah.

If I'd made that decision back then my life would probably have turned out very differently. Margaret was an intelligent woman. She was a solicitor specialising in corporate law. If I'd married her, chances were that I would never have lost the brewery. Not only that but I probably would have ended up with a son like Richard, ready to take over from me when I retired.

But I'd made the wrong decision back then and I would have to live with the consequences of that for the rest of my life.

# Chapter 28

Nigel and Molly decided to tip the contents of the spirit bottles into the sink, just as they had done with those they had discovered in the dining room.

Like the other sideboard this one also contained a variety of glasses, most of which were pretty nondescript and were destined to join the others in a box to be taken to the hospice shop.

One, however, caught Nigel's eye as it was engraved. It was a pint mug. One side had the Chesterfield Grammar School badge on it, with the school motto of *non quo sed quomodo* underneath. The other side said, 'To Miles Goodyear on the occasion of his retirement July 19th, 1991'.

"It's his retirement present," Nigel explained. "I remember that he retired in July 1991, the same day the school closed for the last time."

\*\*\*\*\*\*

In August 1973, I received an unexpected letter through the post. It was from Howard's wife telling me that he had died suddenly from a heart attack. It was like a bolt out of the blue. He was only 48 and had seemed to be as fit as he'd ever been when I'd seen him two months previously at the university reunion.

He was the first of my friends to die and it served to remind me how fragile life can be. Of course, my brother Rupert had died when he was nineteen, but that was war. Howard had died from a heart attack. People don't normally die from heart attacks aged only 48. I was going to be 46 myself the following month and it made me wonder how many more years I had left.

I didn't know Howard's wife, as he hadn't met her when Sarah and I got married. After that the only times we ever met were at university reunions. Naturally, he never brought his wife to these annual events, as it left him free to spend a night of passion with Gorgeous Gail every year.

It seemed his wife got my details from Howard's address book along with several other of his friends who she'd never met. She had written to all of us to let us know.

Howard worked for Berkshire County Council and lived in Reading. So it was with a heavy heart that I caught the train to Berkshire the following Thursday in order to go to his funeral.

The crematorium was packed with his work colleagues and friends, none of whom I knew. The wake was held in a local cricket club, where I went up to Howard's wife and introduced myself. I told her how sorry I was to hear that Howard had died so young. He had left her widowed at the age of only 42 with two sons aged fourteen and sixteen.

I told her the story about how Howard and I had dressed up the statue of William Herbert with a handbag and scarf when we were students. It was one of the few stories about Howard that I could tell her.

The story made her smile.

"You know today has made me realise just how many of Howard's friends I've never met," she said. "You've all got such wonderful stories to tell about him. Somehow it makes this awful situation seem better. But tell me, I've already asked several people, and nobody knows who she is. See that woman over there? She must have thought a lot of Howard, as she hasn't stopped crying since she arrived. But I've never met her before and I don't know who she is. Do you know her?"

She was pointing at Gorgeous Gail and I had only a split second to decide what to say.

"That's Gail, our old cook from university," I replied. "In fact, she still works there as I last saw her when Howard and I went back for the reunion in June. She's always had a soft spot for Howard, always gave him second helpings."

"Well, it's really good of her to come," she replied.

"Gail always bent over backwards for Howard," I continued. "She was always going to come."

It was an inappropriate joke to make at a funeral. But Howard would have loved it.

Howard must have been dealt a poor hand in life since none of my other friends died when they were so young. As for my own life, well I just kept on with my bachelor existence of occasional visits to the pub with Brian and Colin and cultural trips to the Continent during the summer.

In fact in 1974, the five of us went on a tour of Italy when I was finally able to visit Rupert's grave, something my father had never been able to do. It was thirty years since Rupert's death and yet his grave and all the others in Monte Cassino cemetery were in pristine condition, which was thanks to the Commonwealth War Graves Commission of course.

School was an endless struggle as I tried to teach the boys about Caecilius, Matella, Quintus and all the other characters in the Cambridge Latin course. That said, most of the boys I taught ended up passing their Latin O-level. We were a selective school after all. You might not have to pay to go there anymore, but you still had to pass your eleven-plus.

They say that time speeds up as you get older and I can definitely back this up as it didn't seem very long before I'd clocked up twenty years' of service.

It was January 1990 and I was now 62 years old, less than three years away from retirement. However, it was looking less and less likely that I would last that long.

Not that there was anything wrong with me, it was the school where the problem lay. Chesterfield Borough Council had been trying to do away with its grammar schools for years. Mr Price, the headmaster, was fighting a rear-guard action trying to save us, but the council was Labour-controlled and they didn't like grammar schools as a matter of principle. It seemed that the name change, dropping the word 'Grammar' from the title of the school, hadn't fooled them in the slightest.

The headmaster's last chance was a vote by the parents to take the school out of local authority control. But when that failed, the game was up. The school year of 1990-1 was to be our last and the grammar school, which was only three years away from celebrating its 400th anniversary, was to be replaced by a new comprehensive.

Of course, most teachers could have transferred to the new school, but very few of my fellow masters took up that option. I was only just over one year away from retirement anyway, so I was never going to take up a new post. Brian and Colin were only in their mid-fifties, but both of them opted for early retirement as well. After all, both of them were not married and they owned their own houses outright. The two of them also had over thirty years' worth of pension contributions, so they didn't need to work anymore.

My pension was much smaller as I had only been paying into it for twenty years. There never seemed much point in having a pension when we owned the brewery. It was stupid really since all our staff had been in a company pension scheme. But the brewery was a family business and I always assumed that it would continue to support family members after they retired. It had never even crossed my mind that the business wouldn't exist when it came to my turn.

The last day of term was a sad affair as we were all saying goodbye to colleagues we'd known for many years. When all the pupils had left, we held a farewell party in the school hall at which we were all presented with a glass tankard resplendent with the school crest. They were all individually engraved, which was a nice touch.

"You may as well take some of the Latin books from the library with you as well," said Brian. "They won't be needing them in the new school as they aren't going to teach Latin. They've decided that they need a more modern curriculum and so they are going to replace it with Media Studies instead. Personally I find it amazing that you can get a GCSE in watching TV these days."

I went to the library and helped myself to a book of poetry by Catullus and the works of Pliny the Elder. They'd been part of my life for over twenty years, even longer if you included university and my lessons with Hugh Janus before that. Anyway, if I hadn't taken them, they would only have ended up in a skip.

# Chapter 29

"I know the tankard is personalised but it will still probably fetch something at auction being as though the school's closed down," said Molly.

Nigel agreed and placed it with the items waiting to be taken to auction. By this stage, the pile was so high you could barely see the fireplace. Nigel drove a Volvo Estate. It was the favourite car of shopkeepers due to its massive load carrying capacity. But even so it looked as though it was going to take them two trips to take everything to the auction house.

There were only four drawers in the sideboard left to clear out and the first of these contained yet more old coins. Not only that, but this time there were also some ten shilling and £1 notes. All of these were added to the growing collection in the tea caddy.

Two of the drawers were crammed full of old photos, which Molly put into a box so that Emma and Nigel could look through them all at the weekend.

That left only one drawer. They initially thought it contained a variety of programmes, but they turned out to be 'celebrations of life,' from the funerals of people Uncle Miles knew. There were quite a few of them, a sad reminder that Miles had outlived most of his friends and family. Included amongst them were the orders of service for the funerals of Nigel's parents.

"We still have both of these but I'm not going to throw them away just yet as Emma might have misplaced hers," said Nigel, who then put the rest of the orders of service into the nearest bin liner.

\*\*\*\*\*\*

Retirement should be fun. It should be a time for you to do some of the things you've always wanted to do. However, I wasn't enjoying retirement at all. For a start I was lonely. Being single wasn't so much of an issue whilst I was working, but once I'd retired I really started to regret my decision not to find another partner.

Herman had retired shortly after me, but his retirement could not have been more different to mine. Neither of his children was interested in taking over the family business, so he'd sold the shop and got a good price for it. He and my sister now seemed to spend all their time travelling around the Mediterranean on various cruises.

I wasn't travelling abroad anymore as my friends could no longer accompany me. Colin had bought an old chapel near Barlow and was converting it into a cottage for himself. He was so busy that he had no time to travel. Meanwhile, Barry had bought himself a smallholding and couldn't leave his animals. I had no desire to go abroad by myself, so I just went for walks in the Peak District instead.

The only person who hadn't retired was Sprout. By 1999, he was 71 years old and was still head of R and G, still being supported by Carrot. Both of their sons were working for the company in senior positions. However, Sprout showed absolutely no intention of giving up work and handing control over to them. Or so I thought.

I didn't get to see Sprout much anymore, as work took up all his time. Therefore, it came as a complete surprise when he phoned me up one day and asked if I wanted to go out for a drink.

We decided to meet in the Market Tavern at seven o'clock the following Tuesday and I was really looking forward to it. Sprout was always good company. I'd known him for sixty years and we never ran out of things to talk about.

As soon as we'd got our first beer he dropped his bombshell.

"I've decided to retire," he told me.

"Give over," I replied. "I thought you and Georgina would go on forever."

"No Miles, I mean it. We are both going to retire. There's a new millennium about to start and it's time to give the next generation a chance. Richard and Gordon are both in their late forties and have been waiting in the wings for ages. It's their turn now. Don't forget that my father passed the running of the company over to me when he was in his fifties. I was only in my 20s at the time. No, I've delayed long enough. I don't understand things like computers and I'm too old to learn new tricks. I've taken the company as far as I can. We are currently the number four supermarket chain in the UK. If we are ever going to make it to that number one position, it will be Richard and Gordon who will take us there, not Georgina and I."

"Well, I never thought I'd see the day when you decided to give up work. What do you and Georgina intend to do with the rest of your lives?"

"For a start, I'll have more time to spend with you and Herman having a few beers down the pub. But in addition to that, both of us are still healthy so we've decided to see the world. After all, we've got the money and it's something I've always wanted to do. The two of us have never taken that many holidays so we have a lot of catching up to do. In fact, we're planning on making a start by going to Antigua in February to renew our vows on Valentine's Day."

"Really," I said before taking another gulp of my beer. "Personally I've never seen the point of this modern trend to renew vows."

"Don't knock it. I love Georgina just as much as the day I first went out with her and I want the world to know. This is the best way I can think of showing it."

He then added in a hushed voice, "You know we've still got an active sex life."

"I don't believe it, you're both in your seventies," I said, quite aghast at what he'd just told me.

Sprout winked at me and whispered, "You know the rhyme about sex in old age, don't you?"

I didn't but I suspected I was about to find out.

"When I was young and in my prime
I used to do it all the time.
But now that I am old and grey
I only manage twice a day."

He then gave a little chuckle before adding, "Well, twice a month at any rate."

"You always were a lucky bugger, Sprout," I added.

"Anyway," he went on, "both of us want you, Herman and Rebecca to come with us. We'll pay of course. The three of you have been really good friends to us over the past sixty years, even though we've usually been too busy to spend any quality time with you. Well, we've got the time now so we want you to come with us."

"That's very kind of you, Sprout. Excuse me whilst I just check my diary."

He knew I wasn't being serious of course.

"No", I said. "You're in luck. I've got nothing planned for the rest of my life."

I looked at him and said,

"Seriously though, I'd be honoured to go with you and Georgina."

We had another couple of pints and shared many memories of our schooldays and our time together in the RAF. It was the happiest I'd been in a long time and I could tell that Sprout was happy as well. I'd never been outside of Europe before and I was really looking forward to going to Antigua with my friends. But even more than that, I was looking forward to many more evenings just like this one, evenings spent chatting and reminiscing in the pub with Sprout, my best friend.

Just before we left Sprout reached into the bag he'd brought with him.

"Before you go I just wanted to return this to you."

To my complete surprise I saw that he was holding Edward.

"You took him? But why?" I asked.

"It was to protect you," he replied. "Your life would have been absolute hell if you'd kept him. Both Sergeant Dyke and the other lads in the squadron would never have let go of the fact that you had a teddy bear. They would have teased and tormented you mercilessly and I couldn't let it happen."

"But why didn't you give him back to me when we left?" I pleaded.

"It seems silly, I know, but I was worried that you'd stop being friends with me if I told you that I'd taken him. So I just put him in a drawer and forgot about him. I found him the other day when I was clearing out some of my things. I thought it was about time I returned him to his rightful owner."

"I don't think anything would ever stop me from being your friend, Sprout. That's especially true nowadays, as I'm far too old to make any new ones. Thanks for telling me what happened," and then turning to Edward, I added, "And welcome home to you, Edward, I've really missed you, old pal."

That night I put Edward on my bedside cabinet and just before I switched the light off, I said to him, "I'm keeping an eye on you old boy. So don't think that you can disappear again."

We never went to Antigua. Sprout never saw the new millennium as two months later he suffered a massive stroke and died. His luck had finally run out. So, just like my father, my best friend was never able to fulfil his dream of travelling the world.

Sprout's death was major news both locally and also in the wider business community. It was even covered on *Look North*, a fitting tribute for Chesterfield's most prominent businessman. His funeral was a massive affair and was my last chance to say goodbye to my friend of sixty years.

Carrot sat in front of me at the crematorium. She looked to have aged considerably since Sprout's death. Grey roots were starting to show through her ginger hair. She had probably been dying it for years, but with Sprout's death she'd lost the will to continue making an effort.

If her hair was no longer red, then that couldn't be said of her eyes, which were all puffy from sobbing. She looked a shadow of her former self and it came as no surprise to me when she too passed away three months later.

A year after that Richard and Gordon decided to sell up. They never had the same drive as their parents and lacked the desire to push R and G into the number one spot. They accepted an offer for the company from Sainsbury's and both of them went to live in the Cayman Islands as tax exiles.

No sooner had Carrot passed away than I received some bad news from my sister. It seemed that Herman had gone into town the previous week, but couldn't find his way back home again.

With hindsight the signs had been there for some time, but everyone had turned a blind eye to them. However, they couldn't be ignored anymore and so Herman went to see the doctor who diagnosed him with Alzheimer's.

Sprout's death had been a shock to everybody as it was so sudden. But Herman's demise was a long slow slide downhill as dementia took hold of him. Herman had never been a violent person, but as his symptoms got worse, his temper got shorter and shorter. Eventually my sister decided that she couldn't cope by herself anymore. Herman had threatened to hit two policemen who'd brought him home. They discovered him walking the streets dressed only in his dressing gown and slippers. Shortly afterwards Herman was put into a home where he passed away six months later.

I visited him there once, but he didn't recognise me. It was one of the saddest days of my life, as I knew I'd never see him again. In reality, he'd already left this world. My old friend was now just an empty husk with all the important bits removed. It made me wonder if Sprout's luck really had run out in 1999, for at that moment it seemed as if he had been the lucky one. He'd gone whilst he was still at his peak and never had to suffer the ignominy of having somebody wipe his arse for him.

Herman died in the summer of 2002 and, as a result, I found myself at the crematorium for the third time in less than two years. I watched Herman's coffin arrive draped with both the Union Jack and the Swiss flag. It represented the dual heritage of the boy who'd told us on his first day at school that his grandfather was not a Nazi storm trooper, but was a watch repairer who came from Grindelwald in Switzerland.

I got a lot closer to my sister after that. The two of us had something that bound us together, she was a widow and I a widower. I'd go round for lunch on a Sunday and we'd listen to the radio just like we used to do in the old days.

When she died in 2006 it hit me badly. She was three years younger than me. I never doubted for one moment that she would outlive me. After all, women always outlive men, don't they? How wrong I was and her death left me more alone than ever. I was 78 years old, all my siblings and my long-term friends were dead. I'd no children and my only living relatives were all very distant, both in terms of where they lived and in terms of my relationship with them.

# Chapter 30

After clearing out the sideboard Nigel and Molly only had to add the record player, old TV, the pre-war radio and the standard lamp to the auction pile. They then decided they were finished for another day.

Of course they did have to go to the recycling centre a few more times and had one more load to take to the hospice shop. But pretty soon they were heading back to Ashbourne with their uncle's modern television in the back of their car, which they had decided to put in their spare bedroom.

Nigel and Molly had to be back at nine o'clock the following morning as that was when the furniture removal people from the hospice shop were due to arrive.

As it turned out they needn't have worried as the men from the hospice shop were half an hour late. So whilst they were waiting they loaded the Austin 10 onto the trailer they had brought with them.

When the van finally arrived, the outcome was a little disappointing. Nigel knew that the hospice shop wasn't prepared to take all the furniture, but he thought that they would take more than they did.

They wouldn't take either the double bed in the main bedroom or the single bed in the second bedroom because they said they were stained. Not that anybody could see where these marks were, unless you used an ultraviolet lamp.

They wouldn't take the cot because it didn't meet modern safety standards, or the wardrobe because it had been personalised. That was despite Nigel's suggestion that it was just the thing a couple with the names Mick and Sharon would be looking for.

The only items of furniture they took from upstairs were a bedside cabinet and three chests of drawers.

Downstairs the story was much the same. Nigel and Molly had agreed that the hospice shop could take the dining room table and chairs and they were more than happy to take them, since they were antique and of high quality. But they wouldn't take the set from the kitchen as they said they were too tatty. They also wouldn't take the three-piece suite, as it didn't have fire retardant labels. So that left them only taking two sideboards, the desk and chair from the study, and a coffee table, standard lamp and magazine rack from the lounge.

It was less than the two of them had hoped for but at least it was a start. So whilst Molly made a cup of tea, Nigel phoned the council to see if they would pick up the rest of the furniture. In total, they had ten items to be collected including the washing machine, tumble drier, fridge and cooker. Nigel was surprised that it was only going to cost them £30 plus an extra £15 to dispose of the fridge.

The person from the council told him to leave everything in the driveway, explaining that it would be collected sometime during the next week.

Nigel was glad that he'd phoned the council now rather than later, as Molly wouldn't be able to come back on Friday and he needed her help to remove all the bulky items from the house. If the truth be told, he hoped that he wouldn't have to come back on Friday either, but that depended on what they discovered in the attic, garage and shed. It was the attic that worried him the most as he'd already had a look in the shed and garage and had seen that there wasn't too much there that needed to be removed.

Nigel and Molly spent the rest of the morning moving the remainder of the furniture and putting it in the driveway, which left them with the afternoon to tackle the stuff in the garage, shed and the attic.

The house was now empty apart from the fitted furniture and the huge pile of items in the living room waiting to be taken to auction. It felt like a different place, no longer a home, more like a condemned man awaiting execution.

"Well, there's no point in putting it off any more," said Nigel. "It's time to tackle the attic."

The attic was accessed by a set of dropdown steps and Nigel's biggest fear as he climbed them was that it would contain as much junk as the rest of the house.

As it turned out, he needn't have worried. It was actually surprisingly spartan with only two boxes stored there. One of these was a large wooden crate full of old toys and the other was a smaller box full of photographs. Nigel had been expecting to find Christmas decorations and bits of old carpet up there, but was pleased to see that there were none of these things.

The toys were placed on the auction pile and the photos were added to those downstairs waiting to be examined by Nigel and Emma. Most of the photos were loose although a few of them were in albums. However, one was in a silver frame. It was in sepia and depicted a family, a proud father seated with his wife, mother and children. It was very old, probably taken sometime during the nineteenth century.

"Do you know who the people are in this photo?" asked Molly.

"They are almost certainly relatives of mine," Nigel

replied. "But I haven't got a clue who they are. Perhaps Emma will know."

After getting off lightly, the next job was to tackle the garage. Most of the contents were really old, ancient motor oil, an old canister containing Redex, a grease gun, old cans of WD40 and a set of jump leads. One by one they were put into a large cardboard box ready to be taken to the recycling centre. Nigel discovered a few spare parts for the Austin 10, which he kept, placing them in the Austin's boot. But overall, the garage contained mainly junk.

So did the shed. It contained several opened paint pots, an old set of steps, a rusty old saw, a trowel, a hedge-trimmer, several jars containing screws and nails, and a large toolbox. Both the box and the tools it contained were absolutely exquisite. In fact, it was more of a fitted case than a box and each of the tools had its own custom made slot inside. Surprisingly, none of the tools were missing. They were obviously of a far higher quality than the rest of the junk in the shed and Nigel initially thought about taking them to auction. But then he had another idea.

"I'm going to ask John next door if he wants these," said Nigel. "We don't need them and I think he deserves more than just an old lawnmower from us. After all, he was my uncle's executor and he organised his funeral."

"That's a good idea," agreed Molly. So Nigel put the toolbox to one side and the two of them started putting everything else into another cardboard box ready to take to the recycling centre.

By three o'clock they were finished. This time they didn't have anything to take to the hospice shop, but they did have a car full of things destined for the recycling centre. They had to come back again in order to collect the trailer with the Austin 10 on it and to see if John wanted the toolbox. But apart from that they had finished. There was no need for Nigel to come back on Friday. The only thing left to do was to return on Saturday with Emma and Ralph in order for them to choose the item they wanted to keep. After that their final job would be to take everything else to Bamford's Auctioneers in Rowsley.

When they returned, John told them he was happy to accept the tools and once Nigel and Molly had left he looked through the contents of the box. The tools contained inside were beautifully made out of solid hardwood and steel. All of them were inlaid in brass with the initials BG. The tools had obviously been made at the same time as the box since they all had their own place and all fitted perfectly.

"I wonder who BG was," John thought to himself. "It was probably one of Miles's relatives, so I guess I will never know now that he's passed away."

*******

Later that year Bob, my next-door neighbour, moved into a retirement home even though he was only 77. My new neighbours were John and Eleanor Blenkin. He was a retired civil servant and she used to be a nurse. They had downsized from a house in Ashgate, which had become too large for them once their two daughters had left home. So they'd sold up and bought the two-bedroomed end of terrace cottage next door to me, putting the balance of the money from their sale into the bank for their old age.

They were the ideal neighbours, thoughtful, caring and above all quiet. Which was more than could be said for the pub on the other side of me.

The brewing industry had changed out of all recognition since I'd left it. I'd kept abreast of the changes primarily because my landlord kept on changing, but also because I wanted to know who owned the rights to my family name.

Sheffield Brewery had been taken over by United Breweries of Burton-upon-Trent in 1973. Two years after that United had become part of Imperial Brands, a conglomerate based in London. They, in turn, fell victim to Wilson and Bush, an American multinational corporation in 1979.

Things then remained pretty stable for the next ten years until new legislation known as the Beer Orders was introduced. This had the effect of limiting the number of tied pubs that breweries in the UK were allowed to own. As a result, Wilson and Bush sold off all their breweries to CBL of Canada in order to get around the new law.

It was at this point that my two interests went in separate directions, since Wilson and Bush was my landlord, whereas CBL now owned all the rights to the name 'Goodyear's Brewery'.

Eventually, Wilson and Bush decided to sell off all their pubs and the chain was split up amongst various pub groups. After passing through the hands of numerous owners, Sizzling Steak Shacks acquired the George Stephenson in 2001 and became my landlord at the same time.

Sizzling Steak Shacks initially planned to rename the pub the Rodeo Ranch and wanted to demolish my house in order to build an extension incorporating a Mexican restaurant. Mexican restaurants were very big at the time and Sizzling Steak Shacks owned several of them. They were all branded under the truly awful name of Hacienda That. Fortunately though, my lease was watertight and they had absolutely no chance of evicting me, so eventually they dropped the idea. They also dropped the proposed name change after a mass protest by the local residents, which I was pleased to be part of.

In the years that followed, Sizzling Steak Shacks made numerous offers to buy me out. Each time it was to make way for one of their latest hair-brained schemes. But where would I go? I had absolutely no intention of moving into an old folks' home like Bob had done. After all, I'd seen what it did to my grandmother.

The noise from the pub grew louder as the years went by and I became paranoid that it was a deliberate ploy on their behalf to intimidate me. If that was the case it was never going to work, as I was getting more and more deaf as I got older, so all I had to do was to switch my hearing aid off.

I'd always got on well with John and Eleanor, but it was only after Eleanor died in 2005 that I considered John to be a close friend. Our friendship got even stronger when Rebecca died the following year. Suddenly we were both in the same boat. We were both widowers with no relatives living close by. John did have two daughters, but with both of them living more than a hundred miles away he rarely saw them.

We'd go to the pub together, not to the George Stephenson, but to the Nags Head further down the road. We'd chat over the garden fence during the summer, and we'd go for walks in the Derbyshire countryside. It was good to have a friend like John, especially since he only lived next door.

I think I needed him more than he needed me, particularly when I gave up driving. He was ten years younger than me and a lot fitter than I was. That said I'd been pretty lucky with my health over the years, only suffering from arthritis and a degree of hearing loss. Mind you, I think he really enjoyed my company, especially in the years immediately following Eleanor's death.

As I progressed into my eighties, my arthritis got worse and John offered to do the gardening for me. But my garden was quite large and I didn't really want to impose on him. So I told him that I would struggle on, adding that the day I stopped gardening was the day I gave up on life.

# Chapter 31

"Look, there's Mum and Dad," said Emma. "They look so young."

Nigel, Molly, Emma and Ralph were looking through their uncle's photograph collection on Friday evening. Most of the photos were destined to be thrown in the bin, but every now and again they decided to keep the odd one.

Emma and Ralph had arrived in Ashbourne two hours earlier and after the four of them had eaten, they all sat down to look through the photographs.

"Here's one which I presume is Uncle Miles's class at school," said Emma. "I wonder why all the faces are crossed out other than those of Uncle Miles and one other boy?"

"God only knows," replied Nigel.

The four of them were finished looking through the photographs Nigel and Molly had found in the rooms in Miles's house. Next was the turn of the box retrieved from the attic. It was these photos that posed the most questions. They recognised very few of the people in them, just the occasional ones of their mother and uncle as children. They were often with another older boy, who they presumed was their Uncle Rupert.

Emma didn't have a clue who the people were in the photo in the silver frame. She agreed with Nigel that they were almost certainly relatives of theirs. But she didn't have the faintest idea whether they were from their grandfather or grandmother's side of the family.

In the end they decided that there was no way they were ever going to identify who they were and so they agreed to add the silver photo frame to the list of items destined for the auction. They discussed whether or not to include the actual photograph along with the frame. They all felt that this was a good idea, since having a photo in the frame really showed it off to its full potential.

All together, it took them over an hour and a half to look at all the photos. Some of them brought back memories. Some of them were photos of their mum and dad that they had never seen before. But many of them didn't mean anything to them at all.

The 'celebration of life' cards from their mum and dad's funerals brought tears to Emma's eyes. She still had her copies, but hadn't looked at them in years and the sight of them brought the memories flooding back. In the end, neither Nigel nor Emma wanted to throw them away, so Emma agreed to take them home with her.

The following day there was no need to head off early to their uncle's house, as there weren't any big jobs waiting for them there. In fact, the only job was to transfer the items from their uncle's living room to the auction house. Nigel suggested that they take two cars, as the items would not fit into just one.

At a quarter past ten, the four of them set off for the final time, arriving at just before eleven. The first thing that Nigel noticed was that the council had already collected the furniture. They had told him that it would take up to a week, but had actually picked up the items the day after he had contacted them.

The house looked very forlorn with everything removed

from it and after briefly wandering around all the empty rooms, Emma joined the others in the lounge.

"If you want to start looking through the items we are taking to the auction, you can choose something to remember Uncle Miles by," said Nigel

"Actually, I was thinking of going for his Austin 10," she announced with a mischievous look in her eye. "Ralph and I are thinking of touring around Europe when we retire and it would be brilliant if we could do it in a vintage car."

Nigel was speechless for a few seconds, before Emma announced that she was only winding him up.

"I've absolutely no desire to own the car and even if I did then I'd still let you have it. You deserve it for clearing out the house. In fact, I'd like Molly to choose something as well, as a thank you for doing half the work. After all it hardly seems fair that she's only going to get an old car as a reward."

Molly thanked her and said she would like to take the Charlotte Rhead jug if that was okay.

Emma started to go through all the items in the pile before eventually deciding to take her grandfather's medals.

Nigel was almost as shocked as he'd been when she'd suggested that she wanted the car. However, he was secretly pleased, as he hadn't wanted to take the medals to auction. They were a precious piece of family history that really ought to stay with somebody from the family. In fact, he probably would have chosen them for himself if he hadn't discovered the Austin 10.

"You do surprise me," he said to her. "I'd never have guessed that you'd choose the medals."

"Well, they're small. They are part of our family's history and granddad must have been extremely brave to be awarded these medals. I'm going to get them framed and I will put them on the wall in our conservatory."

Once that had been decided, they started to remove the rest of the items from the house and packed them into the two cars. Half an hour later when they had finished, they decided to take one last look around the house, just in case they had missed anything.

"What's this?" said Ralph as he picked up a piece of card from the mantelpiece and handed it to Nigel.

It was an invitation card that they had missed due to the large pile of items that had been obscuring their view of the fireplace.

"Well, I never," said a surprised Nigel as he read the invitation. It was addressed to their uncle and said:

The directors of Goodyear's Brewery would like to invite
Mr Miles Goodyear
To the opening of our new brewery on
Feb 10th 2020 at 11am
At
Unit 27
Storforth Lane Trading Estate
Storforth Lane
Chesterfield
Tel 01246 987643
RSVP

"Well, that's a surprise," said Nigel. "It looks as if someone's decided to open up a new brewery using the Goodyear name. I'll have to look on the internet and see if I can find out anything more about it."

And that was it. The four of them set off to the auction house in order to drop off all the items they had collected. There they would be assessed before being catalogued and put into lots.

Nigel and Emma never went back to Chesterfield again.

They had no cause to do so. Two weeks later boards were erected around their uncle's house with a notice on it, which read:

Koming soon, Kaptain Kustard's Krazy Kids Kabin
Opening May 2020

Alliteration had always been a big thing at Sizzling Steak Shacks and their marketing department had come up with the new name after deciding that Barmy Barn wasn't 'katchy' enough for them.

By the end of that week, their uncle's house and all the memories that went with it had been demolished. It was just as if it had never existed.

******

I was 92 years and 87 days old on December 21st. Nothing worth celebrating for most people, but for me it marked a milestone as it was the day that I overtook my grandmother to become the longest living member of my family ever. I say ever, but of course I don't know what age any of my ancestors lived to prior to my great-great-grandmother. That said I doubt if any of them who'd lived in the eighteenth century or earlier would have been able to reach such a grand old age.

Granny always used to say that old age wasn't for wimps and as I'd got older myself I'd began to realise what she meant.

Not that I could complain about my health, because other than arthritis in my wrists and partial hearing loss I was in rude health. No, it's the fact that you get to see everyone you hold dear pass away if you live to such a fine old age. All my family and friends had died and yet I stubbornly carried on.

It was as if God was determined to punish me for my past misdemeanours.

Barely a week seemed to pass by without people I knew, either from school or from work, appearing in the obituary column of the *Derbyshire Times*. I still had a photograph of my class from the first year at the Grammar School and would put a cross through the faces of my former classmates as they passed away. When Andrew Gleason died at the end of November, it only left one face, other than my own, without a cross through it.

Of course I'd made a few younger friends over the years, John next door for a start. Also I still occasionally met up with Brian and Colin, but they were no substitute for the friends I'd had since childhood. As a result I was still lonely and I really missed Sprout and Herman.

It was four days before Christmas, not that you would have known it from the inside of my house. I'd given up celebrating Christmas many years ago and there was no tree or decorations in my home. There wasn't a wreath on my door or any cards on the mantelpiece either.

John next door had gone to spend Christmas with his daughter in Cambridge and wouldn't be back until Boxing Day. So this year I faced the prospect of having absolutely nobody at all to talk to on Christmas day. Not that it bothered me. I'd decided to spend Christmas day watching TV whilst at the same time waiting for it all to be over. I really didn't like Christmas anymore.

Shortly after lunch there was a knock on the door, which was something that rarely happened these days. Unless of course it was the postman with a parcel too big to fit through my letterbox. Either that or the Jehovah's Witnesses.

I opened the door and was surprised to see a young man standing there. I say young but, in reality, he was probably in his late thirties, but he was young compared to me.

Thinking about it, though, everybody was young compared to me.

"Mr Goodyear," he said.

"Yes," I replied really hoping that he wasn't the Conservative Party candidate for the next council elections.

"My name is Alex Hopkinson. You don't know me but you taught my father Latin at Chesterfield School.

"You're Richard Hopkinson's lad," I said. "In which case, I knew your grandmother as well. But don't just stand there in the cold. Come on in."

I showed Alex through to the kitchen and asked him if he wanted a cup of tea. He said that would be lovely.

"So you didn't go to the Grammar School yourself then?" I asked as I put the kettle on.

"No, I was only born in 1983," he replied. "So the school had closed before I could go there. I went to St Mary's instead."

"I hear it's a good school," I replied. "But tell me, what did your father do when he left school?"

"He became a solicitor just like Granny, as did I."

"Your grandmother was a fine woman. I nearly went out with her twice you know. I really should have done. It is one of the biggest regrets of my life."

"Why don't you go and see her," said Alex. "She still lives in the same house and is very active for her age. I'm sure she'd really like to see you. After all, most of the people she knew from her youth are dead now."

"I'd really like to do that," I replied. "To tell you the truth, I had no idea that she was still alive."

"Oh, she's very much still alive," replied Alex. "But she and my dad aren't the only members of my family who knew you. My grandfather used to work for you. That's my mother's father by the way, not the one who was married to grandma Hopkinson. He was your last head brewer."

"What, Stuart Datcheler?" I asked incredulously. "What happened to him? I lost touch with him after the brewery was taken over.

"Oh, he never got another job in brewing. He was unemployed for over a year before he eventually got a job with Express Dairies. He retired in 1988 and passed away ten years later.

"When I was young he used to tell me stories about the brewery. He used to absolutely love working there. He'd tell me about how the head brewer, Bill Jones, would get so drunk that he couldn't start the brew off. So Granddad would have to do it even though he wasn't fully trained at the time. How it was so hot shovelling out the spent grains from the mash tun that he'd have to do it without wearing a stitch of clothing. They were the happiest days of his life and he always regretted the fact that they didn't go on for longer."

Alex looked at me and said. "I haven't really enjoyed my time as a solicitor, Mr Goodyear, because when you look at it there isn't much fun or excitement in conveyancing. All my life I've wanted to do something that I really enjoy and that doesn't mean sorting out people's wills or their divorce settlements. No, I want to be like my grandfather. I want to become a brewer. I'm already a proficient home brewer, but I want to take it one step further. I want to re-establish Goodyear's Brewery and that's why I'm here. I want your blessing."

"Well, I'm absolutely astonished," I replied. "What makes you think it will be a success? After all, we had problems for years and despite my best efforts I couldn't stop the company from being taken over in 1967."

"With the greatest respect that was in the 1960s and everybody wanted keg beer and lager back then. But CAMRA started in 1971 and with it the start of a backlash against bland fizzy beer. Nowadays, there are more brewer-ies in Britain than there have ever been. Most of them are small microbreweries helped by the introduction of progres-sive beer duty, which enables them to compete with the big boys. Who knows, if only you had been able to hang on for another four years, the original Goodyear's Brewery might still be thriving today."

Alex went on to explain that he had bought a 25-barrel plant and had rented premises on Storforth Lane. Several local businessmen, including a local undertaker, were back-ing him.

"He's been brought in to add body to the beer," he joked.

"Well, I'm absolutely delighted," I said, "and I have no objection to you using the Goodyear name. But it's not me you need to get permission from, it's CBL. They own the rights to the Goodyear name these days."

"Actually that's why I said blessing rather permission. I've already spoken to CBL and they have agreed to sell me the Goodyear Brewery trademark and the rights to all the Goodyear brands for only £1."

I noted that Alex was displaying his training as a solicitor. He was choosing his words very carefully.

"I guess they just don't need them anymore," I replied. "It's not surprising really being as though they never wanted them in the first place. They merely inherited them when they took over Wilson and Bush's brewing interests in the UK. They never had any interest in the Goodyear name or any intention of reintroducing products like Goodyear's Pride."

"No, but we do. My grandfather kept the original brew-ing book so we've got the recipe for Goodyear's Pride. We've even been able to obtain the original yeast strain from the National Collection of yeast cultures. We've already carried out two trial brews and we think that you would be hard pressed to tell the difference between our version and the original."

Alex continued enthusiastically and said that they were planning to have a press launch in the new year and that he would be absolutely delighted if I could attend. I told him that nothing would give me more pleasure.

He presented me with an invitation and then added, "Granny will also be there, but if you want to contact her before that I'll give you her number," and with that he wrote her telephone number on the back of the invitation.

We continued chatting for a while and once he'd finished his tea he made his excuses and stood up ready to leave.

But as he got to the doorstep I said to him, "You know I am really pleased that you're bringing back the Goodyear name. I told you earlier that not going out with your grandmother was one of the biggest regrets in my life, but do you know what my biggest single regret is? It is failing to save my family business, seeing it taken over, resulting in many good people, like your grandfather, being thrown onto the dole. I've always considered myself to be a failure, but now at least I can die knowing that the Goodyear Brewery name is in safe hands."

However, I wasn't quite finished and so I continued. "You know, if things had turned out differently you could have been my grandson or at the very least my step-grandson. You could have been part of the Goodyear family and for that reason I want to give you something."

With that I disappeared back inside the house and reappeared holding the brass plaque that had originally been on the wall outside the brewery offices.

"Thank you very much," he said. "I will always treasure it and I promise that I will fix it to the wall outside the new brewery."

"And I promise that I will phone your grandmother

tomorrow," I replied and with that we said goodbye and he left.

Alex's visit had brought back all sorts of memories. My life had not gone as I had wanted, of that I had no doubt. Later that evening as I put my head down on my pillow I decided that there were three major events that had changed my life.

The first was when Rupert had died. If he hadn't decided to charge a German pillbox carrying only a wooden gun, he may well have come back alive. He should have run the company not me. He may well have made a better fist of it than I did and, as a result, we may never have lost control of the business.

Of course I will never know the answer to that question and, anyway, what Rupert did or didn't do was outside of my control. There was absolutely no point in beating myself up about it.

Another major turning point was that night out with Sprout in 1965 when he told me about lager, but also told me about venture capital. He was trying to advise me to start brewing lager, which was a good idea. But at the same time, he told me how he was going to raise finance in order to grow his business. He never advised me to do the same. That was my idea and it turned out to be a big mistake.

But the biggest mistake of my life was getting married to Sarah. I was dazzled by her good looks. I should never have been so shallow. If I had my time over again I would never choose to go out with her. I'd opt for somebody with similar interests to myself, somebody I could discuss things with, and someone I'd be happy with right into old age. But of course nobody ever gets a second chance at life.

With that I turned my bedroom light off and went to sleep.

When I awoke the next morning, I was feeling odd. I had

a pain in my arm, which I took to be caused by sleeping in strange position, so I decided to ignore it.

I got out of bed and ran myself a bath. After washing, shaving and cleaning my teeth I got dressed and went downstairs for my breakfast.

I had decided to have beans on toast and so I opened a can of beans and put them on the worktop whilst I went to get a small pan.

It was at this moment that I felt an almighty pain in my chest. I closed my eyes and doubled up in agony as I fell to the floor. When I finally opened them again I was surprised to see that I was no longer in my kitchen. Instead, I'd been transported to the living room of our old house. Not the house as it is nowadays, but the way it had been back in the 1930s. It was Christmas Day and Rupert was playing with his train set, my sister was playing with her doll and my father was sitting in front of the fire smoking his pipe whilst listening to the radio. At that moment my mother walked into the room carrying the Escalado box under her arm. She looked at me and said,

"Hello Miles, where have you been? I haven't seen you in ages."

She then added, "Tell me Miles, have you been a good boy this year?"

"Yes Mother," I replied. "I've been really good."

Everything was just as I remembered it from my boyhood, the best, most perfect Christmas ever.

I blinked and in the time it took to close and reopen my eyes I had been transported to the roof of the bike shed at school. I was looking down on the playground of the girls' high school next door. Sarah was there dressed in her gym kit, her long legs going all the way up to her navy blue knickers. She looked so beautiful, no wonder I used to refer to her as Venus in pumps.

Then I noticed that instead of being surrounded by her classmates she had Sprout, Herman and Carrot standing next to her. They were all smiling up at me and beckoning me to join them.

Sarah blew me a kiss before saying, "Aren't you coming to join us, Miles?"

She took off her beret with a flourish before adding, "You know that I forgive you, don't you Miles?"

With that I climbed down the wall into the playground below and ran over to join her.

I shouted out as I ran towards her, "Wait for me Sarah. I'm coming. I am so very sorry, I love you and I never want to be apart from you again."

# Epilogue

Bamford's Auction Rooms, Rowsley,
Derbyshire, Thursday May 7th 2020

"Now we move on to Lot 132," the auctioneer announced. "This is the first of several lots that form part of the estate of the late Mr Miles Goodyear of Chesterfield. It is a mixed lot comprising a Hornby O gauge railway, a Merrythought teddy bear, an assortment of vintage marbles and the *Pip, Squeak and Wilfred* annual for 1934. I have a couple of commissioned bids on this one and I have to start the bidding at £220.

230

240

250

260

270 and I'm out."

There was a couple of seconds of silence before he continued, "If there are no further bids I will sell for £270."

Bang, his gavel went down. A dealer from Uttoxeter bought the lot.

"Lot 133 is a 1930s uniform for Chesterfield Grammar School, complete with matching cap and tie. You also get a beret from St Helena's school thrown in as part of the lot. Who would like to start me off at £30?"

Silence.

"£20 then."

Still silence.

"£10 then, come on it's got to be worth that at least."

Finally, there was a bid.

"Thank you,

12

14

16

18

20," bang. The winning bidder was from Chesterfield Museum.

"Lot number 134 is a 1932 Marconi Radio with a chrome-rimmed speaker and crescent tuning panel together with a 1953 Bush TV and a 1954 Pye Black Box Record player along with the original receipt for £17, 18 shillings and six pence. There has been a lot of interest in this and I have to start the bidding at £320.

340

360

380

400

Are you out, sir?

Yes, then it's with me at £400," bang. The lot was won by a commissioned bid from a shop specialising in vintage radios in Guildford.

"Lot 135 is the first of several breweriana lots. It is an acid-etched Edwardian mirror with Goodyear's Fine Chesterfield Beers written on it, a lovely example. I have to start the bidding at £180.

200

220

240

260

280

300

320 and the book is out.

Are there any more bids in the room?

Well done, you've bought it, sir," bang.

The winning bidder was Alex Hopkinson and he was really glad to have bought the mirror. He continued to buy all the other Goodyear's Brewery lots spending over £1,500 in total. It was only three months since the relaunch of Goodyear's Brewery and it had exceeded all his projections. So much so in fact that he was beginning to regret only buying a 25-barrel plant. By the way things were going, it looked as if they would shortly be brewing at full capacity. In fact, he had already ordered two more fermenting vessels in order to help keep up with demand.

Unlike most microbreweries, Goodyear's of Chesterfield had a history and that history was something that Alex was keen to exploit. This was why he'd been at the auction hoping to purchase all the old memorabilia, including all the old awards, the advertising signs, old bottle labels and pub signs. In fact, the only lot that he didn't buy was the Sheffield Brewery Clock, which was bought by a collector from Rotherham.

Alex left the auction after the last breweriana lot and made his way to the front desk of the auction house in order to pay for the lots he'd just won. In the meantime, the auction continued.

"Lot 146 is a canteen of silver cutlery hallmarked Sheffield 1952 together with a boxed set of silver fish knives and forks hallmarked Sheffield 1950.

What am I bid for this lot?

Start me at £100.

Thank you.

120 on the internet

140

160 on the internet.

Any more bids?

No? In that case I sell to the internet," bang.

The winning bid was made by an artist based in Barlow, near Chesterfield, who specialised in making sculptures out of old knives and forks. He was too busy to attend the auction in person and so had been bidding on the internet instead.

"Lot number 147 is a really nice example of an art deco statue of a nude.

I've got a bid on the book for this lot and I start at £160."

Silence.

"If there are no further bids in the room or on the internet, I will sell to the maiden commissioned bid of £160," bang.

A collector from Leeds bought this lot. He was a businessman who was working in Amsterdam on the day of the auction and so had left his bid with the auctioneer instead.

"Lot 148 consists of a silver photograph frame, hallmarked Chester for 1870 and containing a photograph of a Victorian family. Let's start the bidding at £50.

£50 surely.

Silence.

No, well £40 then.

Thank you.

45

50

55

60

65

If you are all finished then," bang.

The photo frame was sold to a lady from Youlgrave who wanted it for a picture of her cat. She didn't need the picture of Benjamin Goodyear and his family. In fact, neither she nor anybody else knew that it was a picture of the

Goodyear's Brewery founder and so she merely threw it in the bin as soon as she got home.

"Lot 149 is a large collection of pre-decimalisation coins. Also three ten shilling notes and two £1 notes.

Let's say £20.

£20 for the old coins.

22 on the internet

24

26 on the internet

28

30 on the internet

32

The internet is out so I sell to the room," bang.

The winning bid came from a gentleman who ran a shop selling old coins and banknotes in Buxton.

"Lot 150 consists of a silver hipflask hallmarked Birmingham for 1915, and a silver tankard engraved with the words R and G supermarkets, hallmarked for Sheffield in 1962.

What will you start me for this lot?

£200

Silence.

£100 then

Still silence.

£50

Thank you, sir.

60

70

80

Silence.

It's still cheap, but if there are no further bids I give you fair warning and I sell for £80," bang.

This lot sold to a silversmith from Sheffield who would melt them down for their metal.

"Lot 151 is a large hibiscus patterned Moorcroft fruit bowl together with two small candlesticks also decorated with the hibiscus pattern.

I have two commissioned bids on this lot and also a phone line booked and I start the bidding at £250.

260

270

280 and I'm out.

290 on the telephone.

Silence.

I sell to the telephone then," bang.

The winning bidder came from the owner of an antique shop in Tetbury, Gloucestershire.

The lots kept on coming thick and fast. Colin Potter bought the Chesterfield School glass tankard for only £10. He'd wanted it as he'd smashed his own a few years earlier. The clock that Major Goodyear had received on his retirement in 1958 was sold for £40 to a dealer from Matlock. Different antique shop owners bought the Persian rug, standard lamp, Pearson's pottery vase, RAF cap badge, Royal Doulton plates and the copper charger. The various prints and paintings were bundled together into three lots and were bought by three different dealers. However, one of the paintings had been singled out to be sold in a lot by itself.

Finally, the auctioneer arrived at this lot, the last one containing items from Miles's house.

"Now on to Lot number 159.

The one you've all been waiting for.

It's a 1955 oil on canvas painting of Chesterfield Marketplace by L.S. Lowry. This painting comes with the original receipt for £50 signed by the artist. No doubt, we will exceed that amount today.

I have sixteen commissioned bids for this lot, including bids from some of the most prestigious art galleries in the world. There are eleven telephone bidders from as far afield as New York, Johannesburg and Sydney and I also have numerous internet bidders.

You can ignore the guide price on this one, as I have to start the bidding at £3 million.

Do I see 3.1?"

The end

# Author's Notes

There were originally three breweries in Chesterfield, which were Chesterfield Brewery, Brampton Brewery and Scarsdale Brewery. Of these, Scarsdale was the smallest with only 35 tied pubs and ten off-licenses. It was also the one that my father worked for, starting as a junior clerk in 1940 when he was fourteen years old.

My father used to tell many stories about his days at the brewery and many of the events in this book are based on his reminiscences. For example, the incident of the men setting fire to the cellar flaps during the war actually happened. The pub involved was the Walton Hotel on St Augustines Road, Chesterfield. The hotel has since been demolished.

Another thing he told me was that on his first day at work the ladies in the bottling hall stripped him naked and stamped his private parts with the brewery stamp.

Scarsdale Brewery started to go downhill when Major Gerald Birkin took over the running of the family business from his father shortly after the end of World War II. It was never intended that Major Birkin would inherit the brewery, but just as in this story, his elder brother had been killed whilst attacking a German pillbox armed only with a wooden gun.

Major Birkin ran the brewery along with his two sisters,

but he was not a businessman and eventually he sold out to Whitbread's in 1959. They immediately closed the brewery, followed by the offices two years later. My father was one of only two Scarsdale employees who transferred to Whitbread's offices in Sheffield.

When my aunt died in 2016 aged 95 it fell to my wife and I to clear out her house. My uncle had died many years before and the two of them had never had any children. Following his death she never remarried and the house was full of things we had to sort out. Just like in the story we divided everything into three piles, things that we would take to auction, things that we would give to charity and things that were destined for the recycling centre.

We had some difficult decisions to make as a lot of the items had obviously been of great sentimental value to my aunt, but meant nothing to us. Lots of her photos were quite old and since my father had died ten years earlier there was nobody left alive who could tell us who was in most of them.

In fact the photograph described in the story is based on one I discovered whilst clearing out my aunt's house. It is extremely old and the family in the photo must be related to me. But since there is nobody to tell me who they are, I guess I will never know for certain.

During the clearance my wife and I light-heatedly wondered what we would do if we discovered a genuine Lowry painting on the wall. My thinking behind this was influenced by the fact that several years earlier, my father had told me how the artist had once given a painting to Derek Coleman, the manager of the Civic Theatre in Chesterfield. At the time, Lowry was an unknown painter who was exhibiting in the theatre's bar. Derek thought that the picture was amateurish and gave it away.

In 2011, a Lowry painting, *The Football Match*, sold for £5.6 million at auction.

I would like to thank Chesterfield Museum for allowing me to listen to the tapes they have of my father recalling his days at Scarsdale Brewery. It was where many of the snippets in this book came from and was the first time I'd heard his voice since his death in 2006. It brought back some tremendous memories, especially those of the stories he used tell me when I was young.

# About the Author

Ian Walker was born in Chesterfield in 1956. His father was the chief clerk for a brewery in the town and his mother was a ballet teacher.

He went to Chesterfield School before gaining a place at Leicester University where he studied Chemistry and Maths.

After graduating he got a job working in the laboratory at Truman's Brewery in Brick Lane, London. The following year he transferred to Watney's Brewery in Mortlake, where he moved into the sales department eighteen months later.

A variety of sales roles followed until he eventually ended up as Regional Sales Director for Scottish and Newcastle based in Bristol.

All this came to an end in 2006 when, aged just fifty, he suffered a stroke and had to give up work. After twelve months of physiotherapy he felt sufficiently recovered to buy a pub in the North York Moors along with his wife Eunice.

In the eight years that they owned the pub, they achieved listings in both *The Good Beer Guide* and *The Good Pub Guide*. They were also in *The Times* list of the top fifty places to eat in the British countryside.

In 2016, he decided to retire and moved back to Chesterfield where he hadn't lived for forty years. He now lives just around the corner from the house where he grew up along with his wife and Purrdey, the cat.

He has two grownup sons from a previous marriage.

*If only they could talk* is his first novel.